death by the glass

nadia gordon

death by
the glass

a sunny mccoskey napa valley mystery

CHRONICLE BOOKS
SAN FRANCISCO

ACKNOWLEDGMENTS Heartfelt thanks to everyone who helped with the creation of this book, especially Judy Balmain, who read and commented on drafts as they were written. Further thanks to Dorian Asch, Rebecca Carter, Dave Chapman, Derek Chen, Patrick Comiskey, Dale Crowley, Kelly Duane, the folks at Longmeadow Ranch, Lauren Lyle, Erin McMahon, Lore and Maya Olds, Norm Ross, and Jonathan Waters, who variously shared their input, expertise, good company, and opinions on topics from vintage port to police procedure. While their assistance has been valuable, any errors or oversights in the text are entirely my own. I am particularly grateful to my editor, Jay Schaefer, for his patience, insight, and ongoing support. —NG

Library of Congress Cataloging-in-Publication Data:
Gordon, Nadia.
   Death by the glass : a Sunny McCoskey Napa Valley mystery / Nadia Gordon.
      p. cm.
   ISBN 0-8118-4180-4 (hc) — ISBN 0-8118-3678-9 (pb)
1. Napa Valley (Calif.)—Fiction. 2. Wine and wine making—Fiction. 3. Restaurants—Fiction. 4. Women cooks—Fiction. 5. Cookery—Fiction. I. Title.
   PS3607.O594D43 2003
   813'.6—dc21
                                        2003009591
Manufactured in the United States of America

Book and cover design by Benjamin Shaykin
Cover photo by Untitled/Nonstock
Composition by Kristen Wurz
Typeset in Miller and Bodoni 6

Distributed in Canada
by Raincoast Books
9050 Shaughnessy Street
Vancouver, British Columbia V6P 6E5

10 9 8 7 6 5 4 3 2 1

Chronicle Books LLC
85 Second Street
San Francisco, California 94105
www.chroniclebooks.com

For Josephine

*"He had a weak point—this Fortunato—
although in other regards he was a man to
be respected and even feared. He prided
himself on his connoisseurship in wine."*

—*The Cask of Amontillado,*
Edgar Allan Poe

death by the glass

The last of the wait staff did rock, paper, scissors to see who would take Nathan Osborne home. Nick Ambrosi, the bartender, lost. Now he stood outside the restaurant and waited, watching his breath. It was past midnight and cold, the clear night sprayed with white pinprick stars. He could hear Osborne inside talking loudly, ranting about some culinary detail that had offended him, and the soft murmur of Dahlia Zimmerman's voice as she coaxed him to put his arms through the sleeves of his coat so she could button him up.

"If she's so concerned, why doesn't she take him home," muttered Nick to himself. Half an hour round-trip at least, he figured, and that wouldn't put him in bed until after two. He let out a sigh of disgust. After a minute, the door swung out and disgorged Nathan Osborne into the night.

Nick had already pulled the car around. The Mercedes was idling, its diesel engine purring like a sewing machine. Nick held the passenger door for his boss and closed it after him, then went around to the driver's side. He pulled out of Vinifera's parking lot and headed toward the hills that overlooked Yountville. A sliver of moon lit the way.

"Morales is going to fucking ruin me," said Osborne, puffing as he settled his briefcase and groped for the seat belt. "He's trying to destroy my restaurant." He waited for a response but didn't get one. "Who eats Moroccan food, anyway? Who wants to eat Moroccan food?"

"Moroccans?" said Nick.

"Nobody comes to Napa Valley to eat Moroccan food," said Osborne dismissively. "We're supposed to be in Provence. Or Tuscany. Nobody in Napa wants to eat preserved lemon rinds and couscous."

"You're sure about that?" said Nick, tapping his ring on the steering wheel. "Seems to me Andre knows what he's doing."

"Is that what they're teaching you at that phony college of yours?" said Osborne. "How to run a restaurant?"

"*Hire the best and then let them do their job.* Isn't that what they say?" said Nick. "You did the first part right."

"Mafia," said Osborne. "You're all organized against me. That whole staff is like a mafia, with its secrets and its little cliques. I see you with your looks behind my back. I ought to fire every last one of you. I've been in the food and wine business for twenty years. Twenty-five. And I have to fight every one of you on every decision."

Nick looked at him and turned up the volume on the stereo.

"What is that?" said Osborne.

"Red Hot Chili Peppers."

Osborne ejected the CD and tossed it in the backseat. "Have you seen next week's menu?" he said.

"I saw it."

"And?"

"I think it's genius, like always." Nick shook his head, smiling. "You keep badgering him like he doesn't know how to run his kitchen, and one of these days Andre Morales is going to get fed up and walk, and you're gonna have no one to blame but yourself. That is not going to be a pretty day."

"It's a mafia," muttered Osborne, leaning his head back and closing his eyes. "I have been run out of my own restaurant."

Osborne's breathing deepened, and after a pause he started to snore.

Nick felt the sedan take charge of the curves leading into the hills. It wasn't all bad driving Osborne home. At the turnoff to the house, Nick lowered the window and punched the key code into the pad by the gate. It buzzed and swung open, and Osborne snorted awake. They drove up the driveway in silence. At the house, Osborne climbed out and waited while Nick opened the front door and switched on the lights, setting Osborne's briefcase down inside. Osborne moved slowly. His legs were bothering him again.

"Damn gout," he said, puffing.

"What about the car?" said Nick.

"Put it in the usual spot. I'll call tomorrow when I need it."

After Nick left, Osborne rested his briefcase on the counter and removed the bottle of wine, running a finger over the label. His movements slow and steady with reverence, he circled the lip of the foil with a knife, then inserted the corkscrew, being careful to set it precisely enough off center to accommodate the twist. He pulled the cork and took down the decanter, then changed his mind and put it back. It was too late to bother with formalities, and besides, a little sediment wouldn't hurt him. He poured himself a glass and went into the living room, taking the bottle with him. The same Chet Baker album had been on the turntable for a week and he was getting sick of it, but he started it anyway, too tired to make a new selection.

He sat on the couch and drank, then poured himself another glass. He would have expected more sediment from a Burgundy that old, but you could never tell about these things. Every wine was different. Could be the sediment was all stuck together along one side or at the bottom, depending how long it had been standing up. He held up the bottle to see, but the room was too dark. He set it back down and put his feet up on the coffee table and his hands on his belly, trying to relax. Andre Morales took life too seriously. He couldn't wait to be famous, as if that would change anything. He already had everything a guy could want. Osborne thought of what it would be like to be young and handsome and unaware that one day life might be lived in a state of more or less constant pain.

He tried not to think about anything and just listen to the music. The sound of it both lulled and excited him. How could anybody be sick of Chet Baker? Especially when he was playing "Tenderly" the way he did that first time he recorded it in Paris. It would have been around 1955. Baker was what, twenty-five at the time? Younger? Just a kid in Paris with his trumpet.

He poured another glass of wine. When he himself had been twenty-five, he was island-hopping and hanging out in Greece and Key West, and on a little strip of sand and palm trees his girlfriend found just a short boat ride off Samoa. That was some kind of place. Osborne's head grew pleasantly foggy as he drifted into the past.

After a while, a funny feeling came over him and he came back to the present. He couldn't quite place the feeling. He put down his glass and looked around the room as though he expected something to happen. The lamps seemed to flicker and his eyes widened with fear. He gasped once, gurgled, and slid down off the couch. Just that quickly, Nathan Osborne was dead.

PART ONE
Faux Finish

I

Sunny McCoskey had a nose for wild mushrooms. That morning she'd spent four hours collecting a bagful of fresh chanterelles from her favorite spot. Now they sat on the passenger side of her pickup, filling the cab with a smell like damp leaves.

She rolled down the window to let in the cold air. The afternoon sky was a low, velvety gray. It was winter in Napa Valley and the hills were carpeted in new grass, the grapevines bare, yellow sprays of mustard between the rows. She hit fourth gear and the truck sailed down Highway 29, rocking gently on its old shocks.

At Yountville, she turned off and in a couple of minutes pulled into the parking lot of Vinifera. Banging her door shut, she went around to the passenger side to collect her knives, uniform, and bag of mushrooms. The parking lot was mostly empty. Near the front, parked under a tree, was a Mercedes sedan the color of vanilla ice cream. A black 911, too new to have license plates, sat nearby showing a tease of cherry-red disk brakes through the silver wheel covers. At this time of day, they had to belong to the owners, maybe the chef. Sunny peeked in the window of the 911. Could this be Andre Morales's car? She shook her head. She'd made her choices, keeping her own café small and manageable. No eighty-hour work week, no six-figure profits, no racy little Porsche. She glanced back at her 1978 Ford Ranger, with its root-beer side panels and its body nicked up like an ancient whale's. The truck had its virtues: it could hold a cord of firewood, for one thing, or six wine barrels. To each her own.

Inside the grand stone entrance to Vinifera, she slipped past a heavy curtain into the dining room, where a few staffers were getting organized for the night. The scope of the place was impressive, especially compared to Wildside, the ten-table restaurant Sunny owned, and where she was the chef. At Vinifera, a veritable soccer field of tables and booths stretched toward the kitchen doors. A mahogany bar ran the length of the room off to the right. Behind it, an enormous mirror reached for the ceiling, and glass shelves glowed with scores of bottles and their clear or amber liquids. Across the room, a staircase went up to a balcony with more seating. To the left, a catwalk led past several closed doors. Straight above, dangling from the ceiling by cables that looked far too slender for the job, was an aluminum dragonfly as big as a hang glider. Art.

One of the staffers, a sous-chef from the way he was dressed, came up to Sunny and asked her to please wait at the bar. He disappeared back into the kitchen. Behind the bar was a guy with sandy blond hair and big shoulders who was talking intently on the telephone. Sunny sat down. Cradling the handset on his shoulder, the bartender set up a glass of mineral water with a squeeze of lime and slid it toward her, meeting her eyes for an instant. She watched his hands while he went on listening, occasionally correcting the person on the other end of the line. She sipped the water and looked around for someone else, then went on watching the bartender. He was probably a few years younger than she was, maybe in his late twenties. He held himself well, like an athlete, and had a smooth, deliberate way of moving. She was just about to decide which martial art he practiced when Andre Morales walked up carrying a large mortar and pestle. He set it down on the bar and wiped his hands on his apron, then greeted her with both a vigorous handshake and a kiss on each cheek. He smelled of freshly ground pepper, spicy and floral and mineral. She fought the urge to grab him and inhale deeply.

"We've met before," he said, "but I'm sure you don't remember. It was only for a second and you were pretty busy."

"Of course I remember," she said. "It was at the Star Route Farm dinner, about this time last year."

They exchanged the usual pleasantries and small talk for a few minutes, giving Sunny the chance to study him. It would have been difficult to forget Andre Morales. He made quite an impression, and he was making it again. He was a large part of the reason she had agreed to participate in tonight's event, a benefit dinner called Night of Five Stars, when five well-known chefs came together to cook five different courses. There were certainly more noble reasons, such as supporting the Open Space Coalition cause and being part of the community, but the truth, and she would barely admit it even to herself, was that she'd agreed to do it because she wanted to see him again. He was a well-executed interpretation of the tall, dark, and handsome motif. With golden brown eyes lined with black lashes and hair shoved back from his forehead in graceful waves, he reminded her of a Chilean architect she'd had a crush on once, but Andre had stronger, more relaxed features.

"I can give you the grand tour, if you're interested," he said.

"Definitely." She looked at her watch. "How many are we serving tonight?"

"A hundred and forty."

"All in one sitting. We sold out."

He nodded. "That's seventy thousand bucks for the OSC."

That's also one hundred forty plates of hand-cranked fettuccine with wild mushroom sauce, Wildside's signature dish, thought Sunny. That was about a hundred and twenty more than she was used to making. With a pang of regret, she reflected on her decision not to bring pre-made pasta, a decision that could have gone the other way and made her life, or at least the next few hours, so much easier. Almost no one could tell the difference between really fresh pasta and really, really fresh pasta, anyway.

"Don't worry," he said. "We've got you set up with more than enough of everything you ordered, and there's plenty of help if you need it. We have the entire staff on deck."

"It shouldn't be a problem," she said. She imagined a line of plates a hundred and forty feet long.

He started the tour in the kitchen, a setup that made the kitchen at Wildside look like a hot plate and a mini-fridge. Not only was the place enormous, it was immaculate and filled with state-of-the-art equipment. The granite counters glistened. The twelve-burner range was spotless. She tried not to gawk. Andre introduced her to the covey of staff members already busily at work, then she followed him into the walk-in, a chilly wonderland of ingredients almost the size of the entire kitchen at Wildside. She eyed a shelf of white plastic containers labeled "Nathan's Salad Dressing," "Der Wunder Sauce," and "Nathan's Fancy Marinade."

"We have some special needs customers," said Andre, following her glance.

"Vegan?" she said.

"If only it were that simple. Most of that stuff is for regulars who get attached to a certain dish or dressing and keep asking for it after we take it off the menu. It drives me crazy."

"I've had the same problem at Wildside," said Sunny. "There are a couple of dishes that I never want to see again, but every time I try to take them off the menu, people get all upset. Tonight's pasta, as a matter of fact, is the primary offender. Every fall I try to replace it with a slight variation, something just a little bit new so I don't die of boredom, and all my regular customers make a fuss until I put it back exactly the way they're used to it."

"Same deal here, except the biggest offender is an owner," said Andre. "He has a whole menu of his own, and one of his girl-friends is even worse."

"One of?"

"I can't keep track. Anyway, she doesn't eat dairy, seafood, pork, or duck, and when she eats chicken it has to be accompanied by her special sauce or else Nathan comes into my kitchen and looks for it himself."

"Skinless breast of?"

"What else?"

Andre led the way back out through the kitchen and dining room, then down a flight of stairs.

"Now for the complement to any great meal," he said, pulling on the handle of a heavy wooden door. It swung open with a sucking sound and they stepped into the cool, underground air. "This is the secret of Vinifera. A true cellar. We don't air-condition or control humidity. It stays between 58 and 62 degrees on its own. We have a walk-in for whites that keeps them at precisely 52 degrees, but other than that it's completely au naturel."

The room was as big as a gymnasium and filled with wine. There was wine in boxes, on racks, and even in barrels along one wall. About half of the open space was taken up with stacked cases of wine in cardboard boxes; the other half held standing racks of bottles. Lights in wire cages stuck out from the rough walls at intervals, providing puddles of dim yellow light. Otherwise the room was dark, a tableau of cement gray, woody browns, and deep bottle green. On three sides, alcoves blocked with metal grating receded from the light. Andre walked between the racks. Every few steps he extracted a bottle and turned the label for Sunny to see.

"This is the wine that's on the list right now, or most of it," he said, gesturing to the general area where they were standing. "We have about twenty thousand bottles in circulation, and about the same number laying down until they're ready to drink."

"Is that what's in the alcoves?"

"That, and the rare wines that the sommelier handles. Some very old vintages, cult wines like Screaming Eagle and Harlan Estate, a bunch of terrific old Sauternes, older Burgundies. Anything too valuable to leave around where somebody might trip over it. And some exotic stuff. He has a case of hundred-year-old Venezuelan rum that's about the best thing I've ever tasted."

"I don't think I've ever seen a wine collection this extensive," said Sunny.

"There's nothing to compare with it on the West Coast. There are places in New York that have legacy stock that is harder to find, and certainly there are places in France with cellars that make this look like a closet, but they wouldn't have any of the California wines."

They heard the door open and turned to watch a man walk toward them with brisk steps. He was slender, with taut, slightly hawkish features and slate gray hair. He stopped a few feet from them.

"Can I help you find something?" he said.

"Speak of the devil," said Andre. "Remy Castels, this is Sunny McCoskey. I was just telling her about our wine collection."

Remy stepped forward and placed his hand in hers. "Pleased to meet you."

They stood in the half light without speaking. After a moment, Andre said, "We were just on our way out."

Remy gave them a clipped smile and they walked toward the door in silence. Sunny felt his eyes follow her. She and Andre climbed the stairs and emerged into the dining room, its high ceiling and warm light a welcome change from the cellar. Andre cleared his throat and gave her a look.

"Are we in trouble?" she asked.

"I don't think so. Besides, I can't be in trouble, I'm the boss, kind of." He gave a smile of false modesty, lacing his fingers and extending them to crack his knuckles. "However, Remy can do pretty much whatever he wants. He's one of about forty Master Sommeliers in the country. That's pretty good job security."

"Is he always like that?"

"You mean the human iceberg? He's been more aloof than usual lately. We had a weird thing happen last week. A magnum of Champagne burst in the cellar. Good stuff, too. I've never heard of it happening before. Remy said it's bad luck, like when a mirror breaks, only worse because you're out the Champagne."

"What do you mean it burst?" said Sunny.

"It built up pressure for some reason and the cork blew. There was Champagne everywhere."

"What would cause that?"

"An impending brush with evil, according to Remy."

She raised her eyebrows at him. "He doesn't really believe that, does he?"

"I don't think so. Or at least I hope not. But he has definitely been grouchier than usual lately. He'll warm up when he resurfaces. The cellar brings out the inner wine troll."

They stood quietly, Andre ruminating on some thought, Sunny watching a haze of dust motes roll in the afternoon light.

"He's not all bad," said Andre at last. "He's incredibly knowledgeable. The guy can tell Côtes-du-Rhône from Côte de Brouilly from fifty paces without reaching for his corkscrew." He looked behind him to see if Remy was there. "He's just overly territorial."

2

Sunny was in the locker room at Vinifera buttoning up her chef's jacket when Rivka Chavez walked in, her cheeks flushed with the cold. She was wearing jeans, a T-shirt, and a suede welding jacket that didn't look very warm. Rivka didn't like winter and never seemed to dress for it, as if ignoring it might make it go away. Two long braids hung down her back from underneath a navy blue bandanna. Rivka had been working at Wildside with Sunny since she graduated from culinary school a couple of years earlier.

"Fancy," Rivka said, looking around at the sage green lockers and the row of gleaming shower stalls. "I've been to spas that didn't have dressing rooms this nice."

"It's okay," said Sunny. "It doesn't compare to changing in the office at Wildside, of course."

"No, it doesn't," said Rivka dryly. "It also doesn't compare to hosing off in the garden when it's thirty degrees out."

"What doesn't kill you makes you stronger."

"Is that supposed to sound like a perk?"

"Cold water is good for the circulation. The Inuit have known that for years. Helps prevent varicose veins."

Rivka snorted and perused the rest of the amenities. There was a long mirror with a counter in front of it arrayed with an arsenal of blow-dryers and hair products. There was even a pitcher of ice water with slices of lemon floating in it. Rivka picked up a blow-dryer and held it like Angie Dickenson aiming a pistol. "Freeze, scumbag! Hair police!"

Sunny gave her a look.

"Have you seen the resident stud, I mean chef?" said Rivka, putting the dryer down and taking off her backpack.

"Affirmative."

"And?"

"Three words: total monster babe," Sunny said, trying not to blush.

"I like the sound of that."

Rivka stepped out of her jeans and took a pair of ugly cotton pants printed with a black-and-white houndstooth pattern out of her backpack. She swirled her hands, amassing imaginary thunderheads. "The clouds are gathering, I can feel it. The great McCoskey love drought is about to end."

"It's about time. I'm pretty tired of doing the rain dance."

"A bit of advice. Don't wait six months before you kiss the guy this time. Remember the Charlie Rhodes phenomenon."

"I know, we've been over it," said Sunny. "Besides, that was different."

"The man was different but your style stays the same," said Rivka. "You are a notoriously slow mover. The guy gives up from exhaustion before you give him the green light. You've got to let things happen more quickly. On the other hand, I wouldn't sleep with this guy right away. He's obviously an overachiever hotshot type. This is a man who likes having the best of everything, and he knows the best doesn't come easy. He wants to work for it."

"I don't think we need to worry about that quite yet," said Sunny. "I hardly know him."

"You've known him for a year."

"I've known *of* him for a year."

"You're being defensive. That's a good sign. For tonight, I recommend the middle course. Have a good snog and say goodnight. It'll be like you're sixteen again."

"Hello? Rivka Chavez? If you're still in there, stamp your foot twice. Sleeping with him tonight is not an option. Snogging with him is not an option. As far as I can tell, I'll be lucky to have coffee with him."

"Whatever you say," said Rivka, giving her a knowing smirk.

"I can't hook up with him tonight, anyway. I need time to get comfortable. I have trust issues," said Sunny.

"You have mortality issues," said Rivka. "You'll be seventy-five by the time somebody passes all your tests. Trust me, Andre Morales is a good guy."

Sunny looked around to make sure the locker room was empty. "What do you know about Andre Morales? *You've* never even met him!"

"I know he's been on your radar for months, and he's the chef at the snazziest joint in town, and Monty worships him."

"What? I didn't know Monty even knew him." Monty Lenstrom was a local wine merchant who had been a mutual friend for years.

"He doesn't. But that doesn't stop him from going on about how Andre Morales was at this party and Andre Morales was on television and Andre Morales says cauliflower is today's most underrated vegetable. He even told me about seeing him playing tennis at Silverado and how he has *just the right amount of hair on his legs*," said Rivka, making air quotes and blinking meaningfully.

"He said that?"

"Could I make something like that up? Only Monty would analyze the amount of hair on a man's legs. Sometimes I wonder why he doesn't just go ahead and turn gay. It's not like it would surprise anyone."

Rivka finished getting dressed.

"There has to be something wrong with Andre Morales," said Sunny, stuffing her street clothes in a locker and shutting the door.

"Nope, he's perfect," said Rivka. "I say go for it. No credit check, no trunk and glove box inspection, no web searches, no best-friend character references, no phone calls to the parents. This guy is pre-approved for the night."

"You're giving pre-approval to someone you've never met."

"I've never met Sting, but he's pre-approved."

"This is all very interesting, but we have about three hours to make enough pasta to feed a hundred and forty hungry socialites. *On y va?*"

"*Vamanos.*"

They found the kitchen a noisy hive of activity, with white-jacketed cooks busy at every station. Since Sunny's tour, the kitchen had taken on a buzz of controlled urgency. Andre made brisk introductions all around, then went back to managing the flurry of tasks. Sunny and Rivka got started, and were quickly absorbed in the wordless familiarity of cooking. Within a few minutes they were cranking out pasta and simmering an assortment of wild mushrooms, including the ones Sunny had collected that morning.

Everything was going smoothly until she added dried morels to the mushroom sauce. She found a gallon jar of them in the pantry, shook a good-sized mound into a saucepan, and covered them with boiling water. When they were soft, she drained the liquid into a saucepan where a batch of chanterelles was simmering and started chopping the reconstituted morels, which she then added to a large stockpot full of mushroom sauce. She repeated the process with a second heap of morels. She was nearly finished chopping the second batch when she noticed something funny about one of them. The shape looked slightly wrong. Morels ought to be honeycombed. This mushroom looked wrinkled. She pushed it aside and sliced it open. Inside, membranes formed several chambers. Morels are hollow, with just one chamber. She poked through the morels until she found another wrinkled one and sliced that open. Again, multiple chambers.

She turned off the heat on the saucepan and covered it, then did the same with the stockpot. She dumped the morels on the cutting board into a pot and put the lid on.

She sighed and stood looking at the cutting board with her hands on her hips, fuming.

Rivka looked over. "What's up?"

"False morels. Not so good," said Sunny. She caught Andre's eye and waved him over.

Andre concurred without hesitation that all the sauce and all the mushrooms should be discarded. He thanked Sunny sincerely for noticing the problem, said they should send a runner out for more mushrooms, and then moved on to talk with another chef who was signaling for his attention.

"He's pretty calm for someone who almost served toxic mushrooms—his toxic mushrooms—to a restaurant full of his best customers," Rivka said.

"He did the right thing and he did it authoritatively and gracefully," Sunny said with appreciation. "All we can do now is wait. I don't know what they're going to find at four o'clock on a

Sunday, but we can't get by with just these." She poked at the few remaining chanterelles she had picked.

All the runner brought when he returned was a few pounds of supermarket mushrooms and a dank bag of shiitakes. Sunny held up a button mushroom to Rivka.

"This is not good," Rivka said.

"Hang on, I'll bet they've got a few cans of cream of mushroom soup in the pantry," said Sunny sarcastically. "That'll fix it up!" She felt like she was going to laugh or cry, maybe both.

"Let's just hope they keep the wine flowing out there," said Rivka.

Sunny went into the pantry and came back with a bottle of white truffle oil. "White gold to the rescue."

Three hours later, they put up the last serving of fettuccine, upending the stockpot and scraping it to get at the sauce. A waiter came by with glasses of wine. Rivka ticked hers against Sunny's and drank. Her face glowed with sweat.

"Who are we doing this for again?" she said.

"The Napa County Open Space Coalition."

"Let's just write them a check next time."

"Done," said Sunny. She smoothed her bangs to the side with her fingers. "You didn't happen to bring the evil fire sticks, did you?"

"I did."

"Let's go. I can definitely justify one after that ordeal."

They walked through the kitchen to the back patio and pulled up chairs at a long plank table under a tree. A heat lamp hissed overhead, warding off the chill.

"Do you think we pulled it off?"

"Maybe," said Sunny, striking a match. "It was not our best work, that's for sure. But you can get pretty far on heavy cream and butter." She exhaled. "Not to mention truffle oil. I'm just happy we didn't poison anyone. I can't even think of it."

"What if you weren't the one handling the morels? What if nobody noticed before it was too late?" said Rivka. "Somebody could have died, right?"

"Probably not. The potency varies. I've never heard of anyone dying from them, but I certainly wouldn't want to take the risk. Apparently people eat them in Sweden and Norway all the time, but I've always been told they're highly toxic. They actually have the same chemical as rocket fuel. Plus the poison builds up in your system, so maybe you've been eating the occasional false morel mixed in with your regular morels your whole life without a problem, then one day you take a whiff of the steam while they're cooking and drop dead."

"Rocket fuel in your fettuccine," said Rivka, shaking her head.

Sunny sat back, watching the smoke trail up from the cigarette and feeling the short, sweet wave of relaxation wash over her. She called it the squeegee effect, the way nicotine passed through her mind, wiping it clean for a minute or two before a rain of thoughts pattered over it again. They listened to the muffled clatter of pots and clink of dishes from the kitchen. Their dish might have been a disaster, but at least it was over. At least nobody was going to get sick. And who knows, maybe no one noticed that there were hardly any mushrooms in the mushroom sauce.

"I think I might try out one of those showers before dinner," said Sunny.

"What, and waste a perfectly good layer of kitchen funk?" said Rivka, stubbing out the last of her smoke. "I feel like I've been dipped in duck fat."

3

Family meal, as the management called staff dinner at
Vinifera, started late and went later, often transitioning into
a poker game the waiters played until the early hours of the
morning. On Sunday night, after service wrapped up for the
fundraiser, the staff, both front and back of the house, slowly
gathered around the plank tables out on the patio and drank
wine. Wide dishes of polenta, grilled vegetables, and roasted
meat and fish arrived and were passed around. After an event
like Night of Five Stars, there was plenty of good wine left over
from tables that had ordered far more than they could drink,
leaving bottles standing open and full, ready to be spirited out
to the back patio.

Family meal was well under way when Andre Morales finally
joined them. Of the several places to sit, he chose the one next to
Sunny.

"It's cold out here, aren't you freezing?" he said, rubbing her
shoulders briskly before he sat down.

They began a hushed conversation about magical outdoor
suppers they'd been to, and how at the good ones everyone
would linger, talking and sipping wine, tethered to the table in
the failing light and unwilling to go inside even when it got cold
and dark. When he turned to talk to her, his face was very close.

At those moments, her whole field of vision was his eyes. The rest of the table would bubble up with laughter and rowdy voices, then subside into small, quiet conversations, but it was all background noise.

Remy Castels, the sommelier, appeared periodically, carrying a bottle in each hand and walking up and down the two tables, filling glasses. Once he came out with a magnum of ten-year-old Nuits-St.-Georges in one hand and a tasty six-year-old Bandol red in the other. He seemed to have gained weight and color since Sunny had met him in the wine cellar that afternoon. Now his face was almost cheerful as he went around the table urging people to finish off their glasses so he could fill them with something else. Across from Sunny, a woman with short, spiky hair dyed electric blue at the ends leaned forward to light her cigarette from a tea candle. She exhaled and caught Sunny's eye. "I understand you ran into some false morels," she said.

Sunny nodded. "Dried ones. Mixed in with the others in that big glass jar."

"First the Champagne bottle jinxes us, then there are poison mushrooms in the pantry. This place is getting pretty scary," said the woman. "I'm Dahlia, by the way."

"Sonya McCoskey," said Sunny. She turned to Andre. "Do we know where they came from yet?"

"They would have come from our usual supplier," he said. "A guy up in Portland. I left him a message about it."

"I'm not an expert but I can tell the difference between a false morel and a real one," said Sunny. "It would surprise me if a person who makes his living selling mushrooms would make that kind of mistake."

"Yeah, but who knows who he has working for him," said Andre. "He certainly doesn't pick everything himself. Most of the suppliers get their mushrooms from the seasonal crews that come through town every winter. I've always wondered how reliable they are."

"You mean the mushroom gypsies," said Dahlia.

Sunny sipped her wine. "I learned to cook from a woman who said you should always know exactly where every ingredient comes from. That ideally, you would be familiar with the actual place it came from. We always visited the local farms and orchards. She liked to see exactly where everything was grown. She would taste every ingredient before she used it, and taste every dish before she served it. Of course, you can't do that in a place this big."

"Are you talking about Catelina Alvarez?" said Rivka.

Sunny nodded.

"We do that here," said Andre. "The expediter tastes practically everything that goes out."

"Not every plate," said Dahlia.

"Not everything on every plate, but he spot-checks throughout the night," said Andre. He looked at Remy, who'd just brought out a bottle of golden Château d'Yquem Sauternes to general approval.

"Who sent that out, Nathan?" asked Andre.

"No, it is compliments of Eliot," said Remy.

"Eliot sent out a bottle of Château d'Yquem? The same guy who suggested we charge people for extra bread? What's the occasion? Is he feeling okay?"

"I don't ask questions, I just pull the cork and pour," said Remy, his intonation only very slightly flavored by a French accent.

Andre drained his glass and held it out for a splash of the sweet dessert wine. "Where is Nathan tonight? I didn't see him."

"I don't know. He never showed up," said Remy.

"I thought tonight was unusually peaceful," said Dahlia.

"Maybe he's finally decided to leave us alone and go live at some other restaurant," said one of the guys down the table.

The bartender, Nick, who Sunny had seen on the telephone that afternoon, had been sitting quietly at the end of the table for some time. Now he said, "He never called for his car, either. It's still out there where I parked it last night."

"That's odd," said Dahlia. "He never stays home all day. Did anyone try to reach him?"

"Eliot called, but there was no answer," Nick said.

"He never answers his phone," said Andre.

"He's probably hung over," said Nick. "He was feeling pretty good when I took him home."

"If Nathan Osborne stayed home every time he was hung over, we'd never see him," said Andre.

"Who is Nathan Osborne?" asked Sunny.

"One of the owners of the restaurant," said Andre. "The guy with all the special tubs in the walk-in. He got a DUI a few years ago, so now he won't drive his car if he's had anything to drink, which is good, except that it means somebody here has to drive him home practically every night, which is bad."

"The guy needs a chauffeur," said Nick.

"Why does he need a chauffeur when he has you?" said Remy.

"Pipe down, Frenchy," said Nick, reaching for a glass of wine that had been sitting on the table, unclaimed, for some time.

"Wait, I wouldn't do that if I were you," said Dahlia, stopping his hand in mid-air.

"Excuse me?"

"Give me that." She stuck her fingers in the glass and removed what looked like pine needles, evidently from the tree they were sitting under, and dumped the wine out on the ground.

"I was going to drink that," said Nick.

"I know. Did you see what was in it?"

"Your fingers, for one thing. And a little roughage. It's good for you."

"Not that roughage. That's a yew tree," she said, pointing up. "The Celts called it the Tree of Death."

"Dahlia is our resident Wicca priestess," said Andre.

"I'm not a priestess," said Dahlia. "And I'm pretty sure I don't deride your beliefs, at least not to your face."

"I am not deriding anything. You're so touchy," said Andre.

"That's three, you know," said Dahlia.

"What's three?" Sunny asked.

"Three bad signs in a row. The Champagne, the poison mushrooms, and now the yew tree."

"Not that again. You can hardly count a twig in a glass as a bad sign," said Nick. "I'm sure the tree didn't intend to kill."

"Still. It's not a good sign."

"The mark of evil is upon us," Nick said darkly and leaned over to repeat the word *evil* in Dahlia's ear. "The end is near," he hissed, reaching for a bottle on the table and refilling his glass.

Sunny looked at her watch. Indeed, the end was near. It was getting late and she had to be at work early in the morning. She looked at Rivka. "I think I'm going to head home."

"Me too," said Rivka.

"You're leaving?" said Andre.

"I have to be at the restaurant at seven tomorrow," said Sunny.

"Wait a second," said Andre. "I'll walk you out. I just have to get my stuff."

Rivka pinched Sunny's elbow. Sunny ignored her. Across the table, Nick and Dahlia were bickering. Nick had Dahlia's arm twisted behind her back and was trying to bend her over his lap as if for a spanking.

"This is the only way to purge the evil curse on our heads!" said Nick, struggling to contain the squealing Dahlia. "We must

beat a pagan virgin with a willow switch gathered by moon-
light!"

Remy snorted. "At least she's a pagan."

Dahlia's jeans were low-cut, riding just above the cleft of her
bottom. As they wrestled, most of her back was exposed, display-
ing a large, blue butterfly tattoo that disappeared into her jeans.

"Nice ink," said Rivka when Dahlia sprung free, red faced.

"You like it?" she said. "I just got it a few months ago."

The talk turned to body art and the long wait for the best
artists. A few minutes later, Andre reappeared. "*Listas?*" he said.

"I think I'm going to stay for a little while longer," said Rivka.

"I'm *lista*," said Sunny, not looking at Rivka.

They walked through the empty restaurant in silence. The
only person in sight was a man in a suit behind the bar, pouring
himself a glass of wine. Andre detoured to talk to him.

"Eliot, you're here late," said Andre.

"Figured I'd pour myself a little nightcap." He held up a bottle
of red wine and looked from Andre to Sunny and back again, taking in the scene with what appeared to be familiar amusement.

"Eliot Denby, this is Sunny McCoskey," said Andre.

"Nice work tonight," said Eliot, shaking Sunny's hand. "Join
me?" he asked, turning the bottle toward Andre.

Andre examined it, nodding approvingly. "Breaking out the
quality beverage, I see."

"Owner's privileges. Pull up a glass, you two," said Eliot.

"Tempting, but I think we're going to keep moving. Monday
morning comes early."

They said goodnight and walked out.

"Eliot is the other owner," said Andre softly when they were
out of earshot. "Good guy. Stays in his office where he belongs."

A moment later they stood outside in the parking lot, each
with keys in hand.

"You're headed home," said Andre.

"Looks that way," said Sunny.

"It's still pretty early."

"It's past midnight."

"The night is young."

"Is it?"

He smiled at her. "Is sleep really that important?"

She smiled back, thinking about the question. Yes, and no.

"How about you give me one hour of your sleep," he said, reaching for her hand. He turned it over and ran his thumb across the calluses on her palm. "You can have it back tomorrow. We didn't get a chance to finish our conversation."

"We could meet tomorrow," she said.

"I'm here until midnight every night. Tomorrow won't be any different."

She looked at him. How important was a good night's sleep?

"Okay, here's the situation," he said. "I have a bottle of wine at home that I've been keeping for a special night. I say we open it tonight."

She'd woken up at six that morning to go mushrooming. She'd spent hours crawling all over steep, wet, muddy slopes and had barely made it home in time to shower, take care of what needed attention at Wildside, and get to Vinifera. Then there was the disaster with the false morels, and the rush to re-create the sauce. She'd met dozens of people, and had at least four glasses of wine over the course of almost as many hours. The last thing in the world she wanted was another glass of wine. Quiet and solitude and sleep sounded more appealing than almost anything else. Almost.

He was still looking at her.

"One hour," she said.

4

There was no lying to Rivka Chavez. In a glance, Rivka took in the rumpled hair, the dazed look and rosy cheeks, the outfit that hadn't been changed, and no doubt knew somebody hadn't made it home last night. Rivka looked highly amused and smiled broadly without saying anything. Preparing some kind of smart-ass remark, no doubt, thought Sunny.

"Don't say it," said Sunny, giving her the no-paparazzi hand and looking away so Rivka couldn't see her blush.

"What? I was just going to ask why you're late," said Rivka, still grinning.

"I overslept."

"It looks more like you underslept. Anyone I know?"

"No comment."

Sunny looked around the kitchen. Her head was fuzzy with the lack of sleep and she was having trouble staying focused. It was a chore just to decide what to do first. She looked at her watch. Whatever it was, she'd better do it quickly or they'd never be ready for lunch.

Rivka went back to dicing onions, her knife moving with expert speed. "So, where'd you stay last night?"

"I think you know," said Sunny. She went into the office and came back a moment later, tying an apron around her hips.

Rivka smiled and went back to chopping. "What's his place like?"

Sunny pretended to be occupied with a stock list. "Nice. Nicer than mine. The guy has better taste in lamps than I do."

"Uh-oh. Is that a problem? He's not a closeted interior decorator, I hope. He doesn't seem the type."

"I think he just likes his house to look good. Perfectionist."

"So, what happened?"

"We decided to go for a ride on his motorcycle."

"He rides a motorcycle? *Qué macho*," said Rivka. "Harley or crotch rocket?"

"Neither. Some kind of old BMW," said Sunny.

"You ever ride before?"

"Not really."

"Did you have a helmet?"

"He had one for me."

"He carries a spare lid for his bitch," said Rivka in her rapper voice.

"He keeps an extra helmet on hand, in case a friend needs a lift," said Sunny.

"Was it fun?"

She abandoned the stock list and went over to the counter where Rivka was working and leaned against it. "He rides really well. Just right. Fast enough, but polite. Not trying to prove anything."

Rivka looked at her. "You are all glowy."

"I know."

"Come on, spill a few details. You're dying to tell."

"I know. But I can't."

"So you're just going to stand there, bursting at the seams?" said Rivka.

"Yeah. What can I tell you? It was a great night."

Rivka nodded. "Okay, just tell me one thing that you liked about him. Something specific, but not anatomical. It's too early for that kind of talk."

"Just when I was about to get anatomical."

"You know what I mean."

"Not really. What kind of detail are you looking for?"

"I'm just trying to understand what kind of shack-up we are dealing with," said Rivka. "I mean, was it a Barry White scene, with the smooth moves and candlelight, or did you stay up all night swapping recipes, or what?"

"We did not stay up all night swapping recipes."

"Then give me the moment when you first thought, Jesus H. Christ, I can't wait to get a piece of that."

Sunny laughed. "I've definitely got one of those. He wears these leather biking pants over his jeans and they have zippers that go from the hem to the waist on the outside of each leg. So we're standing in the kitchen at his place and it's a little awkward because, you know, what the hell are we doing standing in his kitchen at one in the morning, and he reaches down and unzips one side, and then the other, and then steps out of his leather pants. It was like a tough-guy burlesque. I thought I would pass out."

"What about you? Did you have leathers too, or was he just going to let you get the big nasty road rash?"

"He had a pair for me. He had a second set of everything stuffed in the paniers. Pants, jacket, gloves. It was all way too big for me. Not sexy."

"You never know. Maybe he's into the tomboy look."

Sunny went over to the espresso maker and steamed a pitcher of milk. "You want anything?"

"Cappuccino, *per favore.*"

She fired two shots of espresso. "You know, on days like today I'm really glad I don't have to operate heavy machinery. I don't think I could handle anything more complicated than cooking right now. A day of cooking sounds just perfect."

"Oh, good. You don't feel awake enough to drive a forklift, but you're ready to play with fire and knives."

"I still have all ten fingers after all these years," said Sunny.

She walked to the back window and stood sipping her coffee, looking out at the vineyard that ran up to the kitchen garden. The soil between the rows was black with the recent rain, and the vines stood bare, with a few canes stretching nakedly skyward. Howell Mountain sat to the east, a mixture of wooded green slopes and rusty rock outcroppings. The holidays had been lonely and she had a hunger for the comfort of a new romance. No, that wasn't quite right. She had a hunger for the comfort of an old romance, but the only way to get there was to start with the uncertainty of a new one.

"Looks like it's going to rain again," said Sunny.

Lunch was over and Wildside was closed when Sunny heard footsteps crunching down the gravel path to the back door. Probably Monty Lenstrom stopping by for an afternoon gab. Or one of the restaurant's suppliers running late dropping off an order, or maybe Rivka coming back for something she forgot. Sunny listened from the office, expecting to hear someone come in and announce themselves. Instead, there was a loud knock.

She went to the door and opened it to find Sergeant Steve Harvey and an officer she didn't recognize standing outside. Steve shook her hand and introduced his companion as Officer

Katelyn Dervich, a new recruit who was making the rounds with him. The presence of Officer Dervich, and Steve's businesslike expression, told her this was not a social call. Officer Dervich stood with her shoulders squared and her black hair pulled back in a ponytail, doing her best to appear competent to handle whatever the situation might throw her way. She looked young and tiny beside Sergeant Harvey, who was big, blond, muscular, thirty-five years old, maybe a little older. He had his arms folded across his chest, making his biceps look extra bulky. Sunny had crossed paths with Steve before, when she helped clear her friend Wade of a murder, but she hadn't seen much of him in a few months other than to run into him occasionally at Bismark's, the café downtown.

"We've just come from spending the morning over at Vinifera," Steve said. He watched her face.

She nodded, not sure what he could be getting at. Why would they have spent the morning at Vinifera? She waited for him to go on.

The wait lasted longer than she expected, and after a moment she gathered that what he had to say was more involved than he cared to go into standing in the doorway.

"Why don't you come in and we can talk in my office," she said.

They followed her through a doorway off the kitchen into a cluttered room soaking up the last of the afternoon light.

"Land of chaos," said Sunny, moving her mountain bike out of the way and pushing aside stacks of cookbooks and mail so the two officers could sit down.

When they were settled, Steve said, "Do you know Nathan Osborne?"

"I don't know him personally, but I know who he is."

Steve raised his eyebrows slightly. He was leaning forward with his forearms on his knees and his fingers interlaced. He lifted his thumbs, inviting her to elaborate.

"I've never met him, but I know that he's one of Vinifera's owners. As a matter of fact, I heard his name for the first time last night. I was over at Vinifera cooking for Night of Five Stars."

Steve nodded. "Well, I'm afraid I have some bad news. They found Nathan Osborne this morning in his home at about eleven-thirty. He'd been deceased for a day or so already."

This was the last thing she expected to hear, and she wasn't sure what to say. For a moment, she said nothing.

"The cause of death appears to have been cardiac arrest," said Steve, "but we won't be sure until the coroner's report comes back tomorrow or the next day."

"Cardiac arrest. How old was he?" she asked.

"Fifty-eight," said Steve.

"That's pretty young for a heart attack."

"I guess it depends. Depends on your health, diet, how much you exercise, stress level, family history."

"They must be pretty shook up over at Vinifera," said Sunny.

"Like you'd expect," said Steve. "It's always a shock to have someone die suddenly. No one so far has indicated an awareness that he had heart trouble or any other serious illness, so it was completely unexpected."

She looked out the window, considering the news. He didn't show up for Night of Five Stars because he was already dead. She thought about everyone gathered around the table for family meal last night, and Andre asking where Nathan was. It gave her a chill to think of it.

"Well," she said, "that's a terribly sad piece of news."

She looked from Officer Dervich to Sergeant Harvey with anticipation. They weren't here just to keep her informed of affairs at Vinifera, no matter how grave. She wondered when they were going to get to it.

Sergeant Harvey seemed to think it was time. "We understand you cooked at Vinifera last night," he said, despite the fact that she had already stated as much.

"I did. It was Night of Five Stars," said Sunny. "They bring five different chefs together. Each of us prepares one course."

"Okay, so you're working this Night of Five Stars thing last night," said Steve. "Did anything out of the ordinary occur?"

That was it, the mushrooms. They were here because of the false morels. Was it possible that Nathan Osborne got hold of some? And if he did, would they have been toxic enough to kill him? She thought for a moment, remembering last night and choosing her words carefully.

"Yes, something strange did happen," said Sunny. "I was preparing a mushroom sauce and I discovered several false morels mixed in with the supply of dried morels from Vinifera's pantry."

"What are false morels?" asked Officer Dervich.

Sunny explained.

"How unusual is that, for someone to make that kind of mistake?" asked Steve. "I mean, do the wrong mushrooms turn up now and then in your supplies, so that you're used to watching for them?"

"No, definitely not. I'd say it's extremely unusual. I've never seen it before. Frankly, I can't imagine how it could have happened. Andre Morales, the chef at Vinifera, is looking into it."

"We're looking into it too," said Officer Dervich.

"What did you do when you discovered them?" asked Steve.

"We got rid of the entire supply of morels and everything that had had contact with them, just in case. Andre felt fairly confident that no one else had used any of them recently. There hasn't been anything on the menu at Vinifera with morels for the last couple of weeks."

"Would he know everything that gets used in his kitchen?" asked Steve.

"It's hard to say. Very little happens in my kitchen without me knowing about it, but Vinifera is so much bigger, with a much bigger staff."

"And you don't know what you don't know," said Steve.

"That's true," said Sunny, smiling. For an instant it was impossible to tell if Steve was being funny or serious. A second later, she decided he was serious and replaced the smile with a more appropriate expression of concern.

Officer Dervich looked at Steve as if for permission to speak. He gave her an almost imperceptible nod.

"Several people on staff at Vinifera said Nathan Osborne made frequent special requests of the kitchen," she said. "He was in the habit of asking for things that weren't on the menu. Do you think he could have requested a dish with morels in it on Saturday night?"

"You're asking the wrong person," said Sunny. "I was only there last night. I don't know anything about Saturday."

Officer Dervich looked embarrassed. "I mean, in theory."

Steve cleared his throat. "I think what Officer Dervich is getting at is, how unusual are morels as an ingredient?"

"They're neither common nor rare," said Sunny. "I use them in sauces that I want to have a meaty flavor. I suppose, in theory,

Osborne could have asked for a dish with morels in it, but if he did, somebody on the kitchen staff would certainly remember it."

Steve nodded. "So you don't know if anyone served morels on Saturday."

Sunny was beginning to feel like she was getting the third degree, but considering the circumstances, it didn't surprise her.

"Like I said, I don't know anything about Saturday. All I can say for sure is that there was a gallon jar of dried morels in the pantry at Vinifera on Sunday, and that it was tainted with several false morels. What makes you think he ate bad morels, anyway? I thought we were talking about a heart attack."

"We're just checking out all angles until the coroner's report comes back," said Steve.

"So he ate at Vinifera Saturday night, went home, and died sometime after that. I hate to ask this, but could you tell if he'd thrown up, or if he was in pain? Seems like poison mushrooms would have made him sick to his stomach."

"You would think so," Steve said. "There didn't seem to be any signs of his having been sick, and no signs of trauma."

"You mean no one hit him," Sunny said.

"That, or he hadn't fallen down. He didn't appear to have any injuries. We don't know much for sure right now. We know the bartender drove him home from the restaurant sometime after midnight and returned to Vinifera with Osborne's car. They expected a phone call from Osborne on Sunday, asking for someone to drive his car up to get him. When no one had heard from him by late morning on Monday, the bartender decided to drive up there himself and see if he was okay. He found him collapsed in the living room."

"I met the bartender last night," said Sunny. "Nick, right?"

"Correct," said Harvey. He consulted the little notepad he kept in his shirt pocket. "That's right. Nick Ambrosi."

"Seemed like a nice guy," said Sunny. "Did he say anything about Nathan feeling sick when he drove him home?"

"He said Osborne was moderately inebriated, that's why he needed a ride. Nothing out of the ordinary."

Sergeant Harvey closed his notepad and put it away. He looked at Officer Dervich to see if she was satisfied and then stood up slowly.

"Thanks for your help, McCoskey. Seems like you always land smack in the middle of these things. We'll call you when we hear from the coroner."

5

They would know soon enough if poison mushrooms killed Nathan Osborne, thought Sunny, gathering her things from the truck and heading into the house. His liver was sure to tell the tale. In any case, false morels seemed an unlikely culprit. First of all, there was little chance that he had eaten any of them. They weren't on the menu, and most of the supply had been delivered specifically for her needs just a few days prior. Second, didn't poison mushrooms take a long, terrible time to kill? Osborne would have called someone, gone to the hospital, said something to Nick Ambrosi about feeling sick. It was funny that Steve Harvey was pursuing this line of investigation at all. If it looked like a heart attack, why not wait until the coroner's report came back before pursuing less likely explanations? There had to be something more to his death, something that suggested to the police that there was more at work than natural causes.

She thought about Andre Morales and how he must be feeling, with one of the owners of his restaurant dead and the police sniffing around his kitchen. She'd had the urge to phone him all day, and an equal impulse to check her messages every fifteen minutes to see if he'd called. Now that she was home, she took her time. It wasn't about the excitement of an unexpected romance anymore. An unexpected death had interceded, and any conversation was bound to be awkward.

She showered, changed clothes, brushed and flossed her teeth, started a load of laundry, even swallowed a disgusting multivitamin, stalling as long as she could before she at last picked up the receiver to listen for the pulsing signal that indicated a new message. It was there. She advanced through an amusing but rambling dissertation on the micro-events of the weekend from Monty Lenstrom, then listened to the message she'd been hoping for. Andre Morales's voice sounded sleepy but warm, saying the right things about last night, that he had had a great time and was looking forward to seeing her again soon, and that it had been a strange, foggy-headed morning. Obviously he hadn't heard about Osborne yet. The next message was him again, explaining about Osborne's death, and how the police had been meeting with everyone at Vinifera, and it was all very disturbing. He said he would try to call tomorrow or the next day, when things settled down. She hit save and a second later the phone rang. The caller ID read Lenstrom, Monterey.

"Lenstrom," said Sunny, picking up.

"McCoskey."

"Talk to me."

"Do you want to have a little supper?"

"Absolutely. When?" said Sunny.

"How about now?"

"Perfect. You bringing it over?"

"Not a chance. Come over here. I've got it all ready."

"What is it?" she asked.

"Does it matter?"

"This is supper we're talking about, right?"

"You might be talking about supper. I'm talking about the age-old tradition of friends breaking bread together, in the interest of a more enriched human experience," said Monty.

"And?" said Sunny.

"Spaghetti Bolognese with meatballs, green salad, and garlic bread. Simple fare for simple folk. Take it or leave it."

"Good enough. I'll be there in fifteen."

"What about the girl?" said Monty.

"I'll call her." Monty was easy with his invitations. The three of them ate dinner together at least once a week.

"Okay, but make it snappy. I'm starved," he said.

"Right. Ciao." She hung up, relieved to have a plan for the night, and dialed Rivka Chavez. Three minutes later, Sunny strode out the front door as though on a precision training exercise. Seven minutes after that, Rivka hopped into the passenger side of the truck and they headed for Mount Veeder, where Monty lived in a modest *Sunset*-magazine version of the wine country dream house. Twelve minutes later they were setting the table in the dining nook off his kitchen.

"I've never known anyone who will move so quickly for a meal," Monty said to Sunny.

"Priorities," said Sunny. "I need food, and then I need sleep."

"Ask her why she needs sleep," said Rivka, giving him a wink.

"Do I want to know?" said Monty, running his fingers over his scalp. "Is it going to make me jealous?"

Sunny pulled a loaf of garlic bread out of the oven. "You cook just like my mama, Monty."

"That's me, Mr. Old-Fashioned Home-Spun Goodness."

"Where's Mrs. Old-Fashioned tonight?" said Rivka.

"Yoga. The woman is obsessed. It smells like an Indian bazaar in our bedroom and the last time I got in the car it sounded like I was being attacked by Hari Krishnas."

"Could be worse," said Rivka.

Monty pulled the cork on an open bottle of Cabernet Sauvignon and filled two glasses, handing them around. "You mean she could be addicted to the Home Shopping Network."

"I didn't want to say, but yes."

"You've got it all wrong. She's been off that stuff for weeks now."

"As far as you know," said Rivka.

"She says she can quit watching anytime she wants to, and I believe her," said Monty, trembling his lower lip. "Besides, there's nothing wrong with owning seven bread machines. You never know when we might need a really large quantity of bread, all at once."

"Tell me she didn't buy seven bread machines."

"Okay, two."

"The woman is obviously frustrated in some sector of her life," said Rivka.

"Uh-oh," Sunny said. "Sigmund Chavez is in the house."

"She has a great career, good family and friends, I wonder what it could be? What drives her to garden, shop, and exercise to excess? What is it that's missing? There must be some vital form of release that she's not getting."

"I am officially changing the subject," said Monty. "McCoskey looks like she hasn't slept in two days, but she's not complaining. That can mean only one thing. Let's hear it. Don't deprive me of secondhand thrills. I want to live vicariously through your salacious, single-woman excesses."

"The salacious part is a long story," said Sunny.

"I wouldn't expect anything less," said Monty.

"But it will have to wait. There's something more important. Riv, you don't know about this yet."

Rivka had been slicing marinated artichoke hearts and dried tomatoes into the salad. "What don't I know?"

"Last night sort of culminated in a strange way today. Do you know Nathan Osborne?"

"The guy who owns Osborne Wines?" said Monty.

"I'm not sure. He was one of the owners of Vinifera," said Sunny.

"That's him."

"Did you say *was*?" said Rivka.

"I'm afraid so. It turns out that he died over the weekend."

Rivka gawked at her. "You're kidding! That's terrible. Oh my god, that's why he never showed up for dinner."

"Exactly. He was already dead. After you left today, Steve Harvey and another cop came by to tell me about it." She related the details she'd learned, including, for Monty's benefit, how she'd found the false morels at Vinifera the night before, prompting Sergeant Harvey to come see her. Monty dug his hands into his pants pockets, mulling over the news.

"Wow, that's too bad," he said. "He wasn't very old."

"Fifty-eight. If I actually thought he died because he ate false morels, I don't know what I would do," said Sunny. "Andre must be freaking out."

"Andre Morales?"

"Right. The chef at Vinifera."

"It's not the mushrooms," said Monty. "With mushroom poisoning you go to the emergency room with the worst stomach pains you've ever had, then your liver and your kidneys shut down and you lay there like a gurgling blob for three days before you buy the farm," said Monty.

"Gross," said Rivka.

"What a shame, just when he could kick back and relax," said Monty. "He made a fortune in the wine business. He was smart about it. He'd start a restaurant and then make himself the sole supplier of its wine and booze, so he could double dip. He'd make money as both the wholesaler and the retailer. Remember Denby's in Mill Valley?"

Sunny shook her head. "I don't think I ever went there."

"You might have been too young for the scene. Denby's was at its prime about eight, maybe ten years ago. Riv would have been dating the editor of the high school newspaper about then."

"I was dating the striker on the soccer team," said Rivka.

"I don't even know what that means," said Monty.

"He was also a founding member of the math club."

"The elusive geek-jock combo," said Monty.

"What about Denby's?" said Sunny.

"It was the big scene in Marin for a long time. Eliot Denby, now of Vinifera fame, and Nathan Osborne owned it. Everybody went there. They had every wine you could think of on the menu. This was before wine bars were the hot ticket. They were at least five years ahead of the curve."

"What happened?"

"There was a fire late one night and the place burned down. I would have loved to sell those guys wine, but Osborne wouldn't let anybody else in. Then he cut exclusive deals with a bunch of the producers on the other end. It was all sewn up, start to finish."

"Why don't you cut exclusive deals?" asked Rivka.

"Don't think I haven't tried, my *chiquita* banana. It has not proven to be as easy as it sounds."

"Tell me again how it couldn't have been the mushrooms," said Sunny.

"It wasn't. I know you're going to worry until you find out, but I really don't think it's necessary," said Monty. "I haven't seen him for years, but a heart attack wouldn't surprise me that much. He had all the characteristics even back then. Red face from about forty years of drinking too much wine, carrying around thirty extra pounds, never more than five feet from a pack of Marlboros or a big cigar. Those guys who like to eat and drink and smoke all the time don't live forever. Unless you're a Swedish-farmer type, like Skord. Then you can do whatever the hell you want and live to be a hundred. I'd kill to have that guy's genes."

Sunny and Monty both half admired and half worried about their friend Wade Skord, who seemed to be able to live on fried eggs, Wasa Crisp, and Zinfandel, and still do the work of three men half his age.

"Fifty-eight sounds pretty young to me," said Sunny.

"Not if you live hard," said Monty. "He was having a good time. That's worth something. The nice thing about shaving years off your life is that they get shaved off at the end. That's usually the dull part anyway."

"They were talking about him at staff dinner last night," said Rivka. "Apparently someone had to drive him home practically every night because he drank like a fish."

"It's what he ate that's more important if he had a heart attack, right?" said Monty. "Too much bacon and duck fat, not that I blame him."

"It almost makes me want to reconsider my New Year's resolution," said Sunny.

"You mean the one about eating more bacon?" said Monty. "I want to go on record as not in favor of that resolution. Someday this is all going to catch up with that skinny ass of yours and you're going to wake up looking like Paul Prudhomme. I'll find slabs of cured pork belly tucked under your mattress."

"It's my homage to the noble pig," said Sunny, "tastiest of god's creatures."

"I really don't think the noble pig appreciates that kind of tribute," said Monty.

"I can feel the day coming when I will give serious thought to the plight of the readily comestible sentient beings, and from that day forward, no flesh will pass these lips," said Sunny. "Until then, I'm in denial. It's the year of the pig and I'm going to enjoy it."

"It's true. If we really sat down and thought about it, we wouldn't eat meat at all," said Rivka.

"Let's really sit down and not think about it, how about that?" said Monty, setting a bowl full of spaghetti on the table. They took their seats and Monty poured another glass of Cab all around. He said, "Denial is bliss," and they chimed glasses.

"You know what else about Osborne?" said Rivka, loading her plate with spaghetti. "You're not going to believe this."

"What?"

"You remember Dahlia, the waitress with the blue hair?"

"And the stained-glass butterfly tattooed across her butt?"

"You didn't like it?" said Rivka. "I thought it was beautiful."

"It's beautiful now, but in a few years it's going to be out of style and faded and even more huge. It's reckless."

"You sound like my mom," said Rivka.

"It's not like other tattoos," said Sunny. "I like plenty of tattoos. It's just that this one is really big and really colorful. It's a big commitment."

"How do you know she has a tattoo on her butt?" said Monty. "Is this story about to get really interesting?"

"It's not on her butt, it's on her lower back," said Rivka. "You could see most of it above her jeans."

"This is not a terribly modest girl," said Sunny.

"*Anyway*," said Rivka, "the point is that she used to date Nathan."

"Whoa. For how long?" said Sunny.

"I don't know. It sounded like they were pretty serious. They just broke up recently."

"She must be about thirty years younger than him," said Sunny.

"About that. She's my age. Apparently he's dated loads of younger women. A few of us went to Bouchon after you left and they were talking about how Osborne is such the ladies' man."

"I can't believe that. I had the impression nobody liked him," said Sunny.

"Really? I figured it was just the obligatory boss bashing. He must be sort of okay if Dahlia was into him," said Rivka.

"I'm not sure I like the sound of that," said Sunny.

"Don't worry, you're immune. You're not a boss in the derogatory sense," said Rivka.

"I hate to say it about someone who's died, but he sounded kind of like a jerk to me," said Sunny. "I don't think Andre liked him much."

"I actually thought the one nobody seemed to like was Dahlia. Everyone was ripping on her all night," said Rivka.

"If she was dating the owner that was bound to alienate her from everyone else. It's like being the teacher's pet," said Monty.

"I thought she was interesting," said Rivka. "She's an artist and she lives in a tent cabin way out in the middle of nowhere. I'm going over to her place tomorrow after work to see some of her paintings."

"A tent cabin," said Sunny. "That's fantastic. I love it."

"What does any of this have to do with McCoskey getting her ashes hauled last night?"

"You are so crude, Lenstrom," said Rivka, smiling.

"I'm sorry. What does any of this have to do with McCoskey falling in love in a deeply meaningful, though remarkably swift fashion late at night. I need a name."

"Andre Morales," said Sunny. A sense memory of the night before flashed back for an instant, sending a pleasant jolt through her body.

"The chef?"

"Yes," Sunny said.

"Perfect!" Monty said, rubbing his hands together. "That's going to fit beautifully into my plans. We'll have holidays at your place. Rivka can watch the kids. The food will be impeccable."

"Don't get all excited, it was just one date," said Sunny. "I don't think we need to call the florist yet."

"I'm not sure you can actually call last night a date," said Rivka. "I'd call that a hook up."

"Chavez takes the hard line," said Monty in his baseball announcer voice. "Calls it like she sees it. Now it's up to McCoskey to defend her position."

"He picked me up after work and we went for a drink. That's a date," said Sunny.

"He picked up on you at work and took you home with him. That's a hook up," said Rivka.

"It's Chavez with a deep line drive, she's easily rounding first, second, she's headed for third and looking confident! McCoskey is going to have to come up with something more substantial than that if she's going to stay in this game," said Monty.

"Aren't you the one who was urging me on?" Sunny said. "I think you may have actually said *seize the moment*."

"I'm not saying it was a bad idea," said Rivka, giggling. "I'm just saying it wasn't a date."

"Point taken," said Sunny.

"Can we skip the semantics?" said Monty. "I want to know how he enticed you to stay out after midnight. You're the biggest stay-at-home I've ever known."

"Hot body," Rivka fake-coughed.

"Wrong," said Sunny. "It was much more than that. He said he had a very special bottle of wine that he had been saving and he wanted to open it."

"That makes sense to me," said Monty. "You have to open that stuff while it's still fresh or you might as well throw it out. It was probably due to expire the next day."

Rivka snickered.

"That is absolutely the oldest line in the book," said Monty, "but this is the first time I've ever heard of it working."

"You guys are being mean. It may have been a line, but at least it was true. He had an old bottle of Burgundy I've never even seen before, let alone tasted."

"What was it?"

"1967 Château de Marcclinc St.-Quinisque Premier Grand Cru Reservée by Michel Verlan."

"Tah-tah-tah," said Monty. "I guess somebody has some cash to burn. Give that guy my card, will you?"

"The sad thing is, it was sort of a waste. By the time we got there and opened it I was so tired I couldn't taste anything. It didn't seem like anything special. I'd already had about four different wines and a glass of port. He could have opened anything and I wouldn't have known the difference. And we only drank about half of it."

"Not a big deal," said Monty. "That's around, what, two hundred dollars a glass, give or take a few ounces? Next time, get a doggy bag for me. I tasted a seventy-one a few years ago. That old stuff doesn't come around very often."

"I wanted to soak the label off the bottle for my journal, but I couldn't think of a way to smuggle it out without looking like a complete dork," Sunny said.

"You could have told him you're really into recycling," said Monty.

"At least I got the cork." She groped in her jacket pocket and produced it, handing it over to Monty. He examined it and opened his mouth to say something, then changed his mind and served himself a second helping of salad instead. Sunny looked at him.

"What?"

"Nothing," said Monty.

"There's something. You have a funny look."

"It's nothing."

"What? Tell me," said Sunny.

"You're insane. I'm just getting more salad," said Monty.

"No you're not, you're hiding something. Tell me what it is."

"No way."

"She's right. You have to ante up when you make a face like that," said Rivka.

"For the last time, it's nothing."

"Okay," said Sunny. "You leave me no choice. I am going to throw all of this delicious food on your nice, clean floor in exactly ten seconds if you don't tell me what that look was about. Ten."

"It was nothing."

"Nine."

"Stop counting."

"Eight. Come on, tell me. It makes me crazy when you do this."

"Wouldn't you rather live the fantasy?" said Monty. "Instead of getting it all smudged up with reality?"

"Seven. Of course not. What are you talking about? You know how I am about full disclosure. I always want the whole truth, no matter what," said Sunny. "Six."

"Okay, stop counting. I just hate to tarnish what sounds like a lovely evening."

"What do you mean?"

Monty picked up the cork, turned it a few times, and set it down again. "What you drank was a very good bottle of Château de Marceline St.-Quinisque, but not the Premier Grand Cru Reservée. That particular producer bottles several different wines each vintage, only one of which is estate grown and has the winemaker's signature and all the other goodies. It's like Hess Collection versus Hess Select, or DKNY versus Donna Karan black label. They sell the bridge line and they also sell really high-end stuff. This cork comes from a bottle of their less expensive wine, who knows what year."

"How do you know?" asked Sunny.

"All of these producers do things a bit differently. Some put their name on the cork, some put the year. Some producers put everything on there, the name of the winery, the vintage, distinctions like Grand Cru or vintner's reserve or whatever, their phone number, the web site. I've even seen bin numbers on some corks. There are no rules about this stuff. All the Frog's Leap corks say is *ribbet*. Marceline does everything differently for the Grand Cru. The bottle has green foil instead of red, the label is different, of course, and the cork says Premier Grand Cru Reservée right on it along with the year. And they use slightly longer, higher-grade cork because the really expensive wines are built to last. This cork comes from a bottle of their very good but not nearly so expensive regular release. You can tell because they didn't print the year, and because it doesn't say Premier Grand Cru Reservée, and it's the wrong style of cork. I've probably opened a hundred bottles of this stuff and the cork has always been the same. Like this."

"I don't understand how that could be right," said Sunny. "I made a point of looking at the label. It was definitely the Grand Cru, with the winemaker's name on it and everything."

"Do you remember what color the foil was?"

"I'm not sure. I didn't pay much attention to the foil. Are you absolutely certain, Monty?"

"Completely. This is the wrong cork for that bottle of wine."

"One of us has to be wrong. I saw the label."

"Maybe you saw a forgery," said Monty.

"A forgery?"

"Where did he get it?"

"I don't know. He didn't say."

"Are you going to tell him?" Rivka asked Sunny.

"I don't know. No, probably not. He was so excited about opening it."

"Believe me, he'll be plenty excited when he finds out he paid eight hundred dollars for a sixty-dollar bottle of wine," said Monty. "He needs to go back to the place where he got it and get them to explain where that bottle came from."

"Have you seriously heard of that?" said Sunny skeptically. "I mean, somebody getting hold of wine that isn't authentic?"

"Absolutely, especially at the very high end. I don't think it happens often, but it happens. That's why the industry has traditions like special foil and labels and printed corks and stamped wax. Most people couldn't tell the difference between a 2001 California Pinot and a 1972 Burgundy if all they had to go on was the wine itself, and yet the price difference between those two bottles would be at least two hundred dollars, and sometimes hundreds or even thousands more. Authenticity becomes a matter of packaging, and in wine, the packaging amounts to a hunk of green glass, a square of paper, some cork, and a scrap of foil. Can you think of a commodity worth that kind of money that's as easy to falsify? Every once in a while somebody gets caught doing it. The French are particularly bad on that score. It's always some little old man from Marseilles who looks like he belongs on a bicycle with a baguette in the basket and a beret on his head who's been selling bottles of seventy-year-old St.-Aubin that he happened to have whipped up in his basement about a week ago."

Sunny tapped the cork on the table anxiously.

"Who cares if the wine had red foil or green foil?" said Rivka, looking from Sunny to Monty and back again. "What's important is that you had a great time opening it together. I don't see how it changes anything."

6

At one o'clock the next afternoon, the wait for a table at Wildside was forty-five minutes. The windows steamed up with a cozy heat from a room filled with the bustle and clatter of service. Sunny and Rivka worked quickly. It was days like this when they were at their best. There wasn't time for distraction— no talk or music—it was a clean, straight-ahead hustle, their hands passing over the food with choreographed efficiency. Around two o'clock the sound of flames kicking up on the grill mixed with the heavy patter of raindrops on the roof and patio.

At three, Sunny sent out the last plate of chicken cooked under a brick with celery root dressing, roasted beets, and garlic mashed potatoes. She stopped long enough to down a glass of water and wipe the sweat off her forehead with the sleeve of her jacket. At four, she watched the maître d' carry out a last round of cappuccino, espresso, and doppio macchiato. What was that pleasant sensation washing over her, soothing her tired muscles? Satisfaction. Life felt almost normal again after the flurry of the unusual, the unexpected, the tragic.

The coroner's report had come back that morning and Sergeant Harvey and Officer Dervich had stopped by the restaurant to deliver the news personally.

"The autopsy lists the cause of death as cardiac arrest," Steve had said, looking almost as relieved as Sunny. "No evidence of trauma or suspicious substances, nothing to suggest foul play."

"What was it that made you think there might be in the first place?" asked Sunny.

"There was some evidence at the scene that seemed to suggest that Osborne may not have been alone the night he died. We'll keep looking into it, but it doesn't seem to have had any bearing on the ultimate outcome."

"What kind of evidence?"

Steve smiled at his partner and said, "Sunny likes to spend her spare time doing police work," but he didn't answer her question.

Probably the story about how she'd practically gotten herself killed not too long ago chasing a murderer was still making the rounds at the police station. Her hand went to the back of her thigh involuntarily, touching the place where a shard of glass had sunk in several inches, a lucky break considering she had narrowly missed taking a bullet.

"So you're satisfied with the autopsy?" she said.

"For now," said Steve.

"Is something going to change?"

"You never know."

Steve Harvey was a man of few words, and fewer today than usual. The way he seemed to enjoy withholding information tried Sunny's patience. She suspected he was showing off for his new partner.

By the time Andre Morales called late in the afternoon, everyone but the dishwashers had gone home and Sunny was busy battling paperwork in the office. The workman's compensation people had sent a stack of forms as thick as a dictionary

and about as user-friendly as any of the other government doc-
uments littering her desk. She stared at the jumble of blanks,
boxes, charts, and fine print. The only thing clear about most of
the forms was that not completing them correctly could result in
the immediate or eventual demise of her business. The phone
was a welcome interruption, made more so when she heard
Andre's voice on the other end of the line. Her heart kicked up
a notch or two, and she felt her face get hot and her hands go
cold.

"I've been meaning to call," he said. "I haven't had a second.
It's been chaos over here. Did you get the news? The police said
they were going to stop by and let you know."

"You mean about the autopsy? They came by this morning.
What a relief."

"You're telling me. Now maybe we can get back to work
around here. I thought things were bad while Osborne was alive.
He's twice as much trouble dead."

"Can you say that?"

"You mean is it a sin against the deceased?"

"I guess so."

"Knowing Nathan, he's getting a kick out of watching me
sweat. His final insult."

"He wasn't really that bad, was he?"

"He wasn't bad, he just loved to be a pain in the ass. He loved
to push my buttons and he was very good at it. He wasn't what
you'd call the warm fuzzy type. Not that I like the fact that he
died, but I'm certainly not going to miss having him in my face
every other night."

"I guess I can understand that."

The line was quiet for a moment.

"So, do I get to see you tonight?" he said. "I'm working, but you could come by the restaurant around ten and we could hang out for a while, maybe have a late snack."

———————————

Satisfaction comes in many forms. What she had been planning to do at ten o'clock that night was snuggle up in bed with the tower of books and magazines stacked on the nightstand, and that's exactly what she would have done, except that there was no denying the deeper impulse to return to Andre Morales. Sunday night had certainly brought them together in a way that was arguably too close, too fast. Now the idea of him drew her irresistibly toward him. Wasn't there something about that in physics? How bodies of a certain substance manufacture their own gravity and can't help pulling in anything that comes too close? She had picnicked in his gravitational field and now a subtle, pervasive force was pulling her toward him whether she was ready or not.

She took a bracing shower and put on her best jeans, the ones that could pass for dress clothes, chose a silk blouse and pointy alligator heels, threw her wallet and a lipstick in her good handbag, and drove down to Vinifera. With the Nathan Osborne mushroom crisis behind them, she could give her undivided attention to getting to know Andre better.

At Vinifera, the hostess came back from the kitchen with the message that Andre would be out in a few minutes and suggested she have a glass of wine. It looked like a slow night. Only about half the tables were full and there was plenty of room at the bar. Then again, it was well past the dinner hour. Nick Ambrosi, the bartender, lifted his chin at her when she looked over. She sat down in front of him.

"You're back," he said. He stood with his palms on the bar, like he was about to do a push-up.

"I'm meeting Andre," she said.

"So I heard."

"Did you?"

"No secrets around here," he said. "He's been sending someone out every five minutes to ask if you're here yet. What would you like to drink?"

"A glass of something red sounds good. Whatever you have close by."

He rubbed his hands together. "I just opened a bottle of Au Bon Climat Isabelle Pinot that's drinking really nice."

"That sounds great."

He poured the wine and set the glass down in front of her, then walked to the other end of the bar, returning with a dish of little deep-fried nuggets.

"Green olives stuffed with anchovies," he said.

"Yum."

He leaned into the corner of the bar.

"I was sorry to hear about Nathan," she said. "Steve Harvey said you were the one who found him."

He nodded and took a swig from a bottle of Calistoga water.

"That must have been terrible," said Sunny.

"Not a pretty sight," said Nick. "I'll be glad when things get back to normal around here and I can forget about it. Is Sergeant Harvey a friend of yours?"

"He came by yesterday to talk about the false morels I found on Sunday night. I think initially they were worried that Osborne might have come in contact with some of them."

"They grilled a bunch of us here about that too. The police have been knocking on our door every five minutes to question somebody about something for the last two days. They were here again this afternoon."

"I guess it's good they're being thorough," she said. "Still, I don't understand why there's an issue if the autopsy says he died of a heart attack."

Nick selected an olive out of the little dish and ate it. "They're trying to figure out who was in Osborne's house Saturday night."

Sunny sampled an olive. "What makes them think someone else was there?"

"They didn't tell you?"

"They didn't give me any details."

Nick ate another olive and stared at her while he chewed, thinking.

"Nathan was in the living room when I found him," he said. "It looked like he'd come in, poured himself a glass of wine, and sat down on the couch. He was sort of crumpled on the floor right in front of it, like he'd slid down there when he died. The glass of wine he'd been drinking was on the coffee table in front of him. That all makes sense. What doesn't make sense is that a few feet away, a full bottle of wine was smashed on the floor. Osborne's living room has a tile floor. Somebody dropped a bottle of wine and it broke. There was wine all over the place when I got there."

Sunny raised her eyebrows. "Maybe it was Osborne who dropped it," she said. "Maybe he started to have a heart attack, dropped the bottle of wine, and sat down on the couch."

"No way," said Nick, frowning. "I'm no expert, but my guess is that it was dropped after he was dead. You could tell by the way there were splashes on the pant leg that was closer to where the bottle broke. I'm guessing the police think the same thing, or they wouldn't be looking into it. Plus, the bottle that was broken hadn't been opened. The cork was still in it. It wasn't the bottle he poured his glass of wine from."

He rubbed his neck and tipped his head back, cracking several vertebrae loudly enough for Sunny to hear. She waited, sensing there was more. There was.

"The really odd thing is, they haven't found an open bottle of wine anywhere in the house," he said. "And you wanna hear the kicker?"

"There's a kicker?"

"A good one."

"Let's hear it."

"They ran a report from the security system and somebody disarmed it about two hours after they figure Osborne was already dead. That's why they've been questioning everyone around here. It had to be somebody who knew the alarm code."

"How many people is that?"

"Most of the longtime staffers around here. Anybody who ever took him home knew it. It's the same code that opens the gate on the driveway."

Sunny ate another olive. No wonder Steve Harvey was checking out all the possibilities. This was starting to sound like a very complicated heart attack.

"There's no security tape?" she asked.

"You mean video?"

"Yeah."

"No, there's nothing like that. It's not Fort Knox up there. He's just got a regular alarm system with a motion detector and an automatic gate."

She met Nick's eyes. "What do you think happened?" Sunny asked.

"Me?"

"You were there. You saw it all with your own eyes. You must have a theory."

He held up a finger for her to wait and went down the bar to pour a couple of glasses of wine for other customers. When he came back he said, "I haven't come up with anything that explains all of it. I can imagine him giving his alarm code to a woman, so she could come over late at night and let herself in. He was like that. Did you know him?"

"No, we never met."

"It was amazing the women he brought in here. I don't know how he did it. Osborne loved women. All kinds of women."

"So she lets herself in," said Sunny.

"She lets herself in," said Nick. "It's late. She expects to find him in bed, but he's not there. So she goes through the kitchen into the living room and flips on the light. When she sees him slumped over on the floor she screams and drops the wine she was carrying."

"Then she panics and leaves," said Sunny. "She doesn't call the police?"

"She's afraid to," said Nick. "Maybe she doesn't want anyone to know she was there. There could be lots of reasons for that. If I was sleeping with Osborne, I wouldn't want anyone to know it."

"I'll bet!" laughed Sunny.

"You know what I mean."

"I do. Anyway, the startled lover theory doesn't quite fit. Her prints would be on the wine bottle, the light switch, both alarm key pads," said Sunny. "The cops must have found something by now."

"If they have, they haven't said so."

"And there might be footprints in the wine," she said. "Did you see anything like that?"

"I don't think so, but I didn't really look. There were plenty of my footprints by the time the cops got there, that's for sure. It didn't occur to me to be careful at first. It was a very weird scene to find him like that. I walked around a bunch looking for the phone to call the police."

Nick swigged his water. "There's another hole in my theory. It doesn't explain where the wine in his glass came from. They looked everywhere for an open bottle in the house."

"Everywhere is big. Maybe they missed it," said Sunny. "Maybe he'd already put it in the recycling. Or maybe our lady friend took the open bottle with her."

"Why would she do that?"

"I don't know," said Sunny, chewing another olive thoughtfully. "There are two bottles of wine to account for. We can presume there was an open bottle, because there was wine in his glass and that didn't come from nowhere. And we know there was an unopened bottle, because it's still on the scene. We also know, maybe, that there was someone else present. Since the someone else and the open bottle are both missing, it seems logical that they would have left together. What we don't know is why."

He gave her a grin. "You think like that all the time?"

"Too many *Perry Mason* reruns when I was a kid," said Sunny. She held up an olive. "This is about the most delicious thing I have ever tasted. It's like the best pickled thing and the best salty thing and the best deep-fried thing all in one."

"They're dangerous," said Nick. He looked up the bar, where one of the servers was waiting to put in an order. "Don't go anywhere."

A few minutes later he came back. "You come up with anything?" he asked.

"Not yet." She sipped her wine. "I think we have another
problem. I don't think a lover would bring a bottle of wine to a
guy whose business is wine, especially when she must know that
he would have had plenty to drink by the time she got there.
Besides, she's already playing rent-a-babe delivery service. She
wouldn't bring a bottle of wine on top of it."

"Especially not that wine."

"Why, what was it?"

"Auction house material. It was a 1967 Château de Marceline
St.-Quinisque. The good stuff too. Premier Grand Cru Reservée
made by Michel Verlan. It's a pretty chunk of change for a bottle
like that, if you can even get your hands on one. They never make
much of it, and to find a bottle that old is really unusual. It's definitely not your typical booty-call red. Personally, I usually bring
a six-pack of Corona and call it done."

Sunny nodded. "Can I get a glass of water?"

Nick filled a glass and put it down in front of her, then held
up a finger and went to tend to customers down at the other end
of the bar.

Sunny sipped the water. It was the same wine, the wine she
and Andre drank, the really expensive, old, rare French wine.
The phrase *booty-call red* kept running through her mind like a
mantra of disaster. She was slightly nauseous. There was a possibility, small but growing, that she would regret the dish of deep-
fried olives with anchovy. She needed a moment to think and get
her head together. She decided to take refuge in the ladies'.

It seemed to take forever to cross the dining room, and the
stairway leading downstairs looked impossibly far away. With

each step she became more conscious of the placement of one foot in front of the other, making it more and more difficult to walk. The buzz of conversation in the dining room receded and she heard instead the rasp and click of her heels on the floor. They struck the polished concrete loudly with each step and after a while that was all she could hear.

7

The bathroom at Vinifera had a foyer decorated like a bachelor pad. Sunny sat down on a white leather bench and put her head between her knees, staring at the zebra print rug under her feet and hoping no one would come in. Breathing heavy little breaths, she sorted through the facts, putting them in order, trying to figure out what they could mean.

It seemed to go like this: On Saturday night, Nathan Osborne came home from Vinifera late, died in his living room, and had a mysterious visitor who left behind a very expensive bottle of wine. On Sunday, Andre Morales used a forgery of the same expensive bottle of wine as an excuse to get her to come home with him (not that he needed much of one). Nick Ambrosi didn't find Nathan until Monday morning, but whoever visited Nathan on Saturday night would have known all day Sunday that he was dead. She thought about family meal out on the back patio at Vinifera Sunday night, with Andre sitting next to her. He had seemed relaxed enough. He was the one who asked where Nathan was. She remembered Remy Castels reaching over them to refill their glasses. Remy had been cordial, even cheerful that night, at least compared to his demeanor when they'd met him in the wine cellar. Rivka had been sitting beside her, and across from them was Dahlia, the pagan waitress with the blue hair. Nick had been there. He was the one who'd said Nathan hadn't called for his car that day and that Nathan was feeling no pain by the time he took him home on Saturday night. There were a dozen faces at the table, and more at the other table. There was the guy who made the crack about Nathan going to live at some other restaurant, and there was the co-owner, Eliot Denby, who'd been pouring himself a glass of wine behind the bar as she and Andre left. It made her head thud to imagine one of them might have stood in Nathan's living room Saturday night, witness to his death, and told no one.

The existence of those two very unusual bottles of wine in such close proximity to Nathan's death was too coincidental. The scene in Nathan Osborne's living room late Saturday night was growing darker by the minute. There had to be a connection, and it was ominous. The thing to do was call Sergeant Harvey right now and enlighten him about the existence of the second bottle. It could be the break in the case he was looking for.

But her late-night activities would land center stage in an investigation of what was starting to look a lot like murder, and Andre Morales would be right in the spotlight. New lovers were hard enough to find without turning them over to the local law enforcement agency at the first sign of trouble. He couldn't be involved. But what if he was? What if Andre knew about the wine being phony? What if he was involved in its production? What if he knew more about Nathan's death than he was saying? That Andre might be involved in murder was impossible to even contemplate. What made more sense, if any of this made sense at all, was that Nathan had discovered the fraudulent wine and had been killed to keep him quiet. In that case, Andre might be in danger as well, especially if word got out that he'd had his hands on the bogus Marceline. There were more leaps and assumptions than she was comfortable with, but there were too many coincidences and she had to start somewhere. The important thing now was to find out where the phony wine came from, who knew about it, and if it had anything to do with Nathan's death. If Andre was involved, she wanted to know exactly how before she said anything about it to the police—and before she got further involved with him. Regardless of what she ultimately discovered, the faster she moved, the better. One thing was certain, there was more to Nathan Osborne's death than heart disease.

Sunny went over to the mirror, hoping the ritual of freshening up would calm her down. While she combed her hair unnecessarily, smoothed powder over her nose, and glossed her lips, she wondered how much she really knew about Andre Morales anyway. She knew he was born in September, had a promising career as a chef, and lived in the kind of house where the sheets and towels coordinated nicely with the rugs, duvet, and curtains. She knew he was born in Mexico, had tiger eyes, and wore a leather jacket that smelled like pine pitch and campfire smoke. She knew that one of his kisses could open a view to a wide landscape of desire, and that his biceps, round and full, were good places to let her hands come to rest. All of that was sweet and lovely, the stuff of pleasant daydreams, but it didn't tell her where he got that Premier Grand Cru Reservée or if he had anything to do with dropping the second bottle in Nathan Osborne's living room.

He would probably be waiting for her when she got back upstairs. She foraged for a mint, as though fresh breath would help her think of what she would say to him, and walked out rehearsing excuses. A server coming out of the wine cellar nearly ran into her as he pushed out the door and jogged upstairs without a second look. She looked at the cellar door. Almost before the idea occurred to her, she slipped inside.

She didn't bother checking the racks in the middle of the room. What she was looking for was bound to be locked away in one of the alcoves. Nathan and Andre had at least two things in common, namely Vinifera and Château de Marceline. It stood to reason that both bottles probably came from Vinifera's cellar, which would be the closest, most convenient source. It was worth having a look, at least. Sunny walked around a mountain of boxed cases to the other side of the cellar, where she peered through the grating on the locked alcoves at the bottles laying down inside. All she could see were the logos stamped into the foil at the end of the bottles on the first rack. There was almost no chance she would see anything useful in the gloomy light without a key to the grating, but she looked into each alcove anyway, hoping to find something. She was at the far end of the cellar, near the last of the alcoves, when the door opened and she saw Remy Castels come in with another man walking behind him.

She froze in the shadows, hoping they wouldn't look in her direction and quickly trying to think of a reason for her to be there. If they noticed her, she could always say she was curious about their wine collection in a professional capacity and wanted to make some notes. That might not suggest the best manners, but it was at least plausible. She watched them walk over to the main racks and turn down one of the rows. They wouldn't see her unless they walked to the end of it and looked to the right. She crept over to a far stack of boxes, walking on the toes of her shoes like Catwoman, and sunk down behind them. She listened to them moving around the cave. The man said something she couldn't hear. Remy's reply was too muffled to make out. They rounded a corner and she could hear them more clearly. Remy said, "I'd have to check, but I don't think we've bought any in months. He made those bottles last."

"At that price, I'm sure as hell glad he did," said the other man. His deep voice resonated in the stone chamber.

"He drank very little of that kind of thing lately," said Remy. The man chuckled. "You'd never know it."

They turned down another row and Remy said, "What did you need, the ninety-four?" and the other's voice said, "Ninety-six."

"Take the ninety-four. Tell them it's worth the extra fifteen dollars. If they resist, give it to them at the same price as the ninety-six."

"Will do."

She heard heavy footsteps and then the door, presumably the other man leaving. Remy's shoes made a soft, coarse sound as he moved down the rows of wine. His steps grew louder as he walked toward her, along the corridor that went past the alcoves. She edged further away, crouching low and hugging the cardboard boxes of wine. He stopped and she heard the jangle of keys and a lock opening on one of the grate doors. A few minutes later it shut with a loud metallic clang and he walked back across the cellar to the main door and out. She exhaled with relief and walked around the far end of the cases toward the door.

All that adrenaline was a waste of time. If she was going to find a bottle of Marceline in this place, she was going to need those keys. She was trying to think of ways that that might happen when, off to her left, a stack of boxes caught her eye. Several cases had been set aside on a pallet and secured with the wide plastic wrap used to hold shipments of cartons together. One of the boxes was labeled "Château de Marceline St.-Quinisque." Forget the keys.

She went over to have a closer look. The box on top had been opened. Looking around first to make sure she was alone, she lifted one of the cardboard flaps and pulled up a bottle. The foil was red. The label said "1967 Premier Grand Cru Reservée," with "Michel Verlan" spelled out in red capital letters near the bottom, an etching of a château faint in the background. She lifted the other flap. Two bottles were missing from the case. She let the flaps drop and stepped back. A piece of paper with "Do Not Touch—Reserved for Wine Club" written on it in black marker was taped to the boxes and sealed over with cellophane.

Her heart was beating hard as she went upstairs and walked back to the bar. She waited for Nick to work his way over to her. When he got there, she asked him to tell Andre she wasn't feeling well and had gone home. He said for her to wait just a second and he would go get Andre so she could tell him herself, but she said, no, she needed to leave right now, and would call him later.

He gave her a concerned look. "All right, whatever you say. Are you okay?"

"I don't think it's serious. I just don't want to get sick again," she said. People left you alone when your stomach was threatening, she found.

On the way out she stopped at the hostess stand and introduced herself to the woman on duty, saying she was interested in talking with someone about Vinifera's wine club.

"You'd want to speak to the sommelier, Remy Castels, about that. It's not really a Vinifera thing. All we do is provide the space," said the hostess. "I can give you his card."

"That would be great."

"He has a group that comes in once a month. They do a tasting and he recommends wines for them to cellar."

"And they buy the wines from him?" Sunny asked.

"I believe so, but you'll have to ask Remy for the details."

"Thanks, I will."

Sunny smiled and shouldered her little handbag. As she reached the curtain she glanced back at the bar. Andre still had not come out of the kitchen. In a few steps she was out the door and into the night, where she exhaled a breath she didn't realize she'd been holding.

8

Certain small but potent pleasures made living alone bearable, even enjoyable. High on Sunny's list was the freedom to come home late at night, sit cross-legged on the worktable in the middle of the kitchen, eat corn flakes, and watch bad TV, sans remorse. She sat there for the first bowl without turning on the television, staring at the milky gray screen, thinking about Remy Castels. No wonder he didn't like anyone poking around in his cellar. She was ready to believe he knew all about that case of wine.

She got up to refill her bowl from the box of corn flakes. Was anything really sans remorse? She shook the box doubtfully and poured another bowl. Nothing was simple anymore. What she'd grown up thinking was the most basic food, the corn flake, was not what it appeared to be. For some time now, a person's standard equipment hadn't been sufficient to do its job of identifying what was good to eat and what wasn't. The factories did an excellent job of fooling the senses. It might look like a corn flake, smell like a corn flake, and taste like a corn flake, but it was probably made from a fish-corn Frankenstein hybrid, some part of which had been milled, extracted, mashed, strained, bleached, and irradiated until it tasted like cardboard and lasted twice as long, then doctored up to imitate what it might have started out as in the first place: corn. Gene-spliced seeds, irradiation, fungicides—there was no way to know anymore what you were soaking up even if you grew it yourself. All you could really do was light a candle for the immune system and soldier on.

She hit the flakes with a dose of creamy whole milk, dumped in a tablespoon of sugar, and turned on the TV. PBS was showing a rerun of the *Antiques Roadshow* that she'd seen twice already. She tweaked the rabbit ears. For weeks PBS seemed to be running nothing but *ARS*, or the BBC documentary about George Mallory's final trip up Mount Everest. Sunny could watch the Everest show over and over. What *did* happen to Mallory and his climbing partner, Sandy Irvine? Did they make it to the top? What went wrong?

For years she'd sworn off the glowing box. It was only a couple of months ago, when the neighbors upgraded the mini-set they kept in the bathroom and left their old one on top of the garbage cans, with rain clouds gathering, that she decided to alter her policy. Rather than let the little TV fill with water and take a one-way trip to landfill, she had carried it inside and plugged it in.

Sunny added another spoonful of sugar to her cereal and, riveted, watched a mustached man, probably in his late forties, hand over an African spirit healer's mask from the seventeen hundreds. The priceless mask was assessed to be a skillful reproduction of modest value. The owner tried to appear indifferent, but his cheeks flushed pink and his eyes darted left and right, searching for a safe place to rest. He said he had always liked the mask for its intrinsic virtues anyway, that he had always been fond of the looks of it, regardless of its material value or authenticity. Sunny didn't believe him. It was quite obvious that he had never liked the mask and couldn't wait to get rid of it, and now hated it all the more for its falseness. People would lie spontaneously, almost involuntarily, to escape the most minor of embarrassments.

Catelina Alvarez, the Portuguese grandmother who had lived across the street from Sunny throughout her childhood, had been a tireless hunter of lies. She loved to catch one and expose it.

"A lie is the sound a hollow heart makes," she would say, frowning and waggling her finger in warning. She would look at Sunny with eyes that made it clear that it was no use hiding or twisting words and say, "The truth is like water, Sonya. It might trickle away and hide, but it's not gone. It's just waiting until the right moment to bubble up. The truth is always there, waiting for a chance to get out, and there is nothing that makes it want to come out more than a lie. The more lies, the more the truth pushes and pushes toward the light."

At midnight, Sunny turned off the television. Lies. Who was telling lies? Where was the truth waiting to bubble up?

She'd start with the wine. *In vino veritas.* Truth in wine. But if at least one bottle—maybe a case, maybe more—was a lie, the person behind the wine must be the one doing the lying. She decided it was time to talk to Remy Castels.

She found his address online easily enough. With luck, it was the current one. Buoyed by relief earlier in the day—what now seemed like a far-off, happier time—she'd brought her laptop home to hunt for cheap airfares for a spring trip, possibly to southern Italy. Instead, she was doing exactly what she swore she would never do again, getting involved in trouble that was none of her business. Except that she was already involved and it had become her business the minute she met Andre Morales.

Sunny rummaged in a cabinet for a decent bottle of wine and extracted a Green and Red Zinfandel from a few years back. Too good for a night like tonight, when a glass was all she wanted. Finally she settled on a newish bottle of Turnbull someone had brought to a dinner party.

She opened the bottle and filled a glass with the inky red wine. So, she'd go to Remy's house in the morning, unannounced. That ought to make him very friendly. And she would accuse him of wine fraud or imply as much, another great way to make a new friend. She needed to tread lightly and not alienate him with hasty accusations. She might be jumping to the wrong conclusion altogether. It was possible that he didn't know anything about the wine and was duped himself, in which case he might be grateful for the information. Monty Lenstrom had spotted the mistake just by looking at the cork, but maybe Remy had never had that chance. Since he was reselling it, he may never have opened one. The only way for him to tell would have been the color of the foil, and that could have easily slipped past him. He may not have even looked at the wine. Anyone might have opened the box and removed a couple of bottles. On the other hand, if he was guilty, letting him know she was on to him wouldn't help matters. It could even be dangerous.

The phone rang and she went to have a look. The caller ID said Vinifera, meaning it was Andre wondering where she was and why she wasn't getting back to him. There was no good answer to that question right at the moment. She let it ring.

She wanted to have something to drop off as a pretense for her visit to Remy tomorrow morning, not that it would make her intentions any less obvious. A casserole was the traditional food of bereavement, but that wouldn't be terribly appealing at seven-thirty in the morning. She opened a few cupboards and examined the supplies on hand. There were the basics for baking and not much else. Biscotti was an option, or maybe morning buns. She noticed a Ball jar filled with apricot pits that had been on the counter for several months. Maybe it was time to use them. Remy Castels would know how much work it was to extract the tiny kernels inside the pits, called *noyau*, and he might even appreciate the effort. Well, probably not, but it was hard to imagine anyone turning away a plate of morning buns with *noyau* frosting, which would smell and taste like sweet almond. The project also had the benefit of keeping her hands busy, and it might help focus her thoughts. At the moment her mind was leaping with the kind of questions that would stand squarely in the way of sleep.

She found the nutcracker and went to work. The apricot pits released their seal with a woody crack, revealing the tiny, smooth seed inside. When there was a tablespoon of them in the bottom of the mortar, she ground them into a coarse powder and added it to a saucepan of simmering heavy cream. After cooling and heating the mixture several times, she put it in the refrigerator. The cream would continue to soak up the essence of the ground *noyau* until it was strained away.

The morning buns were a simpler task. She mixed up a batch of the sweet, stretchy dough and set it aside to rise.

With the preparations done, she ran a bath and settled in. Remy was onto a good thing with his wine club, she thought. It would be relatively easy to fake a bottle of wine, especially if you were certain that no one would open it for ten years. All he would have to do is soak the bottle in soapy water overnight and the label would slide right off. She did it herself whenever she wanted to keep a label for her wine journal. Then all he needed to do was scan the label from the more expensive wine, print it out on a good printer, trim it, and stick it on. Up at Skord Mountain, she'd helped Wade put plenty of labels on bottles. There wasn't anything fancy about the process, it was just paper and glue. Some wine labels had gold lettering, embossments, and other flourishes, but Marceline didn't. Its label was very plain, stoic.

She added more hot water to the bath. A certain scenario kept running through her mind. Assuming Remy was the one who doctored the wine, suppose that Nathan Osborne found out about it and threatened to expose him. Remy then silenced him in the most permanent way. But how could Remy induce a heart attack without leaving any trace in the body? If that was the plan, and assuming there was a way to execute it, wouldn't it be smart to create rumors of heart trouble? Maybe there wasn't time. Maybe Nathan had threatened to expose his crime right away. She thought about Remy, remembering the few times she'd seen him, searching for signs of what he was capable of. He had a sour, persnickety disposition, but he was French and a wine connoisseur. An uppity demeanor was practically mandatory. There was more than that. He seemed sneaky and surreptitious. Did that mean he was capable of murder?

It was all speculation, and none of it explained how Andre got hold of his bottle of the phony wine or who smashed the other bottle at Nathan's feet. If she went to Sergeant Harvey, what she knew together with what he knew and wasn't telling her might point to the killer, assuming there was a killer. It might also point to Andre, though, who could be smack in the middle of some kind of get-rich-quick scheme, or look like he was. Even if everyone at the restaurant were innocent, if it was Osborne Wines or the importer who had forged the wine, the publicity was sure to hurt Vinifera and Andre. He would look at her as the one who called in the cops to check out his restaurant.

She couldn't risk going to Steve without a clearer and more convincing reason to do so.

By the time she got out of the bath and put on her fleece hoody and warm-ups, the dough was ready to be worked. She kneaded it into one smooth ball, then into Hacky Sack–sized buns. With each one she rolled and placed on the baking sheet, she thought of another question for Remy Castels.

It was almost three o'clock in the morning by the time she pulled the last tray of morning buns out of the oven, three-thirty when her head hit the pillow, and six when the alarm went off.

9

Meyer lemons were scattered on the lawn under the tree in front of what Sunny supposed was Remy Castels' house, a tidy white bungalow sitting demurely back from a quiet Napa street. She walked up to the porch carrying the plate of morning buns and stood listening, half hoping he would be home, half praying he wouldn't be. She looked at the morning buns with regret, wishing she'd eaten one on the way over, and maybe chosen a different plate. It wasn't her best plate, but it wasn't her worst either, and she was a little sorry to see it go. The buns smelled sweet and buttery. The idea occurred to her that she could still turn around and get back in the truck, eat a couple of morning buns, drink some coffee out of the thermos, and head into work like nothing bad ever happened in Napa Valley. She could forget what she knew about the case of fake Marceline and go on with her life. Of course, that might mean she would never find out where it came from or if Andre Morales had anything to do with it.

She rang the doorbell. The sound of water running in pipes suggested someone was home. She rang again and waited. After a while, she heard footsteps and the door opened. Remy Castels stared at her from his bathrobe and pajamas, both cotton and reminiscent of a Japanese bathhouse.

"Yes?" he said, looking at her blankly.

"It's Sunny McCoskey. We met on Sunday," she said, "at Vinifera."

"I know who you are," said Remy, looking behind her as if he expected to see someone else there. "Why are you here?"

"I know how upset you must be about Nathan's death," she said with determination. "I did some baking last night, and since I was on my way to work, I thought I would stop by and leave you a few morning buns for breakfast."

"Morning buns," said Remy dryly.

"With *noyau* frosting," said Sunny.

"*Noy-au*," said Remy. "Not *no-yau*. Let me get this straight. You drove twenty minutes out of your way at seven o'clock in the morning to try to poison me."

"What do you mean?" she said, smiling curiously at what she was sure must be a joke.

"*Noyau* are toxic," he said. "Poisonous."

"Yes, well, that's technically true," she said slowly, "but only if you eat the seed itself, and lots of them. It's only the flavor in the icing. The seeds are strained away. It's perfectly safe. I've made *noyau* frosting and ice cream for years." She hadn't even thought about the poison seeds, at least not consciously.

"But is it a nice gift, to give someone food that might be poisonous?"

"That's ridiculous," she said, with a small laugh. "*Noyau* is poisonous the way nutmeg is a hallucinogen. If I brought you a pitcher of eggnog, would you think I was trying to drug you?"

"How did you find out where I live?" he said, not lightening up.

"I found your address on the web. I decided to take the risk that you wouldn't mind the intrusion."

He stared at her with a look of appalled disbelief she hadn't seen since she started eating before grace at Heather Prine's house in sixth grade and Heather's parents had gawked at her like she'd driven a knife into the table.

"Is this your usual method of making new acquaintances?" he said, frowning. "Invading their privacy at the crack of dawn?"

He was having a fine time making her feel uncomfortable. Perhaps she deserved it for trying to hide her real motive for coming to see him. All the more reason to get to the point quickly.

"It's my method when I need to speak with someone urgently about an important matter," said Sunny.

"What important matter is that?"

"I was hoping we could talk for a moment about your wine club. Specifically, I would like to talk about the case of 1967 Château de Marceline St.-Quinisque Premier Grand Cru Reservée set aside for your wine club in the cellar at Vinifera."

"An exceptional wine," he said, an icy look in his eyes.

"I wouldn't know. But I am interested in where it came from."

"You can buy it from any distributor. It may take some weeks, but anyone should be able to get it, for the right price."

"I don't want to buy it. I don't think many of my customers would spend that kind of money on wine at lunch. I was just curious about where that particular shipment came from."

"Curiosity," he said, "is a nice word for a nasty habit. In France, curiosity is for old ladies who have nothing better to do than peek out of windows. Don't you have anything better to do with your time? I should think running your own restaurant would keep you busy enough."

She felt the heat of anger rising in her cheeks, but it didn't matter what he said. Snippy was fine. Rude was fine. As long as he kept talking and didn't slam the door in her face, she was in business. She looked over her shoulder. The neighborhood was beginning to stir. She could hear a garage door opening nearby, and across the street a man with a briefcase and a mug of coffee was getting into his car.

"Let's just skip where it came from for the moment," said Sunny sternly. "Because you and I both know the answer to that. The more important question is, how are you going to keep me from contacting the police about it?"

Remy frowned. "I have no idea what you're talking about."

"I can show you," she said.

Her heart was beating fast and her hands had started to shake so that she had trouble keeping the plate of morning buns steady. She fished in her jacket pocket with one hand and took out the cork from the bottle of Marceline that Andre had opened Sunday night and held it up for Remy to see.

"Is this the cork from a bottle of 1967 Château de Marceline St.-Quinisque Premier Grand Cru Reservée?" she asked.

He took it and examined the stamp.

"It is from a bottle of Marceline, I couldn't be sure which one. A red wine, obviously."

"But you think it could be from a bottle of Grand Cru?"

"Who knows? It might be, it might not." He looked at her questioningly and handed the cork back. Was it possible he really didn't know? She didn't believe it.

"I wonder what I would find," she said, "if I visited the people who belong to your wine club and had a look at the collections you helped them build? I wonder what an expert might notice about the expensive wines they've bought from you? Would odd little details jump out at him? Like that the topping foil is the wrong color, the corks aren't quite right, and the wine doesn't taste exactly like it ought to?"

She realized she was getting a little carried away, stretching what she suspected about one case of wine into a whole pattern of fraud, but this was her shot at Remy, and she had the element of surprise.

Remy glared at her and crossed his arms. "I seriously doubt that the members of my wine club would open their front door, let alone a single bottle of their wine, to satisfy your whim."

She put the cork back in her pocket and nodded slowly. She was beginning to regret the morning buns, which had failed to smooth over the visit and were now making it hard to look tough. She was getting nowhere.

"Okay," she said, trying to seem unfazed. She used what she knew was her last bit of ammo. "We both know that that case of Marceline in Vinifera's cellar is fraudulent to the tune of about eight grand. Are you going to let me in, or am I going to go to the police right now?"

Remy stared at her for a moment, then reluctantly stood aside. She handed him the plate of morning buns and entered the house. He led the way into the living room.

"Have a seat," he said, gesturing toward a couch. "I'll be back in a moment."

The room was elegantly decorated but cluttered with artifacts competing for notice. The couch was upholstered in wine-red velvet, the dark wood floor lined with kilim rugs in shades of ruby and purple, and the bookshelves loaded with hundreds of old, unjacketed volumes on the theory and practice of winemaking. Mementos of winemaking covered every surface. There was an old wire wine bottle caddy from a French café, a stack of letterpress menus from nineteenth-century French wine bars, and, on a side table, an assortment of what looked like handblown wine bottles, unevenly shaped and presumably very old.

The walls were painted thunderhead gray, including the ceiling, which sat close overhead, heavy and low. Across from the couch was a gas fireplace with a porcelain log burning orange, and on the mantel, rows of antique corkscrews and absinthe spoons were set out like rusty surgical instruments. Velvet curtains a shade darker than the walls prevented the morning sun from coming in. She wondered if it would feel less oppressive if the purpose of her visit were more pleasant.

The heat felt stifling. She took off her jacket and waited. The kettle piped in the kitchen and several minutes later Remy appeared carrying a tray with two cups of tea, cream, and sugar. He had changed into a black T-shirt and jeans. He put the tray down, carefully set one of the cups in front of her, then took up the other cup for himself. He had apparently brewed the tea and poured it in the kitchen, because there was no pot and there were tiny bits of leaves floating in the cup. Where was the teapot? Why not bring it out? Such a small thing, and yet it seemed symbolic, like he was hiding something. She stirred cream and sugar into her tea.

"This tea was grown on the estate of my mother's family in Ceylon," said Remy. "I think you'll find it unlike any other you've tasted."

She took a tentative sip and put the cup down. "It's very good," she said.

"That is hardly enough to taste it properly," he said. "You won't get another chance for tea like this without taking a very long journey. You can't buy anything like it in the States."

Sunny looked at Remy, sitting across from her with his cup of tea on his lap, playing the part of the pleasant host. "I'd like your opinion on something," she said.

Remy waited, watching her.

"I would like to know," she said, "how you think a bottle of the wine club's Marceline ended up broken in the middle of Nathan Osborne's living room on Saturday night."

"How do you know it was the wine club's Marceline?" he said.

"Isn't it?" she asked.

"It might be, it might not," he said. "If it is, my guess is that Nathan removed it from the cellar himself. He was in the habit of tasting whatever wine interested him, and that wine in particular was of great interest, being relatively unusual."

Remy picked up a silver tastevin from the end table beside him. He turned the little cup in his hands, rubbing its embossed handle with his thumb between revolutions. Sunny waited. Was it a nervous gesture, or the unconscious adoration of a collector for his treasure?

"You mean he would just take wine home from Vinifera's cellar?" she asked.

"Certainly. As owner of both Osborne Wines and Vinifera, he viewed every bottle in our cellar as his to take, which was true in a sense, though not of the wine club stock. But he wouldn't have paid attention to that. Nathan wasn't one for technicalities."

"That would account for one of the two bottles missing from the case. Where is the other one?"

"I see you've made an inventory," he said. "I have no idea. I only discovered that the wine was missing in the first place after the police mentioned the broken bottle on Monday. Naturally, as I have paid for it already, I would like to know. You have the cork, maybe you took it."

She smiled. "You yourself said that cork might have come from any bottle of Marceline."

"So which one did it come from?" he asked.

"It didn't come from a Grand Cru, that much I know for sure," she said. "Let's get back to the bottle in Nathan's living room. Nick Ambrosi says it looked like it was broken after he was already dead, and the police agree. You must know that from talking with them."

"Yes."

"Then Nathan couldn't have been the one who dropped it."

"That seems a safe assumption."

"Who do you think did?"

"I have no idea," said Remy. "What makes you think I would know anything about it?"

She'd thought all this through last night and on the way over, thought about each card she had to play, knowing this would be a game of bluff. It was time to take the plunge and hope he would give her something more to go on.

"I'll tell you what I think," said Sunny, leaning toward Remy. "I think you faked that case of wine. I think you did it for the money. You bought the standard-release Marceline, soaked the labels off, and replaced them with phony Premier Grand Cru Reservée labels. The label on the box was easy. I think you've done it before, maybe you've done it for years. You put, what, an extra seven, maybe eight thousand dollars in your pocket with every case?"

Remy smiled at her coolly. "Don't you want your tea? It's best when it's still hot."

He turned the tastevin in his hands, staring at her. His eyes were dark gray, like the wall behind him, and like the limp strands of hair pushed behind his ears. She lifted her teacup and sipped, looking over it at him. The revelation that she'd found out about his forgeries did not seem to have had much of an impact. She decided to push harder.

"It should be relatively easy to prove what's been going on," she said matter-of-factly. "You obviously don't have invoices for the Premier Grand Cru Reservée, since you never bought it, but you'll have the income from having sold it. And I'm sure there is plenty of evidence on your computer. It might take a recovery expert to get at the deleted files, but the scanned images are probably still on the hard disk somewhere. They say it takes months to write over memory. Even if I can't prove that you perpetrated the fraud yourself, you will still have been caught dealing in forged wine, which I'm sure isn't good for a sommelier's reputation. Eliot certainly won't be amused, and I can't imagine that the people at Marcclinc will enjoy having their name sullied with the publicity this kind of crime generates."

His eyelids were half lowered and he gazed at her with a drowsy expression. If she didn't know better, she would guess he was bored.

"One thing puzzles me," said Remy. "I don't understand why you would choose to make any of this your business. Why do you care? Suppose you're right and the wine isn't what it's supposed to be. What is the harm of a few gullible rich people drinking the wrong grape juice? They don't really care what it tastes like anyway, trust me. The thrill is in the expense. They want to pay excessive amounts of money. It's part of the high. It makes them feel powerful and privileged. In fact, you may be onto something. Repackaging wine might not be such a bad idea. That way, the rich customers get what they want, the repackager gets what he wants, and someone else, perhaps someone who actually understands what he is drinking and can appreciate it properly, gets to buy the real Reservée, of which, as you know, there is an extremely limited supply. I'm starting to like this idea of yours."

She smoothed her bangs to the side with her fingers. Was it getting even hotter? She had the urge to pant, like when she was sick to her stomach. The tea. Did he put something in the tea, or was it just too hot in this room?

"Let me be very clear about this," she said, struggling to keep her voice steady. "I'm going to need some kind of cooperation from you, or else I'm going to have to go to the police with what I know right now. Why I care is irrelevant to you. I have my reasons. But I know something and I can't not know it."

"What interests could you possibly have in anything that goes on at Vinifera? It has nothing to do with you," he said.

"I think you're missing my point," said Sunny, losing her patience. "It's not important that *you* know or understand *my* motives. Someone is dead, someone is committing wine fraud, and unless I get your help, I'm going to the police with my theories, right or wrong."

Remy put his head down and rubbed his temples. After a long pause, he looked up at her. "There is no reason to discuss any of this. It's in the past. It's over. The guilty party is beyond punishment, and the victims never knew what happened and were only harmed in ways they could afford. Nathan came up with the idea a couple of years ago. I was never involved."

"You mean you didn't participate." Sunny tried not to seem too relieved that he had finally cracked.

"No."

"But you didn't stop him."

"He signs my paycheck."

Sunny nodded. "Nathan owned two businesses, both of them successful. You're telling me he risked it all for penny-ante wine fraud? And if that's the truth, why would he involve you in it?"

"Nathan wasn't as financially secure as some people would like to believe," said Remy. "A few thousand on the side every now and then could make a big difference. I have to admire the scheme. You fake a few of the very expensive wines that get sold to an audience that self-selects for people guaranteed to have a great deal of money and no idea what they are buying. Nobody gets hurt and he puts a nice chunk of cash in his pocket." He paused. "That's the only good thing about his death. Now he'll never get caught."

Sunny watched his eyes, searching for signs of whether or not he was lying. She didn't like him or want to believe him, but he seemed to be telling the truth. "He won't get caught, but you might. What if somebody who knows what to look for gets hold of those bottles? Dealing in phony merchandise is a crime."

"I didn't do anything. I don't even know that anything has been done. Frankly, I'm not even sure Nathan ever acted on his idea, I just know he talked about it. I simply chose to look the other way. The forgery you are talking about, if that's what it is, has not been sold, and won't be until I check it out. This is much ado about nothing."

"I wonder if the police will buy that," said Sunny.

Remy walked over to the fireplace to adjust the flame. He turned to her with a smirk. "Go ahead and go to the police if it amuses you. It will only make a sad week more difficult for all of Nathan's friends, and the headlines certainly won't make your boyfriend feel any better. I'm sure Andre would love to see Vinifera and wine fraud splashed across every newspaper in the country."

She tried not to show any reaction. "Tell me more about why you think Nathan would do this. If anyone found out, it would ruin him and both of his businesses. His life in the Valley would be over, and he'd probably go to jail. What you're saying doesn't make any sense. He wouldn't take that kind of risk for what amounts to pocket change to a man like him."

"You didn't know Nathan," said Remy dryly. "He liked to play with people, and he liked taking risks, even foolish, pointless risks. It was how he had fun. The money was just an associative benefit. He especially liked to watch people rave about bad wine. I've seen him do it on a number of occasions. He liked to play tricks on them, especially if they pretended to know something about wine. I've seen him swap labels, funnel one wine into another bottle, lie about what's in a glass. I even saw him put food dye in a glass of cheap Chardonnay and serve it as a fine Burgundy. He loved to mess with people."

"Is that really who Nathan was?"

"That's who he was as long as I knew him, and that's close to six years."

Sunny frowned. There was one piece that didn't fit. She looked at Remy, who was leaning against the mantel with his hands dug in the pockets of his jeans. She cleared her throat. "If Nathan knew the wine-club wine was phony, if he'd gone to the trouble of doctoring its labels, why would he take a bottle of it home?"

Remy smiled as though pleased with the comment. "I'm not exactly sure, but my guess is that he forgot. We can make nice excuses, but in my opinion Nathan was an alcoholic. He drank more or less constantly. The only time he had a clear head was first thing in the morning. He also lied so much that he would forget the truth. After a while, he would believe the lie himself, or at least he couldn't tell the difference."

Sunny's head whirled as she listened to him. She wondered again if the tea had been drugged. The impulse to stretch out on the couch tempted her and it was all she could do to resist it. She focused on Remy's face. Their conversation would be over soon, and she could lie down in the truck. She heard a click like central heat coming on. Already the back of her neck was sticky with perspiration.

"Are you feeling okay? You look ill," he said. "Let me get you a drink."

He was right. She felt so tired. Remy came back with a glass of water.

"I need to go," she said, standing up suddenly. "We can finish talking about this later."

"My pleasure," said Remy with a reserved smile. "You know where to find me."

Outside, the cool air and morning sun revived her for a moment but walking down the pathway to the truck soon became an effort, her feet heavier with every step. She got in and drove a mile fighting sleep before she knew it was pointless, that the desire to sleep would overwhelm her. She pulled over in the middle of the suburban block and killed the engine. Sixties-era stucco houses lined both sides of the streets, each with its carport and allotment of exotic perennial shrubs imported from Southern California. The last thing she remembered was delicious relief as she stretched out in the cab and settled her cheek into her backpack like a pillow.

10

Sunny's mobile phone woke her up. All she knew at first was that a very loud sound had made her jolt upright. She sat stunned in the cab of the truck. There it was again, farther away now. She looked at her backpack, hardly recognizing what it was, other than the source of the mysterious sound. Gradually the world came back together a piece at a time and she remembered that she owned a mobile phone and that the sound was her phone ringing, which meant she was supposed to find it and answer it.

"Where are you?" Rivka was on the other end.

"What?" said Sunny in a dazed voice.

"Sunny? Where are you?"

"I'm in the truck."

"Where? Are you okay? You sound out of it."

"Just a sec." She put the phone down and stared dully at the dashboard, then yawned and looked around at the suburb where she'd parked. She picked up the phone again.

"What time is it?"

"Nine-fifteen."

"Shit. I'll be there in about ten minutes."

Sunny walked into Wildside without Rivka noticing. Rivka had the stockpot going and the ambient flamenco rave music cranked up good and loud, like a nightclub in Barcelona. She was at the big sink sorting through a box of produce and moving to the music. The steamy air and food smells in the kitchen reminded Sunny how good it was to be on familiar ground again. The spicy smell of fresh arugula leaves and the grassy smell of spinach, kale, and basil woke her up, while the smell of onions caramelizing in butter on the stove, the epitome of warmth, soothed her. The stockpot was sending up wafts of salty garlic chicken, celery root, carrot, and freshly squeezed lemon. She went over and ground a dose of pepper into the pot, then stepped into her office to turn down the music a few decibels. When she came back, Rivka looked over her shoulder at her.

"Where have you been? I was worried. At first I thought you were with Andre again, but he called twice looking for you."

"How could you hear the phone?"

Sunny found an apron and tied it around her hips. Rivka shook the water out of a basket of arugula and set it aside. She looked at Sunny again.

"Are you going to spill it or not? What happened to you this morning? You look a little fuzzy around the edges, if you don't mind me saying."

The espresso machine beckoned and Sunny went over to make herself a cappuccino. "It's a long story. I'm not sure where to start."

"Start with why you stood up Andre last night. He said you came by the restaurant but then you left before he could see you, and you didn't pick up when he called your house. He thinks you're mad at him because he took too long to come out of the kitchen."

"I'm not mad about anything. I just needed some time to think. Remember how everything was back to normal yesterday because Nathan Osborne didn't die of mushroom poisoning? Well, today we're back to not normal again. Very not normal as a matter of fact."

She explained what Nick Ambrosi had told her about the bottle of Marceline in Nathan Osborne's house.

"I couldn't decide what I was going to say to Andre, so I had to get out of there," said Sunny.

"I don't get it," said Rivka. "What's the big deal?"

"Two bottles of Marceline, wine fraud, Nathan's death. They have to be related. It's too much of a coincidence otherwise."

"Maybe, but I don't see why that means you can't talk to Andre."

Sunny finished steaming a pot of milk and spooned the creamy foam into her cup. She licked the spoon and looked at Rivka.

"You don't really think Andre is involved in something criminal?" said Rivka.

"How should I know? I hardly know the guy."

"You know. And I think you also know that you're freaking out. This is a textbook example of the power of the subconscious. Your well-documented fear of intimacy is manifesting itself as a literal fear of Andre. You need to get a grip. The best-looking guy in the Valley already thinks you hate him. You stood him up and didn't even bother to phone to say why. McCoskey, you're going to mess up a great thing before it even gets off the ground."

Sunny frowned. "You think so?"

"Absolutely. Trust me on this one. Andre Morales may be a lot of things, but he is not a murderer or a scam artist. Why would he do something like that? He's successful, his career is taking off. He's not going to risk all that for a little extra cash. The guy has everything to lose."

"Exactly," said Sunny, frowning.

"What do you mean, *exactly*?"

"I mean that he has everything to lose, if someone found out about something he did. He has a motive."

Rivka shook her head and went back to washing vegetables. Sunny sipped her cappuccino like it was medicine and watched Rivka work. She was wearing her standard back-of-house uniform: white tank top with a black camisole underneath for sauce, black studded belt, jeans generously cuffed at the bottom, black work stompers. On the backs of her slender arms were swallows tattooed in blue and red, one swooping back, the other forward, circling. It was impossible for Sunny to imagine her without her tattoos. It was equally impossible to tell her about her experience with Remy Castels that morning. Now that it was broad daylight and Rivka was standing in front of her looking perfectly sane and normal, none of it made sense. Bursting in on Remy, imagining he'd drugged her, suspecting he was lying about Nathan. But things she knew to be true didn't always sound right either.

"You know what is happening," Rivka said without turning around.

"What?"

"Your inner control freak is seizing up."

Rivka looked back at Sunny, who raised her eyebrows dubiously.

"You know I'm right," said Rivka. "You let down your guard for a little while on Sunday. You let the genie out of her bottle for the night and she went and had a great time, and now you're vulnerable. You're scared you're going to get hurt because you like Andre Morales too much and you got in too deep, too fast. So the answer is to create a problem. There has to be a problem, because then you can fix it, thereby regaining control of your life. And if you can shove him away in the process, all the better. Competence is your security blanket, McCoskey, and you have to have a crisis in order to exhibit your competence, so you are manufacturing one."

"Go on, doctor. Tell me what you think."

"I've seen it for years now. When things get stressful, you work. It's a decent coping mechanism professionally, but it doesn't work so well when it comes to love. You can't control love. No matter how meticulous and smart and diligent you are, love can still bite you in the ass. There is nothing you can do to make love a safe place."

"Oy." Rivka was sounding old for twenty-four, Sunny thought.

"That is the sound that says I'm right and you know it. Face it, you're risk averse. You have your world set up the way you like it with your restaurant and your house and you're not about to jeopardize any of that. Only there's something missing in your life, and you're going to have to let go of controlling everything in order to get it."

"Are you seeing Doug again?" asked Sunny. Rivka's therapist.

"Not professionally. We had a drink last week."

"He gave you a freebie."

"I said I would cater his kid's birthday party."

"A three-year-old needs a caterer for his birthday party?"

"Egg salad sandwiches, curly fries, and Jell-O parfait."

"Reasonable. What does he say about you and Alex?"

"That we should take a few weeks apart."

"Because?"

"Don't change the subject. You should give Andre a chance. You're perfect for each other. Did you happen to get a look at yourself Monday morning? I haven't seen you that happy since Monty slipped on a banana peel coming out of Bismark's."

"That was such a beautiful sight. I love it when life imitates cliché. If I should die suddenly, I want you to commission a mural for downtown of Monty slipping on the banana peel. Do it for me."

"Fine. No problem."

"So why do you and Alex need a few weeks apart?"

"Cooling-off period before we restart negotiations. You know how I feel. I love him, but I'm not ready to sign up for a lifelong partnership and he is. It doesn't matter how perfect Alex is, I can't make that kind of commitment right now. We need a few weeks to come to terms with the inevitable."

"Ouch."

"I know. That's why it's more fun to think about you and Señor Morales. I have a really good feeling about it."

"His body rocks the house," said Sunny.

"It's more than that and you know it."

"His jacket smells like a campfire and he uses soap that smells like a lumberyard."

"That's good?"

"Very good."

"You can take the girl out of the boondocks, but you can't take the boondocks out of the girl."

"Especially when she never left the boondocks."

"Yeah, but the boondocks went upscale."

"Les Boondocks."

They fell silent and worked for a while without talking. It was one of those sublimely quiet winter mornings, when the whole world was happy to go dormant for a few weeks.

"Okay, how about this," said Rivka finally. "What if Lenstrom is wrong and there's nothing wrong with the wine?"

"No, he's right."

"How do you know?"

"I checked."

Actually, she hadn't checked. There wasn't time. But Remy's reaction to her accusation had proved the wine was fake. She took the caramelized onions off the heat and started a new batch.

"I was up really late last night," Sunny said.

"Baking what?" said Rivka, smiling.

"Morning buns with *noyau* frosting."

"*Noyau* frosting. How long did that take?"

"Not that long. I went to see Remy Castels this morning."

Rivka looked at her. "The sommelier? Why?"

"I figured I would stop by to see what he knew about the two Marcelines."

Rivka's eyes widened. "And?"

"He wasn't very happy to talk about it."

"I'll bet. The man thinks he runs the best cellar in the Western world and you come in and tell him his most expensive wine is a swindle."

"More or less."

The rest of Wildside's staff was starting to arrive. Bertrand, the maître d', had come in and was stocking the wine bar. The two servers came in soon after and started getting the floor ready. Sunny checked the kitchen clock. The lunch rush would start in two hours. She barely had time to get ready. It was time to stop talking and get serious. Besides, what she had to say even she didn't believe. Rivka was sure to think it was paranoia. Still, she had to tell someone.

"Riv, call me crazy, but I think he may have tried to drug me," she said softly.

"Who, Andre?"

"No, no, not Andre. I'm not that baked. Remy. This morning."

"You're kidding."

"No, really. I've never felt like that before, except maybe when I had the flu. You know how I am, I stay up all night all the time. It makes me a little loopy, but not like that. I passed out this morning."

"Are you serious?"

"I only had a few sips of the tea he served, but I barely made it out of there before I fell asleep."

"If you really think that's what happened, we should phone the police," said Rivka.

Sunny put a hand up for her to lower her voice.

"And I can say that I stayed up half the night baking for no particular reason," said Sunny in a whisper, "dropped in on a near stranger at the crack of dawn, then fell asleep for an hour afterward in my car and now I'd like them to arrest him because I think he drugged me. They'll have me locked up in Napa State by noon."

"You're right, it doesn't sound too good. So what are you going to do about it?"

"Nothing, other than politely decline anything Remy Castels pours for me until I figure out what's going on."

"Is there something going on?" Rivka said skeptically.

"I think so. I'm beginning to think it's something pretty bad, too. And I still don't know where Andre got that bottle of wine."

"Have you asked him?"

"No, not until I know more. I've been avoiding him. Besides, how can I ask him without admitting I think he might be involved in fraud or Nathan's murder, or both?"

Rivka scowled. "Now you're sure Nathan Osborne was murdered?"

"It's just a theory. Not even a theory. It's just a feeling."

"And where Andre got the wine is important to your theory?" said Rivka.

"Very."

"Listen, as your best friend, I can personally guarantee that Andre is innocent of any association with fraudulent wine."

"How do you know?"

"I just know."

Sunny narrowed her eyes. "Rivka Marie Chavez, you're holding out on me."

"I swore I wouldn't tell."

"We're not playing secrets. You might have a piece of the puzzle. I have to know."

Rivka sighed and came closer so she could speak softly. "I want it on record that I disclose this information under protest. I wasn't going to tell you, but you're being so weird about Andre and murder that I'm going to do it for your own good."

"Duly noted."

"Okay, I went over to Dahlia Zimmerman's house after work yesterday."

"Who is Dahlia Zimmerman?"

"Dahlia. The waitress at Vinifera with the turquoise hair and the butterfly."

"Oh yeah, right."

"She's a painter and I wanted to see her work. It's amazing, by the way. Pretty dark, but really interesting. I took some pictures. I'll bring the camera in and show you tomorrow."

Sunny nodded. "And?"

"And she told me some stuff about Nathan Osborne. How she dated him on and off for the last year. He sounded like an okay guy, just really bad in relationships and couldn't make up his mind. He was always breaking up with her, then coming back and saying he loved her and couldn't live without her, then breaking up with her again. Total bullshit. Anyway, recently they got back together and things seemed to be going pretty well. She was thinking they might really be falling in love and it's all great. So he invites her to dinner at his house. He says he's going to cook something special, because he has something important to talk with her about and he wants it to be just the two of them, not at a restaurant with everyone around. He says he's picked out a very special bottle of wine and everything. So she's thinking he's going to ask her to marry him or move in or something. She gets all dressed up and excited and she goes over to his house, and before they even sit down to eat, she figures out that he's not going to ask her to marry him, he's actually breaking up with her so he can go back to his old girlfriend again. He thought that if he made a fancy dinner and opened a pricey bottle of wine she would take it better."

"That's awful. But where is this going?"

"She was completely crushed, as well as sizably pissed off. So she tells him to take his dinner and put it where the breeze don't blow and stormed out. On her way out, she saw the bottle of wine he'd made such a big deal about and decided to take it with her. They were going to drink it that night, and she said she figured she was still entitled."

"Makes sense, I guess," said Sunny.

"Right. So, well, she was upset. And hurt. She's crying and angry. She's mad at herself for trusting him again, feels foolish, the whole deal. And it's still early."

Rivka paused, then went on. "She wanted to hurt Nathan any way she could."

"And?" said Sunny.

"Right," said Rivka cautiously. "So she calls up the one person she knows Nathan Osborne is jealous of and asks if she can come over."

"Oh."

"Should I stop?"

"No, bring it on. I can take it."

"Well, there's not much else to tell. I guess there had always been some chemistry there. She goes to his place with the wine, but they don't drink it."

"Because they're so busy."

"Or maybe they're not thirsty," said Rivka, generously. "You never know."

"Maybe they just stayed up late talking it through," said Sunny. "She had a nice cry on his shoulder and he sent her home."

"You wish! She said they got it on in a huge way."

"Riv!"

"You said you could take it! Now it's all out. Besides, it didn't mean anything to either of them."

"Somehow that doesn't make it better. When was this? It couldn't have been that long ago."

"Mm, it wasn't."

"Oh no. When?"

"Friday night before last."

"As in a week before he got together with me?"

"A week and two days."

Sunny shook her head and tried to go back to what she'd been doing, but the knife in her hand suddenly felt like a foreign object that she had no idea how to use. A loud noise seemed to fill her head, like aluminum siding being dragged across asphalt. She tried to think logically. Sure, she might have all kinds of feelings now, but a week ago she hardly knew Andre Morales. How could she be jealous about something that happened before she was even part of his life? Dahlia Zimmerman was a preexisting condition. Nothing to be upset about. So it was a little nauseating. Suggested some excessively flexible standards on Andre's part. Other than that, what was the problem?

"Not that I really want to know, but what happened after that?" asked Sunny.

"Nothing. It was just a night and then it was over," said Rivka, munching on a carrot.

"They're not still seeing each other."

"No, it's over. They're friends. She said they both think of it as an overstep brought about by traumatic circumstances. I wouldn't have told you about it at all, except you kept going on about where that wine came from. Now you know. Andre never knew it was phony."

"And she's not interested in him? Or him in her?"

"Not at all. She's still pretty shook up about Nathan. She was hardly over his last change of heart, then he died. That's all she talked about the whole time I was there. She said there was a point when she actually hated him. Apparently he flip-flopped on her several times. Said he loved her, wanted to be with her, then broke up over some little thing and went back to his previous girlfriend. Then a couple of months later he'd come back saying that she was the one he really loved, yadda yadda. She still wasn't talking to him the night he died. She said she felt horrible about it, that they never got a chance to make up. I think she still loved him. But she's starting to deal with it all now. She made a shrine for him. She built a wooden box and painted little tableaux on each panel, inside and out, and filled it with things associated with him. It's incredible looking. She's really talented."

"A shrine? She's worshiping him?"

"No, it's more like the shrines they make in Mexico when someone dies. You know, with candles and paper flowers and *milagros*. It's to honor the person's memory and wish them well on their spirit journey in the afterlife. She wants his soul to be at peace."

"Or so she says. Are you sure she hadn't made her voodoo shrine *before* he died? The guy dumped her."

"That's jealousy talking. She can't help that she knew Andre before you did."

"Everyone I talk to paints a completely different picture of Nathan Osborne and has a whole other reason to hate him—at the same time they profess to love him."

II

Something about the maître d's tone of voice
made Sunny look up just in time to see Andre Morales walking toward the counter where she was working at the end of
Wildside's lunch rush. It was a snapshot she would remember
for years to come, him unwrapping a black scarf from around his
neck, smiling at her as he approached. She finished firing a
shot of espresso, set a tiny spoon on the saucer, and curled a
strip of lemon zest on top, then put it up for the waiter to take.
When she was done she wiped her hands on a towel and leaned
across the zinc bar to give Andre a kiss on each cheek. Instead
he touched her chin and brought her mouth to his for a real kiss.

"I called you last night," he said, "but you must have been
asleep already. Nick said you weren't feeling well."

He looked into her eyes and she felt her face begin to heat up.

"Or maybe you weren't home yet," he said, giving her a mis-
chievous grin. "You look pretty healthy to me."

"I must not have heard it ring," said Sunny. She looked back
at Rivka, who was giving more attention than necessary to the
arrangement of a poached pear with chocolate sauce and trying
not to look like she was listening. Sunny walked around the
counter and gestured to an empty table.

A few stragglers dotted the room, lingering over coffee and dessert. Andre sat down and she took a seat opposite him, smoothing the sleeves of her jacket. He watched her, not in a hurry to say anything. He looked clean and rested, and she thought of her own appearance with regret. Her uniform was baggy and unflattering in the best of conditions, and now it was sticky with sweat and notably worse for the day's wear. The rest of her was no more presentable. She was covered head to toe in a thin layer of oil atomized from the grill so that the smell of grilled salmon and halibut, duck breasts, and pork loin seemed to ooze from her pores. Her face was shiny with grease and her short hair was tied up in little bunches all over her head, except for the very back, which lay against her neck like she'd styled it with aioli. She had the urge to pull her jacket up over her head and slink away, but a twinge of irritation saved her. Andre knew what a cook looked and smelled and felt like at the end of a shift. He should have known better than to arrive unannounced at the close of a long day, after she'd had a hectic, sleepless night. The fact that he didn't know she'd had a sleepless night or a harrowing morning at Remy Castels' house was no excuse.

He smoothed back his hair with both hands, gazing up at her from his black turtleneck. He was well dressed. She took in the charcoal trousers and the expensive designer shoes. Even his belt was pristine and lustrous. Most guys she knew wore whatever was within reach.

"The place looks great," he said, glancing around.

Wildside had only one room and a weather-permitting patio out French doors at one end, but it was a very pretty room, with stone walls and burnished concrete floors. She'd put up a show of moody but finely rendered oil landscapes by a local artist, and in the entry there was an arrangement of branches decked with kumquats. At one end of the counter, a tall wire vase overflowed with tangerines and a citrus bowl was heaped with Meyer lemons, the deeply saturated yellow of their skins luminous.

"And you look great," he said.

"The place looks great. I look terrible," she said.

"No, you look great. It's good to see you in your element."

The scent of woodsy cologne drifted across the table. Andre looked at her with a half smile and she felt a jolt of sense memory. For an instant, every cell in her body seemed to leap out of its chair at the thought of the night they'd spent together. His face had the creamy look of a very close shave and she would have leaned across and kissed it if she'd had the guts. He was wearing the same watch he'd had on the night they spent together, a heavy one with lots of dials. She remembered him releasing the steel band with a tug and dropping it on the bedside table. It made her catch her breath to think of it, his arm stretching across her to reach the nightstand. She lingered over the memory of the stretch of biceps, the seductive hollow of armpit.

"Are you okay?" he asked.

"Fine," said Sunny. "Never better. Do you want something to drink? Are you hungry?"

"No, I can't stay. I just thought I would stop by since I hadn't heard from you."

She nodded. His face was serious, waiting for her to say something. If she ever wanted to see him take that watch off again, she needed to come up with a decent explanation for standing him up, and quickly.

"I'm sorry I bolted last night," she said. "I thought I was coming down with something, but I think I was just dead tired."

It was his turn to nod silently. They both knew it wasn't much of an excuse. She couldn't think of anything more convincing short of telling an all-out lie, and she didn't want to do that. They were off to a rocky enough start as it was, and that last bit of intelligence about his night with Dahlia hadn't helped matters. She'd assumed Andre was a man of some experience when it came to the ladies, but the close proximity of his last connection was more than a little unsettling. He was waiting for her to go on, but she couldn't think of anything else to say.

"I brought you something," he said finally, taking a small package out of his jacket pocket. He set it on the table in front of her.

She picked it up. It was too light for a book, too thick for a CD. The package was wrapped in brown paper with a brown and tan striped feather on top, sewn in place with red thread. The Valley was full of peregrine falcons. The feather looked like it might be from one of them, or some other predatory bird. She often saw them standing watch from telephone lines and fence posts along the highway.

"I found that in the vineyard up at Mayacamas," he said. "Have you been there?"

"Once, a long time ago. Did you sew it?"

"I did," he said, sheepishly.

"Very crafty."

She eased the paper open. Inside was a glass-framed butterfly with gray and violet wings edged in black. It was very pretty and she was about to say so when she remembered another butterfly. Her expression froze.

"You don't like it," he said, looking worried.

"No, I absolutely like it. I love it. It's beautiful."

There was another silence while she tried to figure out how to respond to what seemed to be a symbol of his night with another woman. Was it just a coincidence? Her head filled with images of Dahlia Zimmerman lounging next to Andre, his fingers tracing the outline of wings. She knew it was silly to get upset about it, but it was too vivid to ignore.

"You really have a thing for butterflies, don't you," she said.

"What do you mean?"

"Nothing. Just that you seem to really like butterflies."

"This one is beautiful. What others are you thinking of?" he asked.

Why not just come out and ask him about Dahlia? Find out what that night meant to him, if anything? She couldn't do it, just like she couldn't ask him about the wine. Too many suspicions, too many seeming accusations so early in their relationship. It was a lose-lose undertaking. Either her fears would be justified, or he would be insulted.

She turned the butterfly to the light and examined its intricate wings dusted with color. Despite the complications, something about Andre Morales made her happy. Why was she rushing to condemn him based on extrapolation, inference, and hearsay? She had accepted Dahlia's story, told to her secondhand, as irrefutable truth. Of course Rivka wouldn't lie, but accepting such an account secondhand meant she'd lost the opportunity to watch Dahlia tell her story. She'd missed the details and the tone that would have told her what to make of it. A secondhand account was practically worthless. It was gossip. What Rivka said might not be entirely true, or might be missing some important piece of information that could change everything. As far as she knew, it was even theoretically possible, though she couldn't imagine why, that Dahlia had made the whole story up.

Andre sighed. "I knew it, it's the animal cruelty issue. I worried about that. You're not a vegetarian, are you?"

She laughed. "I'm not a vegetarian. Far from it. But you don't expect me to eat this, do you?"

"Not unless you want to."

"I think I'll pass."

"And the animal cruelty doesn't bother you?" he said.

"Was this butterfly tortured?"

"Well, not intentionally."

"You mean it may have been inadvertently tortured?" she said.

"Well, it is dead. It probably didn't go willingly."

"Yes," she said tentatively. "What exactly are we talking about here?"

"We're talking about why you don't like my present."

"I do like it. I love it."

"No, you don't. I can tell. It's the morbidity, isn't it? I knew that would be a problem. Taxidermy is always a risky gift, especially at the beginning of a relationship."

She laughed again. It was reassuring to see him worry. "It's beautiful. I love it. Really. It's perfect."

"I'm glad. I thought of you when I saw it. Its wings are the same color as your eyes."

She frowned, then gave him a wry smile. "That would be true if this butterfly were green," she said slowly.

Andre cleared his throat. "Let me see."

She looked at him intently, widening her eyes.

"Um, I see what you're saying. Did I mention I'm color-blind?"

"I don't think so."

"I am. I swear. You can ask Nick. That's why I always wear black."

"Then that was a pretty risky line to use."

"I thought there were more colors in the wings. But it really did make me think of you—and actually, to me, the wings *are* the same color as your eyes."

She laughed and he leaned across the table for another kiss. There seemed to be a good deal of kissing in this visit, and not without effect. This last one convinced her that there couldn't be anything to the butterfly. It was an unfortunate coincidence, that was all.

They chatted easily for the next few minutes, Sunny watching her own feelings with dismay. A few hours earlier she'd felt miles away from him. He'd seemed so unknowable as to be capable of anything, of lying, stealing, even of murder. Now it was like she knew everything there was to know about him, and that anything wrong had to be an accident or a misunderstanding. How quickly the love goggles descended, how securely they fell into place, making everything look so sweet and easy. Another silence seized them, a romantic one this time. It was interrupted by Bertrand, the maître d', who came over to whisper in her ear. Apparently one of the customers had cut his tongue on a piece of caramel lattice and was demanding something be done about it.

"Badly?" asked Sunny, not in a whisper.

He looked at her with the flat expression of a man accustomed to dealing with the public.

"He is still breathing," said Bertrand dryly. "I thought we could comp his dessert and offer him a digestif to ease the mental and physical anguish of his experience."

"That's fine," she said. "What do you think? There's that bottle of pear brandy from Nîmes that's really nice. I'd forget just about anything after a glass of that."

"My thoughts exactly," said Bertrand.

"I guess we probably ought to warn people about the caramel," said Sunny.

"We do." Bertrand stalked away and Andre raised his eyebrows inquisitively.

"Someone cut himself on a shard of spun sugar."

"Eating is dangerous," Andre said.

"It is like glass until it melts," Sunny said. She lowered her voice. "Still, what happened to the days when people who injured themselves eating dessert were embarrassed to admit it? We have lost all dignity. Sometimes I think there will actually come a time when I have to ask my customers to sign a waiver stating that they understand and accept the hazards of fine dining."

"You think you're joking," said Andre. "Eliot wanted the wait staff at Vinifera to warn anyone ordering the Caesar salad that it has raw eggs and they could get salmonella."

"And?"

"I said no way. It's ridiculous. Next we'll need plates printed with a warning that the food could be hot, and it must be chewed in order to be digested. You can't worry about that stuff. This is America, we'll all end up in court someday."

"I think full disclosure printed on the menu is the way to go," Sunny said. "Warning: The stuff under the peppercorn sauce is actually a hunk of dead cow. Warning: Organic carrots are grown in dirt fertilized with chicken poop."

"Warning: This cheese has been made from juice squeezed out of a goat's ta-tas and left to mold in a musty cave," Andre countered.

"Warning: Earwigs, ants, and spiders were crushed along with the grapes that made your wine," said Sunny.

Andre's brown eyes sparkled. "When?" he said, holding his hands out for hers across the table. "When do I get to see you again?"

There was no denying it, the guy made her melt like gelato on a warm night. After some scheduling back and forth they agreed to meet Friday night at Vinifera after he finished work. That gave her just over two days to figure out what was going on at Vinifera and how much Andre knew about it.

As they stood up and Andre put on his jacket, she realized she couldn't wait any longer. She certainly couldn't wait until Friday night. She had to ask, even if it was awkward.

"That Marceline was a remarkable bottle of wine," she said, as casually as possible. "I can't stop thinking about it."

"They don't come along very often," he said. "I'm glad you were there to share it with me."

"Had you had it a long time?"

"Not that long. I don't cellar wine at home. I'm too impatient." He gave her a conspiratorial smile. "A good bottle of wine doesn't last a week around my house, let alone years."

"Where did you get it, anyway?" she asked, watching his eyes.

"Oh, it just appeared one day. Strangest thing. Happens sometimes with very old, good wine," he said.

"That's funny, the exact opposite seems to happen at my place," she said. "Wine, especially good wine, seems to disappear before you know it."

"Unfortunately, I'm familiar with that phenomenon as well."

She bit her lower lip and studied him. "So the wine fairy up and left you a bottle of forty-year-old Burgundy from one of the best terroirs in France, just like that."

"Hey, hey, hey, watch the calculations there. That wine was not forty years old. Far from it. It was born the same year as me."

"I'm sorry," she laughed. "I mean, what exactly did you do for your wine fairy that led her to leave you a thirty-something-year-old bottle of the world's best Burgundy?"

He gave her a charming smile. "If you must know, I guess you could call that bottle the fortuitous product of a mutually beneficial exchange."

Evasion. She'd learned from running a business that the best way to get someone to answer your question is to say nothing yourself after their lame answer. They would feel compelled to say more, if only to fill the silence.

"It doesn't matter where I got it," he said a moment later. His tone was serious. "What matters is that we had fun drinking it together."

He wrapped his scarf around his neck and kissed her on each cheek, then put the back of his hand to her forehead, feeling her temperature. "You better get some rest before Friday," he said. "You look pale."

PART TWO
Still Life

I2

Muscular types like Steve Harvey didn't generally sit in
the full lotus position, at least not comfortably.

"The man has incredibly open hips," Rivka said to Sunny,
peeking in the window of the corrugated metal Quonset hut
where Sergeant Harvey was practicing yoga. The class was
almost over. From the cinder blocks they were standing on, they
could see Harvey sitting in the front row, his legs crossed with
each foot on the opposite thigh and his eyes closed, a peaceful
expression on his normally tense face. Rivka stepped down and
brushed off her hands.

"How did you know he'd be here?" asked Sunny, doing like-
wise.

"He's always coming out when I'm going in. He does the four-
thirty full primary series every Monday and Wednesday. I do
rocket at six. You'd know that if you came more often."

"What, and get all relaxed?"

"It wouldn't kill you."

"I need my stress to keep me motivated."

Rivka shook her head and they waited in silence. After a few
minutes the door opened and a handful of flushed and sweaty
participants walked out.

Rivka shouldered her mat. "You sure you won't come?" she asked.

"No can do. I've got to get all up in Harvey's business."

Rivka flashed her the peace sign and went in. A few minutes later Sergeant Harvey emerged looking satisfied. His expression changed when he saw Sunny waiting for him.

"Sunny."

"Steve."

"Don't tell me," he said, continuing up the sidewalk. "You're here on official police business."

"More or less," she said, following him.

"McCoskey, do the words *day off* mean anything to you?"

"Two of my favorite words."

"Mine too. I happen to be enjoying my *day off* right now. Or at least I was."

"I'd love to leave you in peace, Steve. Really, I would. But it's important." She looked around to see if anyone was within earshot. "It'll only take a minute. It's about Nathan Osborne, and that bottle of wine that was broken at his house the night he died."

Steve frowned. "What about it?"

"Well, for one thing, I wondered if you'd figured out how it got broken. If somebody dropped it, and if so, who."

"No comment. Next question."

"Okay, how about fingerprints? Did you find any on the broken glass?"

"I'd rather not talk about that stuff, Sunny. In fact, I can't talk about it."

"Does that mean you didn't find anything or you didn't check or they didn't match anybody we know?"

They stopped in front of Steve's car, an old GMC Jimmy from the late seventies painted primer gray. His dog, a chesty mix of what Sunny guessed was black lab and pit bull, with markings like a black-and-white cow, barked at him from the cab, and he held up his finger for her to be quiet. The dog transferred the bark into zealous tail-wagging. Steve stood in the twilight holding his car keys. Sunny could tell she wasn't going to get much more of his time.

"It means I can't give out information about a case like we're going through the daily sports wrap-up," he said. "Listen, you got lucky last time helping Skord, now you need to keep out of police business. I hate to be rude, but you're way out of your league here, McCoskey. You don't have a league. You've got no business in this matter whatsoever, as far as I can tell. We've got your information about the mushrooms. That's the extent of your involvement as far as I'm concerned."

"What about the alarm?" she said. "Do you have any leads on who might have disabled it that night?"

Steve shook his head. "How'd you know about that?"

She smiled. "I have my sources. It's no secret anyway. Your people told everybody at Vinifera about it."

The dog yipped and Steve opened the door and let her out. She wagged and panted back and forth between them and he squatted down to greet her with rough scratches and swats, putting powerful shoulders on display in the process. Sunny wondered if he lifted weights or if yoga did more than she thought. He said, "That's a good girl! Zuma, meet Sunny."

Steve stood up and Zuma trotted off, nose to the ground.

"What's got you interested in all this, anyway?" he said.

"I'm just curious," said Sunny. "I mean, you must be curious too. About who dropped that wine."

"I'm definitely curious. It's my job. I just wonder why you are."

"Because the more I learn about Nathan Osborne's death, the more I wonder if there wasn't some foul play involved. Don't you?"

Steve stared at her intently. "That depends. What exactly have you learned?"

"Nothing you don't know already."

He nodded.

She rationalized not sharing everything she knew with Steve by telling herself that she wasn't actually lying, she was only delaying telling what may or may not be the truth. What she knew about the wine might not mean anything.

Steve gave her the short version of his community reassurance speech. She'd heard it before. He went on about how they were looking into all aspects of the case, being very thorough. If there was anything to find, not to worry, they would find it.

"So you're still working on the case," said Sunny.

Steve looked off toward the craggy bluffs of Mount St. Helena to the north, squinting. "We're certainly ready to follow up on any new leads."

"So you've stopped working on the case."

Steve shook his head, smiling. "Cut me a little slack, McCoskey. The coroner's report says the guy had a heart attack in the privacy of his own home and died, just like Mother Nature intended. End of story. Dying is not a crime. Who exactly am I supposed to investigate?"

"Couldn't the coroner be wrong? He's human like the rest of us. Maybe he made a mistake," said Sunny. "Maybe he missed something."

"She hasn't been wrong in about twenty years," said Steve.

"Sorry, she. She hasn't made any mistakes as far as you know. It's not like Nathan is going to stand up and point out any oversights."

"What is it that you think she missed?" said Steve. "I know you've butchered your share of animals, but I don't exactly think that makes you an expert in forensic medicine."

Sunny frowned. "I don't think of it that way. Anyway, I don't know what she could have missed. I just think the whole thing is sort of fishy. I don't buy the heart attack. It's too convenient."

"Too convenient for who?"

"Well, the murderer, for one."

"Look, Sunny, there is no murderer. There was no murder. Nathan Osborne died of a heart attack. I already asked the coroner for a more detailed report than usual, given the circumstances of Osborne's death and considering there were no witnesses. We requested that they look for anything unusual, such as any signs of trauma or injury, and that they check for indications of mushroom poisoning specifically. The team that worked on him is very experienced, very thorough. If the coroner says Nathan Osborne died of complications resulting from massive heart failure stemming from the fact that he took lousy care of himself for about sixty years, I'm prepared to accept that and I don't see why you aren't."

"I'm not saying he didn't have a heart attack," said Sunny.

"What are you saying?"

"Just that perhaps a bit more poking around might be warranted."

Harvey didn't reply. His face was stern and hard to read. They watched Zuma make her rounds, dutifully sniffing the base of each tree and bush in the front yards abutting the sidewalk.

"You can't tell me you don't think there's a connection between Osborne's death and whoever broke into his house that night," said Sunny. "Especially since there was no open bottle around anywhere. That just doesn't make sense."

Harvey nodded. She couldn't tell if he was agreeing with her or nodding to some thought of his own.

"Sounds like you're pretty well informed," he said, crossing his arms over his chest and stepping his feet apart. "If you have any information you'd like to share with me, I'm all ears."

"What I have is mostly questions," she said. "Like what color the foil was on the bottle that was broken."

"The foil?"

"The topping foil. You know, the stuff that protects the cork. I was wondering if it was red or green."

"Christmas is over, McCoskey. I have no idea what color the foil was on the bottle. Why?"

"I was just curious."

"That's a very specific thing to be curious about," said Steve.

"I just wondered if it was the wine I thought it was. Could you check?"

Steve chuckled stiffly. "I don't think examining the color of topping foil is a good use of my time, even in Napa. Besides, I'm not sure we kept that stuff."

"You mean you might not have?" said Sunny incredulously.

"It's possible. After the death warrant is issued we don't have to keep the physical evidence around. We'd be up to our necks in garbage if we kept everything from every scene where somebody died."

"Well, could you check anyway? As a special favor for me?"

"I'd be more motivated if I knew why you wanted to know."

"I have a theory I'd like to confirm."

"Which is?"

"Too half-baked to come out with. But if I'm right, it might mean something."

"You're a cryptic one, McCoskey." He whistled to the dog, who froze in her tracks, looked back at him with apparent enthusiasm, and came running full bore. Steve greeted her with more pats and rubs while her tail whacked his legs. "Give me a call tomorrow and remind me. I'll go over and have a look if it's really that important."

"It might be."

"And if it will keep you from stalking me on my days off."

"It might."

He opened the door and got the dog situated, then closed it again. She barked and he put his open hand on the window to silence her. He looked back at Sunny. "Why don't you just tell me what this is all about. You obviously have something on your mind."

"If it comes to anything you'll be the first to know," she said.

They walked around to the other side of the truck and Steve got in. Sunny lingered by the door and he rolled down the window.

"Did you notice how nobody seems to be too upset about Osborne's death?" she said.

"Single guy, plenty of bad habits."

"Still, it's strange. Didn't he have any close friends or family?"

"No family has turned up yet, but it seems he had his share of friends. More than most, you might say."

"Such as?"

"The guy who takes care of the wine at Vinifera, for one."

"You mean Remy Castels?"

"Him, and Eliot Denby. They knew each other for years, ran a couple of businesses together. And there was that couple he had dinner with the night he died."

"Who's that?"

"I thought you knew everything, McCoskey. Your sources didn't come through on that one?"

"Very funny."

He grinned, obviously enjoying his remark. "The Rastburns. Pel and Sharon. Wine transplants from South Africa."

"What about a girlfriend?"

"There are some women in the picture, but nobody I'd call a girlfriend. More like friends, but the kind wealthy bachelors have."

Steve pointed and Sunny turned to look. The last of a fiery sunset lit the sky. The ridge to the west was already in deep shadow. It would be dark in a few minutes.

"One more thing," she said. "Did you happen to check around to see who might benefit from Osborne's death?"

"Yep."

"And?"

"Plenty of folks, particularly the IRS, but they're usually pretty patient. If they started getting proactive we'd all be in trouble."

"Just the rich ones. I'll call you tomorrow."

"Can't wait."

He started the engine and she went back to the sidewalk. Steve lifted his hand to her as he drove away.

13

St. Helena came and went as Sunny drove south on Highway 29, and with it her chance to go home. It was not so much a conscious decision to pay Eliot Denby a visit as it was the force of momentum carrying her forward, whether she liked it or not. She scrolled through the incoming calls on her mobile while she drove into the deepening twilight, hoping the number would still be there. He'd called on Saturday morning to see that she had everything she needed for Night of Five Stars. There was only one number she didn't recognize. She tried it and a moment later Eliot picked up sounding frazzled. She explained that she'd like to stop by the restaurant to talk with him if he could spare a moment.

"Talk about what?" he asked.

"I'd rather explain in person if that's okay," said Sunny.

"Nothing serious, I hope. It's not about the mushrooms, is it?"

"No, nothing like that. It's just that what I'd like to discuss is somewhat, well, delicate, and I think it will be easier face-to-face."

"I see. Then we'll meet by all means. Tell Sofie at the host desk when you're here and she can come get me."

Getting in and out of Vinifera without Andre knowing about it would be tricky. He would know if Nick knew, and it would be nearly impossible to get past Nick unseen if he was behind the bar. There would be no way to go up the stairs and along the catwalk to Eliot's office without catching Nick's attention.

"I can be there in about ten minutes," said Sunny. "Any chance I could buy you a drink across the street?"

"You mean Bouchon? What's the story, you don't want to come in?"

"It might be simpler to meet there."

"Sounds more complicated to me, but suit yourself. I'm easy. I'll be at the bar in ten."

It was more like twenty, not that she minded. Eliot took off his jacket and adjusted the cuff links on his pale pink shirt before he shook her hand. He hadn't shaved and a growth of beard darkened his cheeks, making him look slightly seedy and very masculine, as in a glossy Italian magazine advertisement. He was handsome if a bit gaunt, close to sixty, with a smile that snapped on and off like a light and a slender build that suited the well-tailored clothes he wore. His black hair was neatly styled and distinguished by a sprinkle of gray at the temples. He looked at his watch as he sat down, no doubt allotting a certain number of minutes to their meeting, thought Sunny. She was drinking a glass of Bonny Doon Le Cigare Volant. He ordered the same.

"So, Ms. McCoskey, what can I do for you?" he said with subtle but evident annoyance.

Sunny thanked him for meeting her on such short notice, then got right to the point. "I know you and Nathan Osborne were friends as well as business partners, so this may be a difficult question, but are you at all bothered by the circumstances of his death?"

Eliot scowled. "I'm not sure what you mean."

"I mean, do you believe he died of natural causes like the police say?"

"Why shouldn't I? It wasn't anything to do with the mushrooms, if that's what you're thinking. They checked and it wasn't that, thank god."

"No, it's not the mushrooms that bother me."

"What then?" He lifted his wineglass and chimed it against hers before he drank. "The coroner confirmed that Nathan died of a heart attack. Didn't anyone tell you?"

"They told me. It just doesn't make sense, not entirely."

"What about it doesn't make sense?"

"Well, for one thing, isn't it kind of sudden? He didn't have a history of heart disease, did he?"

"I don't think he was ever diagnosed, but just because you don't know you have a problem doesn't mean you don't have one. He fit the profile perfectly. All you had to do was look at him and you could see he was a heart attack waiting to happen. They might have been able to do something about it if he'd gone to the damn doctor, but he never went. In the thirty-eight years that I knew him, he never so much as set foot in a doctor's office. He knew what they'd say, and he wasn't about to quit doing the things he loved."

Eliot stopped, contemplating some point. He took pains tasting his wine, swirling and sniffing and examining the color assiduously as if a roomful of producers were awaiting his pronouncement. After a moment he said, "That's Nathan for you. He wouldn't listen to anybody about anything. Always thought he knew best. Anybody could see that he was overweight, drank way too much, and probably had a cholesterol count that would bring a healthy horse to its knees. I wouldn't blink if someone told me Nathan had diabetes, an enlarged prostate, emphysema, gout, and who knows what else."

Sunny nodded encouragement to keep Eliot talking.

"I tried to get him to exercise for years. Decades, actually. The last time I saw him break a sweat over anything more strenuous than a heavy meal, I was studying for finals and smoking reefer. He'd golf now and then, but that was about it, riding around in a cart. You didn't know him, did you?"

"No, I never even saw him. What was he like?"

"Like Falstaff," he said with a cagey smile, "only not as fun to have around. Is that what you wanted to talk to me about?"

"More or less. I just thought you might have some insight into his character that would help explain how this could have happened. Nobody seems to have known him very well. It's sort of sad that there weren't more people close to him."

Eliot looked at her sternly. "That's ridiculous, plenty of people knew him. And it's not sad. In fact, it's disrespectful to pity him, he wouldn't have wanted it, especially from a stranger. Nathan died exactly as he would have wished. Well, that may not be entirely true. He probably would have wanted a more exotic death if he could have chosen, like falling out of a hot air balloon onto the front lawn at Beringer. But at least it was quick, painless, and unanticipated. Nathan lived the way he wanted to the very end, consequences be damned. He didn't want to live a moderate life, and believe me, he wouldn't have wanted to endure illness and old age. You might even say death did him a favor. It was merciful. We all wish he could have lived longer, but better too soon than too late in my view, and I'm reasonably certain Nathan would have agreed. It could have been much worse. He died well fed, at home, with his toes dipped in Château Marceline, for god's sake."

That silenced them. Sunny stole a look at his face as he stared vacantly across the room, avoiding her glance. It was a challenge to reconcile the man in front of her with the elegant figure she'd met on Sunday afternoon. His appearance now was decidedly frayed, even disheveled. His skin had a wan, sleepless hue, and there was a sadness about his eyes, accentuated by the purplish tint of the skin underneath. He seemed to be taking Nathan's death hard. He sighed and, as he did so, made a soft, involuntary whimper that he tried to cover by clearing his throat. She watched him turn away and wipe the corner of his eye brusquely with the edge of his hand. There was little she could do to assuage his sadness, other than silently give him permission to feel it. She was suddenly awash in remorse for having barged in on his evening, hitting him with a list of questions perfectly suited to pique his grief. The emotion welled up in her, too, encouraged by the wine on an empty stomach.

"You two were close," she said softly.

"At times. A friendship that lasts as long as ours had ebbs and flows. He was like family, with all the good and bad that kind of closeness implies. You shouldn't let yourself get too upset about it," he said, turning on his smile long enough to punctuate the admonition with the outward sign of goodwill. "He lived better than just about anybody. I suppose it might look like a sad life to you, coming into it when you did, and his experience at Vinifera was not ideal. He never got along with Andre, and their bickering had alienated most of the staff. I think people felt they had to take sides. I have some guilt about that. I'm the one who insisted on keeping Andre, even though he was actively turning the staff against Nathan. It was a bad situation for both of them. I would have cut Andre in as a partner if it weren't for Nathan. And Nathan wasn't about to let himself get bought out."

"You tried?"

"Andre did. At this point, Vinifera is more Andre's vision than either mine or Nathan's. He's always wanted to own a piece of it."

"But Nathan wouldn't do it."

"Nathan said there wasn't enough profit to support three partners."

"And Andre knew that?"

"Definitely. They fought about it more or less constantly. It's all moot now, I guess. With Nathan gone, Andre will be able to become a partner. I've always believed a chef should have a stake in the business, no pun intended. In any case, the point is that Vinifera was a small part of Nathan's life, which was otherwise full of successes and friendships. And girlfriends. I could never keep track. Nathan had plenty of people outside Vinifera who cared for him. I'm having dinner with two of them tonight, Pel and Sharon Rastburn. The four of us have been friends longer than Andre Morales has been alive." He checked his watch. "In fact, I'd better get going or they'll be waiting for me."

Eliot stood to go. There were still several questions Sunny wanted to ask. And she wanted to think of a way to get Eliot to introduce her to the Rastburns, the couple Nathan had dinner with the night he died. She swallowed a mouthful of fermented courage and forged ahead.

"One more thing," she said. "What do you make of the bottle of wine that was broken?"

"What about it?"

"How do you think it got there?"

"Isn't it obvious? Nathan dropped it when he began to have chest pains."

"But Nick said he could tell that Nathan had been on the floor already when it was dropped. He could tell by the splash marks."

"Nick Ambrosi, bartender, is now Nick Ambrosi, crime scene analyst? I politely submit that Nick has so idea what he's talking about."

"What about the missing bottle?"

"You're just full of questions."

"Do you have a theory?"

"I don't think it's too difficult to imagine an explanation."

"Such as?"

"You're really concerned about all this. Nathan would be flattered."

His smug manner was beginning to irritate her. "If you have a theory, I'd love to hear it," she said.

"Well, let's see," he said, sitting back down. "Let's say somebody's wife comes by for a little shag time around the witching hour. That certainly was not an unusual occurrence chez Osborne. She lets herself in and finds him keeled over. She's fond of him, maybe even in love with him, and she sits down on the coffee table and begins to cry. Being one of Nathan's lovers and therefore statistically inclined to be extremely fond of the juice, she takes a swig or two out of the bottle next to her. Finally after she's had a good sob, she realizes she can't tell anyone she's found him, can't call the police, unless she wants to see her name in the newspaper next to his. She has to leave, and remove any sign that she's been there. She's upset, so she's not thinking straight. She takes off her sweater and steps on it to erase her footsteps and wipe her fingerprints off the keypad and door handle. After that, all she has to do is go home, keep her mouth shut, and wait for someone else to find him. Only in all the fuss she forgets she's still holding the bottle of wine, but she doesn't want to go back in, so she just takes it with her and gets rid of it."

"That is a very detailed theory," said Sunny.

Eliot chuckled. "Overactive imagination."

"So you're assuming she didn't drop the bottle that was broken."

"Right. Nathan dropped it."

"Would she drink from a bottle of wine that was in front of a dead man? And take it with her? That's very risky."

"You mean, she might think the wine killed him?"

"She might wonder."

"I don't think so. She would have thought the same thing we all did, that he had a heart attack. But what do I know? I'm not omnipotent. Maybe there was no woman. Maybe it was the plumber. Or a burglar."

"A burglar with the pass code."

"An inside job. The pass code wasn't a big secret. Everyone at Vinifera knew it. Listen, none of this matters because I don't know what happened. I wasn't there. I do know that there are all kinds of ways to explain things that go missing, and none of them change the fact that Nathan had a heart attack. One black sock vanishes every time I do laundry, but it doesn't mean someone is trying to poison me. Just because a bottle of wine is missing doesn't mean there was anything nefarious about Nathan's death, or that I appreciate being grilled about it, for that matter, which I certainly don't. Now if you don't mind, I'd like to get to my dinner engagement."

He left and Sunny paid the bill, then jogged across the street to the parking lot. She got in the truck and waited. She figured the Rastburns wouldn't be too hard to identify, assuming she hadn't missed them already. It was cold in the truck and she pulled the sleeves of her jacket down over her hands, shivering as she sat and watched the entrance to Vinifera. What was left of her toasty wine buzz dissipated swiftly, leaving her feeling drained and increasingly grouchy. If she didn't eat something soon the whole evening could go south in a low blood sugar and fatigue–induced collapse. Unless of course she drank more wine. There was a thermos on the floor of the passenger side from the morning. She reached across and poured what was left into the lid that served as a cup. It had started out as strong black coffee with a splash of Merlot the way she liked it, but now it was cold and gritty. She opened the door and poured it out, then settled back into her vigil.

Eliot had looked like a man under a tremendous burden, but he'd lost his best friend and business partner, and was running Vinifera with a police investigation going on. She must have seemed insensitive with her questions.

A burgundy sedan pulled into the Vinifera parking lot and a man got out. He went around to the passenger side to open the door. Anniversary, possibly birthday manners, thought Sunny, and the car is a rental. Not likely to be locals, not my target couple. Another car pulled in, but she decided the couple who got out looked too young to be longtime friends of Eliot and Nathan. The next several arrivals seemed safe to eliminate for various reasons—two businessmen, a wine-maker type on his own probably going to meet friends, a trio of thirty-something girlfriends, a couple with a teenage daughter, an Asian couple. Rastburn hardly sounded Asian. She was on the point of concluding that the Rastburns had already arrived before she got there when a Land Rover pulled in and an elegantly dressed couple of about Eliot's age got out. The woman walked gingerly across the blacktop in modest heels, her long evening jacket skimming the pavement. Her companion, dressed conservatively in a navy dinner jacket and neatly pressed tan trousers, took her arm protectively. His height and posture accentuated a trim, athletic build. Sunny got out of the truck.

They were nearly at the door to the restaurant when she reached them.

"Excuse me, Mr. and Mrs. Rastburn?" she called out.

Mr. Rastburn let go of his wife's arm and turned around sharply. His body language was relaxed but his face looked tense. He eyed Sunny with an aquiline fierceness that made her uneasy, assessing her as if she had already failed in his esteem somehow and would have trouble making it up. His eyes were the pale hazel of beach pebbles and his fair complexion was lightly freckled with copper spots the same color as his hair, which he wore short, in the style of military officers and airline pilots. His face was oval as opposed to round, and his long forehead and the deep vertical line between his eyebrows gave him the intense look of a raptor. Mrs. Rastburn was breezy. She seemed to glide. Her silvery blond hair was cut in a blunt bob just below her ears and a shimmery gloss of pink brushed her lips. A diamond pendant sparkled at her throat, and the matching earrings set off her blue eyes, which must have been magnificent in her youth and were still striking. She had a fragile beauty as she looked from Sunny to her husband and back again.

"I'm sorry, have we met?" asked Mr. Rastburn.

"No, not yet. I'm Sonya McCoskey. I'm a friend of Nathan Osborne's. Or at least I was."

"How did you know to find us here?" he said.

Sunny felt her eyes flick to the left, hunting for an answer. She didn't want to outright lie, but she was willing to stretch the truth as far as she could. "I ate here earlier and I happened to notice your name in the reservation book when I was talking with the hostess. I'd heard you mentioned so many times I wanted to meet you." Sunny paused. "You had dinner with him the night he died, didn't you?"

"I don't remember him mentioning you," Mr. Rastburn said, "but it was nice to meet you." He put his hand on his wife's elbow to guide her toward the restaurant.

"I was just hoping I could talk with you about that last dinner. I'd just like to hear a little more about his last few hours. I don't know why exactly, but it's important to me."

That at least was true. Pel didn't reply right away. Sunny watched him study her, deciding what kind of person was accosting them in a parking lot and what she really wanted. She had the impression he was tempted to hand her a dollar and walk away.

"I think it would help me, help us, deal with his death," said Sunny, "if we could talk with other people who were close to him, share a few memories. I have a restaurant in St. Helena, Wildside, and some of my staff have been pretty upset. There's a need to process the experience. He was an important part of the restaurant community even for those who didn't know him directly."

Sharon Rastburn's tentative expression warmed to a tender look of compassion. She reached out a bejeweled slender hand to Sunny.

"We can understand that, can't we, Pel," she said, looking back at her husband. "It's been a terrible shock for everyone. Why don't you come in and we can all have a drink together. You must know Eliot, too? We'll all raise a glass in Nathan's honor. He'd like that."

Sunny froze. It wouldn't do to walk in with the Rastburns and run right into Eliot.

Pel looked at his wife. "I don't think that's such a good idea," he said. "Not tonight. There's been enough mourning in my opinion for today. I personally would like to leave behind this morbid talk for a few hours."

"Pel, I don't see what . . ."

"Sharon, I think not. Listen, Miss . . . ? I'm sorry—"

"McCoskey," said Sunny. "Sonya McCoskey."

"Ms. McCoskey, my wife and I have had several very tiring days. Why don't you give me your number and we will phone you with an appropriate time and place to meet later in the week. My wife is right, Nathan's death has been difficult to accept. Tonight we do not wish to discuss it. I'm sure you understand."

Sunny, feeling tremendously relieved, assured them that she did. She patted her pockets as though a pen might materialize where she knew there was none. A moment later Mr. Rastburn produced a gold pen and a business card from his coat pocket and Sunny wrote her name and number on the back.

"We'll telephone you tomorrow or the next day," said Pel.

"I'd appreciate that. Enjoy your dinner."

They parted and Sunny walked back to the truck, wondering if Pel was the kind of man who would type her name into a search engine before he called, and decided that he was. What he would find would only set his mind at ease. There was nothing to suggest she was a crazed stalker. Her online persona was almost exclusively culinary, except for the page an ex-boyfriend had posted a few years ago with pictures and notes about a camping trip to the High Sierra.

She sat in the truck with her hand on the keys. It was still relatively early and she had a great deal to think about. The question was where. Home was an option of course, but it wasn't calling to her. A swim sounded nice, but the drive was a motivational challenge even though it was all of about ten minutes down to the gym. She looked at her watch. Rivka would be getting home from yoga about now. If she called ahead, whatever Rivka was making for dinner would be ready right about the time she got there. That plan won points for efficiency.

Sunny stared at the entrance to Vinifera, held in place by inertia. After a moment Nick Ambrosi came outside wearing his long white apron tied low on his hips. He took a pack of cigarettes out of his shirt pocket and lit one, leaning against the wall beside the door. He smoked with obvious relish. She hoped he couldn't see her sitting in the truck in the dark, but he only looked up at the stars. He'd smoked most of the cigarette when a woman came out to join him. Sunny recognized the spiky hair immediately. Dahlia swayed her hips like a hula dancer and Nick nodded, chuckling. He handed her his cigarette and she took three long drags, staring out at the night, smiling at what he was saying. When she was done she flicked the butt into the parking lot and turned to Nick, putting her arms around his neck and looking up at him. Like someone waking from a daydream, he seized her head in both hands and kissed her full on the mouth. A moment later they parted and she went inside. Nick paced for a moment, hands on his hips. He raked his fingers through his hair, then went in after her.

14

In her office early the next morning, Sunny felt alert and energized. She'd chosen the quiet of home, a hot shower, and bed over the companionship and probing questions of a dinner at Rivka's. Dinner was a perfect cup of hot cocoa, her winter obsession, made with milk, cream, sugar, and loamy Scharffen Berger powder. She'd slept hard and dreamed of an accusing face, distorted and menacing, and Dahlia's pornographically writhing hips.

Sitting at her cluttered desk, she waited until exactly eight o'clock before she dialed the number for the police station. She was transferred to Steve Harvey's desk, and a female voice said, "Sergeant Harvey's desk, Officer Dervich speaking."

Sunny identified herself and they exchanged polite greetings. She explained that Steve had suggested she phone about the bottle of wine found at Nathan Osborne's home, specifically the color of the topping foil.

"He left a note on his desk this morning, asking me to look into that. Luckily we still had it in evidence. It's green with a gold M stamped in the top."

"Are you sure?"

"I looked at it myself just a few minutes ago."

"We're talking about the bottle of wine that was broken, the one with the cork still in it, right?" asked Sunny.

"That's right. The neck of the bottle broke off in one piece. The cork and foil were still in place because it hadn't been opened. The foil was definitely green. Is that significant to you for some reason?"

"I had a theory, but it sounds like it was wrong," said Sunny.

"What kind of a theory?"

"Oh, I just had an idea about where that wine could have come from, but I was wrong. Thanks for checking. Any word on the wine he was drinking and where that bottle went?"

There was silence on the other end of the line. Finally Officer Dervich said, "I'm afraid I'll have to refer you to Sergeant Harvey with any further questions."

Sunny thanked her and hung up. When she looked up, Rivka was leaning against the doorjamb, watching her and eating gingersnaps out of a plastic container.

"Who was that?" she asked.

"Are you going to eat all of those?" said Sunny, eyeing the container.

"They're last week's. You said you were going to talk to Steve yesterday and then butt out."

"And I did talk to him."

"But you didn't butt out. Don't you remember a certain traumatic incident that I spent about a grand on therapy trying to process? And how you promised never to get involved in that kind of thing again?"

"Yeah, I remember," said Sunny. "I think it had something to do with one of my best friends not being tried for murder."

"Point taken, but no one needs rescuing now. How about giving Wildside some of your attention for a change? We haven't done any of the stuff we talked about at New Year's. The garden is still a mess, the back fence needs replacing, we haven't gone out to see the suppliers, and racks in the walk-in need to be rebuilt."

"We still have plenty of year left."

Rivka let out an exasperated sigh and flopped down on the couch. "If you won't give it up, at least fill me in. What's all this business about foil?"

Sunny came around from behind her desk and moved aside a stack of cookbooks so she could sit down on a café chair next to the couch. She was about to explain when her mobile phone vibrated against the desktop, caller unidentified.

"It's too early for the telemarketers." She picked up and Pel Rastburn greeted her in the polished tone of a lifelong executive.

"Ms. McCoskey, I wanted to let you know that my wife and I have discussed the request you made last night and we would like to invite you to lunch with us today, or at your convenience."

Sunny thanked him and explained the difficulty of being away from work at lunch time.

"Then you could come for tea this afternoon if you like, around four o'clock."

"Perfect."

She took down directions to their house and hung up. Evidently they hadn't mentioned her name to Eliot, who would certainly have taken the opportunity to tell them she'd never even met Nathan.

Rivka raised her eyebrows. "Okay, spill."

Sunny looked at the clock. "Let's get on it. I'll explain while we work."

They dug into the morning prep routine. Between making sure the day's beets were roasted, trays of vegetables were caramelizing, and potatoes and celery root were well on their way to a rendezvous with the food mill and more butter than anyone cared to admit, and checking deliveries of produce, wine, cedar planks, and salmon, it was well after nine before Sunny had a chance to say anything more about Nathan Osborne. Finally she recounted what she'd learned the previous day, including how Remy had accused Nathan of forging the wine, and what Eliot had said about Andre wanting to buy into the business.

"The green foil this morning was a setback," Sunny said.

"Because . . ." asked Rivka.

"Because the phony Marceline has red foil. The Grand Cru should be topped with green foil according to Monty, not red. But the bottles I saw in the cellar at Vinifera had red foil, even though the label said Grand Cru. There were two bottles missing from that case. We know where one went. I presumed the other was on the floor at Nathan's. I figured it had to be the other bogus bottle."

"But it turned out to be the real thing."

"Right."

"So what does that mean?"

"It means that somebody didn't get to drink a seven-hundred-dollar bottle of wine. Beyond that, I'm not exactly sure," said Sunny.

Rivka ran a bulb of fennel across a mandoline meditatively while Sunny prepared a tray of winter squash and slid it into the oven. She tossed a handful of walnuts in a saucepan with butter, sugar, and spices, thinking. Finally she said, "If we choose to believe Dahlia, then we know that Nathan took possession of one of the forged bottles last week. That bottle eventually made its way from him to Dahlia to Andre and me. It stands to reason that Nathan might have taken a second bottle. He knew where they were kept, and he didn't actually get to drink the one he took home for his breakup dinner with Dahlia. So let's imagine that he opens forged bottle number two, pours himself a glass or two or three, has his heart attack, and dies. Then the mysterious stranger lets himself in, smashes the unopened bottle, and removes the open one."

"And why would they do that?"

Sunny removed the walnuts and set them aside to cool, then loaded the saucepan with another batch. "The smashing, I think it is safe to assume, occurs unintentionally. I don't see why someone would set out to do it. It doesn't seem to serve any purpose and it lends suspicion to what would otherwise be a perfect murder, in the sense of not appearing to be murder at all." She flipped the walnuts in the pan with a deft flick of the wrist.

"So the real bottle gets broken by accident."

"Right."

"And the fake bottle, forged bottle number two, is removed."

"Yes."

"Because?"

"I can only think of two reasons: because it was phony or because it was poison. The poison argument doesn't hold up because they left wine in the glass Nathan had been drinking from. If it had poison, it seems logical that they would have gotten rid of the glass. So it had to be because the bottle was phony and the crook was scared Nathan would figure it out and bust them."

Rivka thought about it. "They were hoping to sneak in and replace the fake bottle with the real one, only they didn't plan on finding Nathan dead."

"Exactly," said Sunny, removing the second batch of walnuts and tossing more in the pan.

"If that's the case, Remy has to be lying about Nathan forging the wines," said Rivka.

"That's what I'm thinking. He has to be lying. How convenient is it to be able to blame the dead guy? It's ideal. Only the dead guy has no reason to commit the fraud. If Nathan was behind the forged wine, he wouldn't have been running around taking bottles home with him, that would be a waste of time and valuable counterfeiting profits. Would he go to all the trouble and risk of doctoring up a case of wine, then drink a couple of bottles himself when he could drink any wine in Vinifera's cellar or Osborne Wines' warehouse? Remy said Nathan was out of control, drinking all the time, and a chronic liar who forgot what was real and what wasn't. I don't buy it. You can't run two businesses of that magnitude if you're totally out of control. I can barely run this place, and I think I have a pretty solid grip on reality."

"Except when it comes to Andre," Rivka said.

"Stick to the subject," Sunny replied.

"Wildside is so small you have to do everything yourself Nathan probably only handled big-picture stuff and could get by being bombed."

"Even the big-picture stuff gets out of control if you're drunk all day. If we accept that Nathan perpetrated the fraud, I don't think we can also accept that he forgot he'd done so. Replacing those labels was the work of someone meticulous, refined, and obsessed with detail."

"Remy."

Sunny threw in more walnuts. "It fits. Since Remy and Osborne are the only two who could profit by selling fake wine to the wine club, I'm prepared to bet that Remy forged that wine himself unbeknownst to Nathan. When he realized Nathan had taken a bottle home, he decided he had to break into his house to get it back before Nathan sobered up and figured it out."

"Because if Nathan found out and fired him, Remy wouldn't be able to get a job serving grape juice at a Taco Bell."

"He could go to jail."

"So he probably assumes you'll get this far in your thinking eventually. Don't you think that might make him a little edgy?" Rivka said.

"I'd say he's already about as close to the edge as a person can get without going over," said Sunny. "I've been wondering if he's going to stick around. I bet a beach blanket in Rio is sounding pretty good to him right about now."

Rivka looked at her. "You expecting a really big crowd for lunch?"

"Not especially, why?"

"You just candied enough walnuts for every frisée salad north of Los Angeles."

There was just barely time after lunch service for Sunny to change into jeans and a clean T-shirt and race up-Valley to the Rastburns'. The directions said to turn at the sign marked "No wineries this road," a narrow lane that ran straight west through bottomland vineyard. Just visible at the end was the terra-cotta roof of a terra-cotta home mostly shielded by a grand eucalyptus. Sunny pulled up in front of the house and got out. Off to the right, an assortment of Defenders and Four-Runners with the Rastburns' galloping Morgan motif stenciled on the doors were parked under a carport, a vine-clad shelter that looked more suitable for a bacchanalian feast than a fleet of four-wheel drives. To the east, vineyards filled the view for a hundred and eighty degrees. The house sat back invitingly from the drive, sheltered by rosemary and lavender hedges with cedar trees overhanging the western edge of the garden and Diamond Mountain for a backdrop. It was all more Tuscan than anything she'd seen in Tuscany. Napa was getting just a little big for its knickers, Sunny thought. Pel Rastburn opened the front door as she reached the landing.

"Ms. McCoskey, welcome. You found it without any trouble, I hope?"

"None at all. Please, call me Sonya."

Pel was dressed in jeans and a plaid shirt, tucked in tidily and finished with a smooth leather belt. Sunny followed him into the living room, where Sharon Rastburn appeared as they were settling into seats. She seemed greatly invigorated by the passage of a day, her smile much more youthful than the night before and her cheeks touched with a blush of color to match her pink turtleneck. She sat down in an armchair between them and said it would be just a moment for tea. A grandfather clock ticked from the wall behind them. Sunny glanced at a side table loaded with family photographs showing a trio of handsome blond daughters at various ages. Sharon gave Pel a meaningful glance and he cleared his throat.

"Ms. McCoskey," he said. "I'm afraid I must apologize for my manner last night. I assumed you were one of Nathan's lady friends. We've had some trouble in that department in the past and I do not wish to make any further associations." He smiled at Sharon. "Over dinner, my wife assured me that she has comprehensive knowledge of Nathan's romantic affiliations and you are not among them."

"That's true," said Sunny. "I never dated Nathan." She paused, considering how to continue. Coming clean would not be easy, but the world, or at least the wine country, was too small to start complicating it with lies.

"Since we're apologizing," she said, "I think I owe you one as well. I said I was a friend of Nathan's. I'm not. To be perfectly honest, I never met him. But I am a friend of Andre Morales."

They stared. "The cook?" said Sharon.

"Yes. And because of that friendship, I've learned some things that have made me wonder if the police have taken all the possibilities into consideration regarding Nathan's death."

"What do you mean by that?" said Pel.

"She means she thinks Nathan was killed," said Sharon breathlessly.

"I wouldn't state it that categorically," said Sunny. "I'd just feel better if I knew a bit more about his last night."

"What makes you think somebody would want to hurt Nathan?" said Pel.

"I can't tell you everything," said Sunny carefully. "There may be other crimes involved, and I don't want to make trouble for anyone, especially if I'm wrong."

"That's very convenient for you," said Pel. "We invite you, a complete stranger, into our home, and you tell us you are in fact not a friend of Nathan's, and yet you can't tell us why you misrepresented yourself, or why you want to worry my wife and me by introducing the hunch, and I suspect that is all it is, that our dearest friend was murdered."

"I know it sounds strange," said Sunny. "I assure you I have only Nathan's interests—the interests of Nathan's friends—at heart."

"What about your interests?" said Pel.

"If Nathan was killed, it's not exactly wise to let the murderer continue to go about their business like nothing happened—especially if it has to do with the restaurant business, which is my business. Others could be at risk. I don't think all the facts have come out yet, and I'd like to know all there is to know."

"A purist," said Pel, skeptically. He stood up and walked across the room to a Japanese cabinet with stair-step drawers and removed a pipe and a pouch of tobacco. He turned to Sunny, holding up the pipe. "Will it bother you?"

"Not at all."

He pressed a pinch of tobacco into the bowl and returned to his armchair. Sharon leaned forward, squeezing her hands together as if to wring the truth from her guest by force of will.

"So," he said, stopping to give his full attention to lighting the pipe. "Why come to us? You could talk to Eliot. He knew Nathan as well as we did."

"Because I want to know everything about the night he died," said Sunny. "There may be some clue in his behavior, something he said. You were the last people to spend any time with him, other than Nick Ambrosi, the bartender who drove him home."

"This sounds like a conversation better had with the police," said Pel, "and we've already had it. Twice, to be accurate."

"It's nothing official. I'm just like you, a friend of those involved who wants to understand what happened."

They were silent. Pel puffed on his pipe, staring at the ceiling.

"Let's hear what she would like to know," said Sharon gently. "We don't have to answer. I don't see what harm it can do."

"Go ahead," said Pel.

Sunny ranked the list of questions in her head. Knowing she might not have the opportunity to ask them all, she set the most important on top. "For starters," she said, "what kind of trouble did you have with his girlfriends?"

Sharon glanced at Pel for reassurance, then leaned toward Sunny. She gave her an introductory smile, then addressed the topic with unabashed enthusiasm, like a witness describing a dramatic accident. "Nathan was a very generous man. He had the habit of reaching out to people and helping them, giving them money, finding them jobs, letting them stay at his house, and they would then expect that assistance to continue indefinitely. When he eventually got tired of supporting them, they would come to us, hoping, I assume, that we would intervene on their behalf and persuade him to rekindle the friendship, romance, employment situation, or what have you. Generally we are talking about a romance of one sort or another. As you know, no friend can change a man's heart, even if they wanted to. The worst was that waitress at the restaurant. I knew she was trouble from the moment I laid eyes on her. She's still around. Delilah? What was her name?"

Sunny looked anxiously at Pel.

"Dahlia," said Pel, exhaling a nicely formed smoke ring. "Like the flower."

"Yes, that's right. I scolded Nathan for getting involved with a girl who worked for him, not to mention one who was half his age. It always leads to trouble, and sure enough."

"She wasn't anywhere near half his age," said Pel, winking at Sunny.

"Age was not the issue. She was dreadful regardless," said Sharon. "You would think she would have found another job after they split up, but she was around more than ever. She waited on us the night Nathan died, which I found excruciating. Nathan hardly seemed to notice. A pretty girl, but with self-esteem problems. Personally, I felt sorry for her with the garish tattoos and crazy hair. All pleas for attention. Nathan broke it off with her after a very short time, I'm glad to say, but she never got the picture. She practically stalked him. I suggested he get a restraining order. It was his own fault. He would never end it cleanly. They went back and forth for months."

"Sharon, please, surely that's enough. I don't see what gossip has to do with Nathan's death," said Pel.

"It isn't gossip," said Sharon. "We were there."

"The definition of gossip is not the dissemination of speculative information, it is the dissemination of information that is none of your affair in the first place," said Pel. "I'll add that I don't think you're being at all fair to Dahlia. I didn't care for the art direction, but she seemed a nice enough person to me, intelligent, and clearly in love with him, though I can't imagine what a girl that young could see in a man who gets the Tuesday discount at the cinema. We must remember that Nathan was not known for his fidelity and good manners, especially when it came to matters involving the fairer sex."

"You're as bad as he was," said Sharon, scoffing. "You can't see beyond the bosom."

Sharon excused herself to make tea when the kettle whistled. Silence settled over the room with her departure. Pel, who seemed in no hurry to speak, puffed on his pipe, gradually surrounding himself with a haze of fragrant smoke. The thick Berber carpet underfoot seemed to suck up every sound, leaving them suspended in a conversational void that gradually intensified until it extracted even the saliva from Sunny's mouth. Her mind scurried from topic to topic, scavenging for an appropriate segue to Remy Castels. She settled on waiting for Sharon to return with the tea before she said anything more. Pel scratched his head with three crisp, audible strokes. Her stomach responded with a long, loud groan, like a sailboat creaking in its mooring. At last, having failed to uncover a less direct approach and despairing of Sharon's speedy return, she said, "Do you know Remy Castels, the sommelier at Vinifera?"

"Yes. Do you?"

"Not very well. Would you say he's trustworthy?"

"You mean as a sommelier?"

"I mean in general."

Pel considered. "I can't say I've had enough dealings with him to make a judgment one way or the other. He certainly knows his wine. That cellar at Vinifera is packed with more gems than the queen's castle."

"How much did Nathan have to do with that?"

"Nathan certainly helped, but Remy took Osborne Wines to a new level. He has connections in France that made it possible for Nathan to do things no one else could do. He brought in wines that nobody else had, made exclusive deals. Remy went a long way toward making Osborne Wines what it is today."

Sharon emerged from the direction of the kitchen bearing a tray with a teapot and cups. Pel stood to take it from her and she went back for another, this one loaded with cream, sugar, and a plate of cookies.

"What did I miss?" said Sharon.

"We were just talking about Remy Castels," said Sunny.

"Oh, that horrible man!" cried Sharon with a high, zealous laugh. "Pel and I both loathe him, don't we."

"I wouldn't say I loathe him," said Pel. "I wouldn't say I know him well enough to use such a strong term. I'm not drawn to him."

"Well, I loathe him enough for both of us," said Sharon, whose personality had undergone a transformation not dissimilar to that of her appearance since the night before. It was as if she had worn a suitably demure persona to match her evening dress, and now that casual attire was the order, her manner had relaxed accordingly.

"Don't get me started on him," she said, arranging the teacups.

"Yes, let's don't," said Pel. He put his pipe aside in a little brass stand on the end table next to his chair.

"I never liked him from the day I met him," said Sharon. "I remember when Nathan introduced him to us. He was so delighted. Nathan thought Remy was a genius."

"When was that?"

"He hired him to take over as the sommelier at Denby's, so it was probably about six, maybe seven years ago. It would have been around the time we bought this property."

"What is it about him that you don't like?" asked Sunny.

"What do I like about him is a better question. You've met him?"

"Yes, several times."

"And? What did you think?"

"He seemed reserved. Hard to get to know. And very protective of his wine cellar," said Sunny.

"You can say that again. He'd keep the whole place under lock and key if he could. He forgets who is working for whom. Once he got the flu and wouldn't let anyone use the keys to the alcoves except Nathan. All week long, Nathan practically lived in the cellar, running bottles back and forth for the waiters."

"Why do you suppose he is so distrustful?" asked Sunny. "Does he think the wait staff would steal from the restaurant?"

"I think he is more concerned about having his very meticulously arranged world intruded upon," said Pel. "That someone might handle a wine that ought not to be moved. That some mistake might be made. So much of the stock at Vinifera isn't on the menu. Remy is the only one who would know what to charge for it, for example. But I think his fears are largely less rational. The thought that someone might put a Meritage in with the Merlot is enough to make his hair curl."

Sharon poured the tea and handed it around. "You're right, there," she said. "He is a total control freak."

She used the term uneasily. It was probably a semi-recent import from the vocabulary of one of her daughters. They sipped their tea. Sunny said, "Let's go back to Saturday night. You're at dinner with Nathan. What was it like? Did he seem himself?"

"It was great fun, like always," said Sharon wistfully. "I'm glad we have it to remember him by. Now that Nathan is beyond hearing, I think it's okay to tell you that I have never cared overly for the food at Vinifera. I like a restaurant's menu to be either more elaborate or more simple. Somehow they seem to strike the middle ground and lose the advantages of both. We eat there because of Nathan and Eliot. That said, our meal was very good and the company and wine excellent."

"Did he say or do anything out of the ordinary?"

Sharon doctored her tea and sipped, considering. "Not that I recall. He was in good spirits, very jovial. Nathan knew how to have a good time. As I mentioned earlier, that woman Dahlia waited on us, but even that was merely uncomfortable. It was a good night."

"He didn't seem tired or sick?"

"Not at all," Sharon said. "It was late by the time we left, and he stayed on. There was nothing about his behavior to suggest he was having any kind of health problem. His death came as a complete shock."

"That's true, he wasn't sick," said Pel, "but Nathan was hardly a specimen of good health. He looked and acted like what he was, a man at the end of a life of rampant excess. Everyone else stopped that business after college. He kept on, and it eventually killed him."

"Do you remember your conversation that night?" asked Sunny. "What you talked about over dinner?"

"I don't think we spoke of anything in particular," said Pel. "Nothing noteworthy that I can remember. It was a long dinner. Andre sent out a number of dishes for us to try. We talked about the food, what we liked and didn't like and why. We talked about the wine. Nathan had an incomparable passion for wine, and he spoke very well on the topic. He knew everything there was to know about wine and loved to share the information. He would tell us about whatever we were drinking, where it came from, who made it. That would inevitably segue into a story about a visit to the château—he especially loved French wines— and one of his romantic conquests. You know, some highly embellished tale of how the wine maker's wife slipped into his room in a white silk gown and dared him to ravish her. Other than that, we talked about our girls, a few mutual friends, Sharon's trip to Prague."

"I went to do Christmas shopping," said Sharon. "They make marvelous glassware."

"Then we went home," said Pel.

"What was he doing when you left?"

"Standing at the bar, talking to Remy, as far as I remember."

"Was he drunk?"

"Not drunk, but not sober either. We had cocktails before dinner, and a bottle of wine, and Remy came around several times with wines he thought we would like to taste."

"He didn't mention any troubles he might be having?" asked Sunny.

"If there had been anything odd about that night, we would have told the police," said Sharon. "It was just an ordinary dinner. We do it every other week or so."

Sunny nodded. "So he didn't seem worried or anxious?"

"Not that I noticed," said Pel. "I'd say he seemed quite relaxed."

"What about enemies? Was there anyone angry at him, who hated him, or who had threatened him?"

"The police asked us that too," said Sharon. "As far as I know, everyone loved Nathan. He was a hoot to be around, always cheerful."

"But you said Dahlia had issues with him, and there were others."

"Yes, I suppose that's true. I never think of estranged lovers as enemies. I still think you're looking for something that isn't there. Nathan seemed fine. There were no problems in his life as far as I know. And while I don't particularly like Dahlia, I hardly blame her for his death."

"What about people who stood to benefit by his death?"

"Your friend would be at the top of the list," said Pel. "Andre must have been torn between joy and sorrow when he heard. He would have been out of a job in a heartbeat if it were up to Nathan."

Sunny frowned. The people who frequented expensive restaurants talked about chefs in that proprietary way other people talked about celebrities, as if they actually knew what was going on in their lives or had any business doing so. "If that's the case, why did Eliot want to keep him on? If it caused so many bad feelings, why not replace him? Certainly Andre could find another post."

"It's anybody's guess. Mine is that Andre embodies what Eliot imagines a chef ought to be," said Pel. "You might say he personifies the spirit of Vinifera, or you could be less kind and say he fits with the decor."

Sunny felt a surge of anger in defense of Andre, which she decided not to indulge. "Surely there were others who stood to gain more directly. Nathan was a wealthy man. Someone is going to inherit all that, aren't they?"

"We'll find out soon enough. They're reading the will tomorrow," said Pel. "Not that it affects us."

He glanced at the grandfather clock and Sunny put down her teacup. The interview was over. As they said their good-byes, the Rastburns assured Sunny they would phone if they thought of any significant detail about Nathan's last night. Sunny felt confident they would not. They didn't seem in the least suspicious about his death, and she imagined they would not give her visit a second thought.

15

It was about to be one of those magic twilights that made Sunny want to put on a down jacket and a stocking hat, grab a bottle of home-brew No Cal Red, climb a mountain, wait for night, and get to know the stars. A sliver of moon as white as porcelain sat on top of Rattlesnake Ridge already, and Sunny felt the pull of Mount St. Helena.

Instead, she was staking out the Quonset hut of yoga—again. She figured that since Rivka's romance with Alex Campaglia was on hold, the odds improved considerably that she would show up for the six o'clock yoga class, even though it was a Thursday. Rivka's compulsion to practice yoga increased dramatically when you took the boyfriend out of the picture. Sunny was parked across the street, watching. Sure enough, Rivka walked up the sidewalk a few minutes before six carrying her mat. Sunny got out.

"Hey, you're coming!" said Rivka.

"I wish. I just needed to intercept you."

"I'm intercepted. Now come have a stretch. You'll feel great."

"I'd love to, but I have an errand I want to run before it gets any later."

Rivka frowned. "What errand?"

"I need to see Dahlia Zimmerman."

Rivka considered. "She's probably at the restaurant by now."

"I just called and she's not working tonight. I was thinking I would try to reach her at home if you have the number."

"She doesn't have a land line at her house, and there's no cell reception up there."

"So there's no way to contact her?"

"No. She likes it that way. You can leave a message on her mobile, but she won't get it until she drives out to the highway."

Sunny sighed. "Riv, it's important."

"Is it?"

"I think it is. Is that enough?"

Rivka nodded. "It is. Still, the only way is to drive out there and hope she's around. It's a long way. Do you want me to come with you?"

"You don't have to. It might actually be better if you didn't. She might say more if you're not there."

"She might say less."

Sunny didn't reply.

Rivka looked at her watch and sighed. When she spoke, her voice sounded matter-of-fact, the mock-helpful tone of someone taking pains to make her irritation known.

"Go up to Jimtown and make a right where you would normally make a left if you were going to Healdsburg. I don't remember the name of the road. You know where I mean? Go for about three miles, until you pass a big white barn on your right. It's going to be harder to notice in the dark, but it's not far from the road so you should be able to see it. After that, watch for the first road on the left. It's not marked, but there's a row of mailboxes with a red one on the end with a thunderbird painted on it. Take that all the way to the end. You'll think you've gone too far, but keep going. You're the expert at that, so it shouldn't be a problem."

"Very funny."

"Stay right at all the splits. There are two or three, but just stay right. She lives in the little cabin on the far right once you get to a group of houses. There's a tent out back that she uses for her painting studio. She might be in there if she's not home, but you'll see the light on."

"Does she live on a commune?"

"I don't know what they call it, but it's a cluster of little cabins."

"Out in the middle of nowhere."

"Pretty much."

"Great. You free for dinner later?" asked Sunny.

"I thought I'd call Lenstrom after class. I'll leave you a message if we make a plan. Hey, beware of the hippie dogs up there. There's a bunch of them running around all lawless."

"Wonderful. Ferocious, I assume."

"All bark and no bite, at least when I was there."

The drive didn't take as long as she thought it would. The road marked with the thunderbird mailbox got steep as it headed up Black Mountain. She downshifted to first gear to let the old Ford take it easy. It was just as well to travel slow. The headlights didn't light up much beyond the immediate road ahead and she was worried she'd drive right past the houses without knowing it. Rivka didn't say if the road dead-ended or not. She drove on until the pavement dropped off to dirt, giving her that uncertain feeling of having gone too far or the wrong way, just like Rivka said.

The truck crawled ahead over potholes and gullies for fifteen minutes in the pitch black. She checked the cell phone. It was searching for a signal without luck. At last the road dropped down and flattened out, revealing a scattering of identical cabins, small and rugged, the sort hunting clubs used to build. Each had a single window over a tiny front porch, a steep shingle roof, and a black smokestack rising up like a sturdy feather in an enormous cap. There were lights on in three of the cabins. Sunny stopped and killed the engine. An entourage of barking dogs quickly emerged from the shadows to surround the truck, edging toward it with paws braced, as if drawn against their will. The teeth were bared, but several tails were wagging despite a ferocious din of barking. She took this as a good sign and opened the door cautiously. The barking intensified when she stepped out and all five of them surged around her. She stood still, attempting to exude an air of benevolent confidence. Like a pot removed from the flame on the point of boiling over, they subsided.

"It's okay, dogs," she said, holding out a hand. "It's just me."

That seemed to satisfy them and the barking settled down to afterthoughts and chatter. Tail-wagging and leaps replaced attack mode.

"Who's there?" called a voice from the darkness.

"Dahlia?" said Sunny.

"Who's there?"

"Sunny McCoskey."

"Who?" said Dahlia, walking up.

"Sunny. McCoskey. From Night of Five Stars. Rivka's friend."

"Oh, Sunny! My god, what are you doing out here?" She stood still, not entirely inviting.

"I needed to see you. I called the restaurant, but they said you weren't working tonight. I got directions from Rivka and hoped you'd be here."

"I can't believe you found it."

"Neither can I."

Dahlia met Sunny's eyes curiously. "I gave away my shift. I wanted to finish a piece I started late last night. Come on in, I'll show you."

Shivering with cold, Sunny followed her down a trail crowded with tall grasses. Now that the dogs were quiet, she could hear the twangy sounds of the Grateful Dead coming from one of the lighted cabins in the other direction. They passed two dark cabins and came to a third, set back from the others and lit by a faint glow through a gauzy orange curtain. Behind the cabin a white canvas tent glowed floor to ceiling with bright light. Dahlia led the way to the tent and held open the door. Sunny stepped into the warmth, the effect of the potbellied stove hissing in the corner.

The tent had been set up on a wood frame with a plywood foundation and a little porch outside. Cozy. Several shop lights, the kind with clips at the base, had been aimed into white photographer's umbrellas, filling the room with soft, bright light. A large wooden worktable in the middle of the room held dozens of silver tubes of paint, variously dented and folded and rolled down to squeeze out the last of the pigment. An array of jars, some of them filled with brushes like stark bouquets, crowded at one end. In front of the table was a large easel holding the canvas she had been working on, a still life of a knitting project in progress, with two bamboo needles in the foreground over a luxuriously folded heap of scarf, and a large round ball of paprika wool behind it. The background was dark and the project had the feeling of having been abandoned mid-stitch. Behind the easel, the same scene was repeated in a half-knit scarf tossed on a chair.

Other pictures were leaned up several deep against a small desk and sagging armchair. The one in front seemed to be a minimalist landscape rendered in somber shades, but as she looked at it she realized it was a muscular forearm stretched across an erect penis, the hand tucked out of sight between the legs. She looked at Dahlia.

"I have a fondness for male autoeroticism," she said.

"And the knitting?"

"Female autoeroticism."

Another worktable set up behind the door was stacked with books liberally decorated with pentagrams and hieroglyphics. *The Complete Holistic Herbal Companion, Celtic Rites and Rituals, The New Paganism, Wicca: A Guide for the Solitary Practitioner, Power of the Witch,* and *The Art of Essential Oils and Aromatherapy.* Above the desk several narrow plank shelves held jars of powders, herbs, and seeds, as well as dozens of tiny dark vials with handwritten labels.

Dahlia took a bottle of wine from the table and pulled the cork. "Have a glass with me?"

"Love to."

She poured the wine into a couple of old jelly jars and handed one to Sunny. Their eyes met for a moment. Sunny thought she detected a hint of bashfulness. Was Dahlia embarrassed by what they shared? Did she know? Dahlia was pretty. Somehow she hadn't noticed it before. She had a wide, full smile and warm brown eyes set in a golden complexion. She was wearing paint-splattered jeans and an olive green Shetland sweater with a large moth hole at the shoulder. It had obviously been washed many times and was now too small and felted.

"To surprise visitors," Dahlia said.

They touched glasses and drank. Sunny raised her eyebrows and turned the bottle toward her. It was a 1998 Flowers Camp Meeting Ridge Pinot Noir, hard to find outside restaurants, expensive, and worth it.

"You live pretty well out here," said Sunny.

"Thanks to Nathan, in several ways. But I'm dying of curiosity. What on earth brings you all the way up the mountain tonight? Not that I mind. Company is always welcome when you live in the sticks."

Sunny moved toward the worktable where bundles of herbs hung from the underside of the bottom shelf, drying. A stone mortar had been used to prop one of the texts open. A dense foliage of notes had been scribbled in the margins. Papers littered the desk, all heavily marked with fine black writing. Dahlia walked over quickly and snapped the book shut. She scooped the papers into a stack and stuck them in the book, then shoved the whole business into a cardboard box under the table.

"I use this place as my workshop, so I don't worry too much about cleaning up. This is where I experiment with all kinds of things. Paintings, tinctures, whatever. No inhibitions. I can do anything my imagination can dream up."

"What is all that?" asked Sunny, motioning to the vials.

"Essential oils, mostly."

"For aromatherapy?"

"And other things. Lotions, soap, candles."

"It looks like you made them yourself."

"I did. My neighbor and I share a distiller out back. You can distill just about anything. Leaves, flowers, bark. Anything that holds moisture will release it when you pass steam through it. Some of that moisture will be water, but mixed in with the water will be the vital essence, what rises up. That's the essential oil. They're incredibly potent. People think of fragrance when they think of essential oils, but it's so much more than that. It is the distillation of the substance, including all its best and worst properties, its fragrance, flavor, everything. It's the undiluted spirit. If it were a person, it would be the soul."

Sunny leaned closer. The labels on the little bottles said Pine Needle, Golden Freesia, Farmers' Market Oranges, Timo's Pale Pink Roses, Wild Blackberries, Fresh Cedar Chips.

"I've been doing it for a few years now. It fits with the way I paint. There's a certain alchemy to mixing pigment. You can burn and dry all kinds of things, pulverize them, and blend them for different colors. You can press certain juices for color. Beets, pomegranate, and blackberries, for example. Essential oils capture a different aspect of a substance. Not the exterior color, but the interior, volatile nature."

"You put the essential oils in your paints?"

"Sometimes. Mostly I put them in candles and soaps."

"So they aren't edible?"

"They're mostly too potent to be safe to cook with. It's all a matter of dosage, and that can be tricky, since you never know how potent the material you start with is. Lots of plants are medicine in one dose and poison in another. Like foxglove. A little bit is good for your circulation and heart function, too much will kill you."

"My neighbors have foxglove planted all along their fence."

"Just because it's poisonous doesn't make it a problem. Most gardens are full of poisonous plants. Luckily most people don't go around making tea and salad out of everything they find growing beside the house. It's like the cleanser under the sink, ammonia is terribly poisonous, but it has its uses."

"You know a lot about poisons," said Sunny.

"I know a lot about medicine. Medicine and poison are two sides of the same coin. Same as what you do. Cooking is as much about what isn't edible as it is about what is. You know not to use the leaves of rhubarb and potato, for example. And that certain molds on cheeses and meats are desirable, while others will make you sick."

"Of course. The interesting part is walking a line between what's good and what isn't. Steak tartare, for instance." Sunny studied the wall of vials. "I know a few cooks who are really into infused oils. Everything is brushed with some kind of infused oil. Even vanilla-infused oil for desserts."

"Andre loves infused oils. He uses them all the time."

Sunny flinched slightly, and she hoped unnoticeably, at the mention of Andre's name. "Does he? I didn't notice."

"He mostly uses them for the hard-to-please, sensually challenged customers. He has a garlic-infused oil that would grow hair on your chest. He used it on Nathan's food, because Nathan was always complaining that everything tasted bland. Nathan's taste buds, like so much of him, were hard to please."

Sunny tried to recall if she'd seen any infused oils in the Vinifera kitchen.

"Here, sit down and relax," said Dahlia, gesturing toward the tatty couch. "I'm just going to put the finishing touches on while we talk. If this paint dries it will take me forever to get the color right again." She added more wine to their glasses, then took up a brush and turned to the painting. "So, you didn't come all the way out here to talk about my interest in herbal medicine."

"No, I came to talk about Nathan. To get your opinion."

"Of Nathan?"

"Of his death. Do you think he died of natural causes, like the police say?"

Dahlia looked at her. "You don't?"

"I'm not convinced."

"Why? The coroner said he had a heart attack. That's a natural cause in my book."

"There must be substances that can cause a heart attack."

"There are plenty. Cocaine, for example, but Nathan didn't do coke. He was into the narcotic effects of alcohol, not uppers. He was about as far from a speed freak as you can get. It never occurred to me that somebody could have dosed him."

"I'm not saying someone did."

"Yes, you are. You just don't like saying it. So what's got you on the trail this time?" She smiled. "I heard about that other case you solved. Apparently you're quite the sleuth."

"That was different. A friend of mine was in jail for a crime he didn't commit."

"And this time around you think a friend of yours isn't in jail for a crime he just might have committed."

"What are you saying?" said Sunny.

"What are *you* saying?" said Dahlia, raising an eyebrow and giving her an enigmatic smile. "The coroner says heart attack and Sunny McCoskey smells murder. Why?"

Sunny took a long sip of the very good wine. Dahlia kept answering questions with questions. "I guess the thing that bothers me most is that smashed bottle in the living room."

Dahlia nodded. "I thought about that too when it first happened. The trouble is, so many people went through that house, night and day. Housekeepers, the people who maintained the pool, the water guy, the plant guy, friends, lovers, accountants. That's why he had the security system installed, so he wouldn't have to keep making dupes of keys. He just told everyone to punch 1111 into the keypad. Nathan didn't like to be alone. That's why he never got married, incidentally. That's my theory, anyway. He had to have somebody with him at all times and no one person could be there every minute. I dated him for a while and there were several occasions—I'm not kidding—when we were in bed together and some woman slipped into bed next to me. It scared the living crap out of me. Other times, I'd go out into the kitchen and some guy Nathan befriended in a bar would be sleeping on the couch. He was the most trusting man I've ever known."

"So you think some guy he met at a bar, a guy who happened to be wearing gloves so he wouldn't leave prints, let himself into Nathan's house, broke a bottle of wine worth half my mortgage payment, failed to notify anyone that Nathan had bought the farm, and managed to get out of there without leaving so much as a footprint?"

"All I'm saying is that so much goes on behind closed doors. A death is like a snapshot or a still life. It takes a moment and freezes it. Who knows what exact sequence of events led up to that snapshot? There are plenty of times in my life where if I were to drop dead, the police would have one hell of a time trying to figure out what I'd been doing. Nathan's life was not clean and tidy. What was most lovely about him was that he was totally without rules. He was the only genuinely guiltless, lawless man I ever knew. He was governed, if you can even use that word, entirely by passion."

She stopped talking and looked away, trying to control some emotion. After a moment she regained her composure. "Are you familiar with William of Occam?" she asked.

Sunny shook her head.

"He was a fourteenth-century philosopher. He said, essentially, that you shouldn't make things more complicated than they need to be. Presuming that the universe is a logical place, the simplest explanation of a phenomenon ought to be the right one. In relation to Nathan, knowing his philandering ways and lifetime of associations with dubious characters, I think we can safely shave off the broken bottle as extraneous to the focal event, which is that he had a heart attack. Anybody could have dropped that bottle and run for it."

"Couldn't one of those dubious associations have brought trouble his way?"

"Absolutely. Just not this time. If there was a knife in his back, I'd say you were onto something. But considering that all the evidence suggests heart failure, the simplest explanation is exactly that."

"Heart failure, yes. The question is, did something trigger it. You yourself said it could have been any number of substances. What would you use if you were trying to give a man a heart attack?"

Dahlia smiled. "In Nathan's case? Stiletto heels and a Wonderbra." She held up the wine bottle. Sunny declined. She could see what Rivka liked about Dahlia.

"What about Remy? Do you consider him dangerous?" Sunny asked.

"Dangerous? Not at all. Bitter, certainly, but harmless. Remy is still pissed off that he's not landed gentry. He has a post-colonial hangover. His mother's family used to own about half of Sri Lanka, but he managed not to inherit any of it. He can't get over the fact that he has fallen into a state of disenfranchisement so profound that the only way he can afford to drink good wine is to kowtow to a bunch of retired yuppies with a napkin over his arm."

"So his father was French."

"I think his father is actually Belgian, but Remy grew up in Dijon. Or so he says."

"That explains the connections in the French wine business."

"It doesn't hurt that his older brother is one of the most respected wine critics in France. All Remy has to do is mention his last name and every cellar door in Bordeaux swings open."

"So why does he live in California? Wait, let me guess. They hate each other."

"You got it in one. A nasty, chronic case of fraternal animosity. From what I hear, Patrick is good looking, rich, and successful.

Whenever Remy isn't getting under my nails like little slivers of bamboo, I have to feel sorry for him. You can tell he's lonely, but he's so angry he never makes any friends. Anger is the only emotion he has left. That, and the perverted glee you can see him feeling whenever somebody orders one of the crappier bottles of wine we have to carry as a favor to somebody. Nathan was his only friend as far as I can tell, and Remy never shed a tear over his death."

"You never know what he felt once he was home alone. He doesn't seem like the kind of guy to reveal his emotions in public, no matter what."

"That might be so. Everyone is more vulnerable than we imagine."

Dahlia turned back to her painting, and after a minute of silence Sunny stood to go. She lingered awkwardly, trying to find an appropriate way to introduce one last question. Dahlia turned. "Is there anything else? I don't mean to rush you, but I need to get this picture done tonight and I've already lost most of this batch of color."

"I'm sorry, I'll go. I just wanted to ask you one more question."

"Fire away."

"When was the last time you were in Nathan's house?"

Dahlia blinked. It was the first time her façade slipped. "I'm sorry, that's just none of your business. Thanks for the visit."

She put down the brush and walked Sunny to the door without saying another word. Sunny stepped outside and heard the latch drop in place behind her.

16

The truck rattled and bounced on the fast trip back down Black Mountain. Sunny didn't bother to engage the engine. In neutral, the truck picked up just enough speed on the downhills to coast up the gentle rises. She hardly touched the brakes and made good time back to the main road, where the cell phone found four bars of reception as she pulled onto Highway 29. It felt good to be back in touch with civilization. Even better, there was a message from Rivka saying that dinner was on at Monty's house for seven-thirty. A relaxing evening with friends and Monty's cooking were exactly what she needed, assuming she could get there before they were done. Monty's place was half an hour's drive past her house, and she was twenty minutes from home at least. She would be late even if she went there directly. Then there was the grisly thought of sitting down to dinner without showering away the day's work muck. The stoplight on the way into St. Helena was red, a clear sign that she was meant to make a right and head for home and the world's quickest shower.

Her hair was still wet when she pulled into Monty Lenstrom's driveway. He opened the door with a glass of red wine in hand. "McCoskey, you're late."

"Look at the positive side: I'm here. And I could have been much later."

Monty peered at her from behind his gold spectacles. "I'll count myself lucky. Get in here."

She followed Monty into the kitchen. Rivka was dressing a salad. She looked at the clock on the oven when she saw Sunny. "Damn, ten minutes after nine. Didn't you have an errand or two to run on the way here? Check out a few books at the library? Round or two of miniature golf?"

"Wow, the 'tude is thick in here tonight. I came as fast as I could. I was way out in the middle of the woods when you called."

"The funny thing is, for once you're too early," said Rivka.

"What do you mean?"

Monty picked up a notepad from beside the phone. "We had a lottery going to see who could guess how late you would be. Annabelle won. She said nine o'clock."

"Let me see that."

Monty had guessed eight-thirty. Rivka put her money on nine-thirty. "Thanks for the vote of confidence, Chavez. I'll remember that at your next performance review," said Sunny.

"Never bet against the boss," said Monty.

"How much was in the kitty?"

"Fifteen bucks."

"Speaking of, where's the lady of the house? Don't tell me she's actually going to grace us."

"Not a chance. She's at Unwatchable Movie Club with Paul. They get together and rent Werner Herzog films and the early Roman Polanski stuff. Tonight is the third installment of the Elliott Gould festival."

"And yet she took the trouble to place her bet."

"In absentia. The woman loves easy money."

Monty handed Sunny a glass of wine, then donned a pair of oven mitts. He opened the oven door and slid the rack out, laying hands on a bubbling casserole like he was delivering a baby.

"Tonight's meal is a tribute to Merle and Joanna Lenstrom, pillars of the wholesome Midwestern way of life that is the backbone of this nation."

"Is that Stroganoff à la Joanna?" asked Sunny. "My oh my."

"None other. And I don't mind telling you it makes tasty leftovers."

"And a tidy profit for the cardiologists."

"Haven't you heard?" said Monty. "Fat is the new skinny."

They moved to the whitewashed pine plank table set up in Monty's dining room. A pot of white tulips sat in the middle between tea-lights in chunky glass holders. Rivka served the casserole while Monty refilled his wineglass and Rivka's. They passed around bread, endive salad, and sautéed carrots.

"Monty, you do things to a carrot that can't be explained by god or science," said Sunny. "How can a sliced carrot taste this good?"

"Very simple. Don't add water. You have to make the little buggers sweat."

"How was your trip out to see Dahlia?" asked Rivka. "Didn't you love her place?"

"I didn't see the house. I only went into the tent cabin. She's into some interesting stuff."

"What did you find out?" asked Monty. "I'm up to speed. Rivka filled me in on the case."

Sunny shot Rivka a look. "The case?"

Rivka stopped buttering her bread, knife in hand. "What? I figured it was okay."

"Don't edge me out, McCoskey," said Monty. "You need me. I'm the one who spotted the fake Marceline in the first place. So what's new?"

"Well, she didn't confess," said Sunny. She sighed and pushed at her food. "I don't know what to make of any of this anymore."

"Don't poke," said Monty. "Dig in before it gets cold. Make Joanna proud."

She took a bite of the wide egg noodles and creamy sauce layered with mushrooms, ground beef, and bell peppers.

"This really is my favorite," said Sunny.

"I wish we could serve this kind of thing at Wildside," said Rivka.

"We might be able to. I've been thinking about making one day a week, like maybe Tuesdays, a very basic prix fixe menu with fewer courses and more simple dishes. We could turn the tables several times and get the people who can't take a long lunch to come in."

"Why not just add that kind of option to the everyday menu?" said Monty. "If you have three hours for the full Wildside treatment, great. If not, sit at the bar and have the prix fixe quickie."

"That is great idea, comrade," said Sunny. "You are like genius smart guy."

"*Danke, liebchen.* That's one problem solved. Now let us turn the light of my genius on the case of Nathan Osborne. The situation seems perfectly clear to me. Remy Castels decides to make a little cash on the side and fakes a case of Marceline. Very clever, as long as he doesn't get caught. It's all great until his boss totters home with one of the bottles. Osborne notices the forgery and decides to have a little fun blackmailing Castels. Remy thinks, I'm not going to put up with this bullshit. So he takes a bottle, injects some kind of stimulant into it through the cork, and sends Osborne home with it. He ODs and no one is the wiser."

"There are about a dozen holes in that story," said Sunny. "But injecting the poison through the cork is sort of interesting."

"Saw it in a movie. What holes?"

"Well, for one thing, why would Nathan take a second bottle home, especially if he'd figured out it was fake? He would need it as evidence if he was to continue his blackmail scheme."

"Exactly. Osborne was planning to hold it hostage. Like when the blackmailer puts the grainy black-and-white photographs of misconduct in the safe, in case the blackmailee gets tired of paying."

"Then why would he drink it? He wouldn't drink his bottle of evidence."

"Chavez, help me out with this one."

Rivka shook her head. "Can't do. I think you're both nuts."

"And none of that explains the broken bottle," said Sunny.

"That part we covered. Remy the murderer had to remove the bottle with the poison in it. His plan was obviously to replace the fake bottle with a real one, thus covering both crimes, only he dropped it."

"I agree with that last part," said Sunny, "but the other stuff doesn't make sense. If there was poison in the fake wine, it would have been in the wine in the glass Nathan was drinking from as well. If Remy went to all that trouble to replace the bottle, he wouldn't have left the wine in the glass where it could be tested."

"He got rattled when he dropped it and hightailed it out of there. I'm sure his intention was to get rid of all the evidence, but he panicked."

"I still don't see why he would doctor one of the fake bottles of wine. That doesn't fit. He had no way of being sure Nathan would drink it, or that he'd drink it alone. Besides, if you were blackmailing somebody over fake wine, would you accept their gift of fake wine? It doesn't make sense."

"Sun's right," said Rivka. "He would have put it in one of the glasses he served Nathan at the restaurant. He had plenty of opportunity to slip him a Mickey whenever he felt like it."

"You are absolutely right," said Monty, his eyes flashing. "I was so fixated on the broken bottle that I completely overlooked the obvious. From what I understand, he drank constantly at the restaurant. Anybody on staff could have dosed his drink. The bartender, the servers."

"Sure, anybody could have poisoned him, but you're overlooking the most important part," said Rivka. "He wasn't poisoned. He had a heart attack."

"Maybe he was poisoned with something that can give you a heart attack," said Sunny. "Like a fat dose of coke, for example."

"It would have to be huge to take effect like that," said Monty. "He was relaxing in his living room when he checked out. That doesn't sound like a cocaine high to me. They would have found him polishing the kitchen floor with a Q-Tip."

"There has to be other stuff that can do it," said Sunny. "Dahlia mentioned foxglove, and I was thinking maybe nitroglycerin. They give people with heart trouble nitro tablets to kick-start their heart if they go into cardiac arrest, but I wonder what happens if you take too many."

"Ka-boom!" said Monty.

Rivka settled her brown eyes on Sunny thoughtfully. "What about her work? Did you get a chance to see her paintings? Aren't they amazing?"

"I was too preoccupied. I couldn't appreciate them properly. She certainly has talent. I'm not so sure about the choice of subject matter."

"I think it's genius," said Rivka. "She captures the primal essence of the men she knows."

"I think they call that a succubus," said Monty between bites. "Climbs in the bedroom window at night. Makes a meal by ripping your heart out of your chest at the moment of orgasm. She'd better not come after my primal essence."

"You should be so lucky," said Rivka. She paused, twisting one of several piercings in her right ear, a nervous habit that meant she was thinking of something else. "So what did you guys talk about?"

"Not that much. She was pretty evasive, kept talking about everyone else. I'd swear she was trying to hide something. I looked at her desk and she practically ran over to put away all the papers on it. They were covered with notes."

"I'm surprised you two didn't get into a full-on cat fight," said Monty.

"Is there anything you didn't tell him?" said Sunny indignantly. "Was there a presentation? Ten quick slides explaining the most intimate aspects of my life?"

"I didn't think you'd mind," said Rivka sheepishly. "We're all family. Actually, I didn't think Lenstrom would be foolish enough to let on that he knew." She punched Monty. "Big dork."

"Perhaps Monty would like to know the real reason why you won't marry Alex," said Sunny.

"Revenge just keeps the wheel of pain turning. You're above the petty bitterness of retaliation," said Rivka.

"Yes, but I might do it anyway."

"Ladies, please. Dinner is a love thing. Besides, you told me already, not that I couldn't have guessed."

"Sunny!" cried Rivka.

"Kidding," said Monty.

"Can we stay focused, people?" said Sunny. "I am trying to get to the bottom of all the weirdness at Vinifera and I'm telling you Dahlia was really defensive, in an assertive kind of way."

"Honestly, what did you expect?" said Rivka. "You drive out to her house unannounced and ask a ton of questions. It had to be obvious that you were there to snoop around."

"That implies a guilty conscience. If there was nothing to hide, it wouldn't occur to her that I was snooping. She obviously didn't want me to see what she'd been writing."

"No, I happen to know she didn't."

"What do you mean?"

"The notes on the desk were part of a project we were working on together."

"How do you know?"

"I was out there just this afternoon before yoga."

"What project?"

"And it has nothing to do with Nathan Osborne, at least in the way you imagine."

An uneasy silence gripped the table. Rivka sighed. "Fine. I'll tell you. It was a love potion. I know it sounds stupid. We were working on a sort of cleansing ceremony and a potion. You put it in a tiny vial and wear it around your neck in one of those little leather pouches. It was partly for you, partly for her. She was trying to cleanse her heart, and in doing so set Andre free of any connections he might have to her, and vice versa. And to set Nathan free so he could proceed through the afterlife in peace. Part of the process is to write down everything about the person that still connects you to them, good and bad. Obviously, she didn't want you to see a bunch of writing about Andre."

"Was that her idea or yours?"

"She was talking about cleansing her heart of past loves, in relation to Nathan, mostly, but also Andre. She suggested we do something to encourage things between the two of you. She really does wish you well."

"Like some kind of spell?"

"You could call it that."

"Monty?"

"Pass. The whole witch's brew–love tonic concept renders me speechless. You're talking to a man who can't believe literate adults still read the horoscope column. It's more proof that people will believe absolutely anything."

"Just because you can't explain a phenomenon doesn't mean it doesn't exist," said Rivka. "So what did she have to say about Osborne?"

"Well, the broken bottle didn't bother her," said Sunny. "She thought there could be an innocent explanation. Then she brought up this philosopher Occam."

"Occam's razor," Monty said.

"Which is?" asked Rivka.

"Basically, whatever looks like the most obvious solution is probably the right answer," said Sunny. "It reminded me of what Catelina used to say, 'If it looks like a duck, smells like a duck, and walks like a duck, don't expect it to taste like a pig.' Dahlia figured since it looked like a simple heart attack, it probably was. I think that solution leaves too many questions unanswered."

The dinner got the best of them and they ate in silence, each possessed by thoughts. After a while, Monty heaped more stroganoff onto his plate. "I think we need a new approach. We don't know what happened, let alone how. We can only guess, and that's not going to do us any good. What do we know about who and why?"

"We'll know a lot more about that tomorrow," said Rivka. "Dahlia is going to hear the reading of the will."

"Do you think she'll tell you what they say?" asked Sunny.

"I don't see why not."

"I still say Remy has the real motive, regardless of inheritance or lack thereof," said Monty. "He is clearly the purveyor of false wines. There's a connection between that wine and Nathan's death. Nathan got in the way somehow and had to be eliminated."

"What bothers me is that case of wine in the cellar at Vinifera," said Sunny. "If Remy did it, why wouldn't he get the rest of that wine out of the cellar before somebody like me or the cops found it? That strongly suggests his innocence."

"Or carelessness, or brazenness," said Monty. "Or intelligence. Maybe he figured the cops would think like you. If he didn't get rid of the wine he must be innocent."

"The more information I get, the bigger the knot becomes. I'm not untying anything. But I still think there is more to those essential oils Dahlia makes. She said most of them are toxic. That gives her the means and the know-how to poison the guy who's been jerking her around for who knows how long. She's bound to have plenty of animosity for Nathan, and possibly a financial motive as well."

"She doesn't have animosity toward Nathan," said Rivka. "Or at least not a lethal dose of it. He was a bad boyfriend who dumped her. Several times. But she doesn't hate him, and it certainly wouldn't be enough to make her want to kill him. And if anything, she was financially motivated to keep him around."

"The Rastburns said she practically went postal on him," said Sunny.

"Who are the Rastburns again?" asked Monty.

After Sunny explained, Monty ran a hand over his scalp, smoothing the nonexistent hair. "You know, Sun, I think you might have to face the fact that you may never know exactly what happened. It is entirely possible, in my opinion, that somebody put something in a drink or a plate of food that eventually made its way to Nathan Osborne's doomed lips. But it could have been any number of people, including just about anybody on staff at Vinifera, or the Rastburns for that matter. We've got your studly chef boyfriend there in the kitchen. He needed Osborne out of the way in order to become a partner, and he knows which plate is his because Osborne always special orders. Means and motive. We've got Dahlia out there on the floor. She's been burned by him more than once and she's still bringing him his evening cocktail. That's got to piss her off no matter what she says. Not to mention that she has a chemistry lab back at her Unabomber shack. Plenty of means, plenty of motive. Then we've got Remy, my personal favorite, the embittered sommelier with a criminal event to protect. He's on the floor, behind the bar, bringing over special drinks. Plenty of means, plenty of motive. And we've got our bartender who takes Osborne home the night he dies. Talk about means. Still, we can probably eliminate him at least. Unless Osborne secretly willed him his fortune, I don't see a motive."

Sunny bit her lip. "He could have a motive. Last night when I was hanging around outside Vinifera waiting for the Rastburns, I saw him kissing Dahlia. It looked like he meant it."

"For the love of a good woman?" said Monty. "It could be that as easily as anything else. Or it could be a busser or a barback or a line cook with a vendetta as far as we know. It could be anybody or nobody. Or two people working together—Dahlia and Andre, if you'll both forgive me."

"I don't think we'll ever know the absolute truth," said Rivka, "but if we have to guess, I'm going to agree with Dahlia. Looks like a heart attack, and was verified as a heart attack by the people who know about such things. I think I'll call it a heart attack. So Remy forged a case of wine. I don't think it's worth ruining Vinifera's reputation over, do you? And as for Dahlia's essential oils, it's a hobby, and a very interesting one in my opinion. She makes her own perfumes, her own candles, her own soap. She mixes her own colors. It's not a crime to be creative. Sunny, you ought to understand that better than anyone. And besides, you yourself said there are tons of poisonous substances around. They're everywhere. Even that tree in the backyard at Vinifera. Just because somebody has foxglove in their garden and ant spray under the sink doesn't make them dangerous."

"It does if you're an ant," said Monty.

"I forgot about that," said Sunny.

"What?" said Rivka.

"The yew tree. Dahlia called it the Tree of Death that night when we all ate outside," Sunny said.

"I know what you're thinking, but it can't be that," said Rivka. "She wouldn't have said that if she'd just killed him, or even if she knew he was dead. No one knew yet, even though he'd been dead a whole day."

"I'm not so sure," said Sunny, shaking her head. "I have a hunch somebody at that table knew. I think somebody from Vinifera visited Osborne late that night, but they kept it and what they saw there to themselves. Bottles of 1967 Marceline don't grow on trees. The most logical place to find one is the cellar at Vinifera, and it's that much easier if you work there."

"The person who knew exactly where to look was Remy," said Monty.

"The Rastburns mentioned something else that's strange. They said Remy is the only one with a key to the alcoves where the more valuable wines are usually kept."

"That can't be true. In a place the size of Vinifera it's totally impractical," said Rivka. "Imagine if Bertrand was the only one with a key to the wine cage at Wildside."

"It's worse than that," said Sunny. "I'm the only one with a key, and I can never find it. But there is usually plenty of warning when somebody is going to crack open a magnum of Morgon over lunch. From what Andre said, the stuff in the alcoves at Vinifera is very high end or not ready to drink yet. And almost none of it is on the menu. Basically, Remy is the only one who sells those wines, so he's the only one who needs access. Still, none of this proves anything. That bottle of wine has been kicking around since 1967. In theory, it could have come from anywhere. It could have nothing to do with the case I found at Vinifera. And so the Tree of Death presides over every family meal on the premises. It may be nothing more than an intriguingly macabre but irrelevant detail. My conclusion, lady and gentleman, is that we're back where we started."

The rest of the meal was spent in the discussion of blander topics. After dinner, Monty served wedges of apple pie with vanilla ice cream while they lay on the Turkish carpet in front of the fireplace in the living room. Conversation was gradually replaced with drowsy silence. They tackled the cleanup with professional efficiency and then said a prompt and sleepy goodnight.

17

Had it been time to get up, the sky would have been
tinged with the pale light of dawn. Instead, Sunny opened her
eyes to heavy darkness. The house was perfectly silent except
for the faint buzz of the old clock radio on the nightstand, a pre-
digital relic yellow with age. She made several attempts to go
back to sleep, turning over and wiggling deep under the covers,
warm and comfortable but thoroughly awake. She tried to set
her thoughts aside and sink into the oblivion of sleep without
success. Voluntarily and involuntarily, her mind analyzed the
previous day's activities with methodical determination. She
went over conversations with the Rastburns and Dahlia, replay-
ing bits and pieces, obsessively hunting some new insight.

The memory of a dream washed over her. It was tantalizingly
close. She lay very still, reaching for each image. She was in a
Gothic-looking workshop or laboratory, dense with dark vials
and menacing, twisting contraptions. Dahlia stood over a cauldron, ripping out her knitting and letting each length of wool
drop into the bubbling water. She tossed the ball of yarn and
bamboo needles in last. Sunny said, "That won't help. You'll ruin
it." Dahlia stirred the pot and said, with almost cheerful non-
chalance, "The needles give it soul. Anything will release its soul

in the right conditions." Sunny lay in bed chasing more of the dream, sensing there was more, but nothing else would come.

Finally she got up and went into the dark living room, where her laptop was set up on a narrow table against the wall. She turned the machine on and headed to the kitchen to put water on for coffee. The clock read just after four. She tried to remember people's reaction at staff dinner Sunday night when Dahlia mentioned the yew tree. There had been a shifting in seats and the exchange of glances around the table when she fished the needles out of the glass. They'd heard her Tree of Death speech before. Everyone knew the tree was poisonous.

She left the water to boil and returned to the living room, where the blue glow emanating from the computer screen filled the dark room with a futuristic aura. She typed *yew* and *poison* into the search engine, which promptly pulled up thousands of entries. Yew's toxicity, like hemlock, was apparently notorious. Dozens of web sites described how the yew tree had been worshiped by the Druids and the Celts, especially at winter solstice. There were accounts of assassinations, suicides, and murders going back thousands of years using infusions and extracts of yew. Ancient arrows had been tipped with poisonous extract of yew. Legend warned even of sleeping under a yew tree. Then she read how Roman soldiers had died after drinking wine that had been stored in casks made of yew wood.

The water in the kettle had almost boiled away when she finally went back to the kitchen, and she settled for a strong cup of coffee instead of a whole pot. Palms moist with a mixture of dread and excitement, she went back to the computer. The more scientific of the sites described the effects and attributes of taxine, the poisonous compound in yew, and taxol, the miracle cancer drug recently discovered in the same branches. The description of poisoning by yew made the room sway, and she had to remind herself to keep breathing as she read. Wrote one researcher, "Yew exerts its toxic action upon the heart. The primary (and often the only) sign of poisoning is sudden death. All parts of the tree are poisonous, particularly the needles." According to the same site, death could occur within a few minutes or a few hours later, depending on the dose. If the dose was high enough, the heart simply stopped.

She typed up her thoughts and printed them out, then waited while the computer ran through its signing-off ritual. Her toes felt icy on the wood floor. She shivered, noticing for the first time her bare arms and legs.

The sun was just beginning to light the eastern horizon as she pulled up in front of the St. Helena Police Station. To the west, the last of the stars persisted in a cobalt blue sky. A layer of frost silvered the sidewalk. Inside the station, a monastic hush pervaded the dimly lit receiving room. Sunny waited for the clerk to turn her attention to her. Behind the clerk, a dispatcher reported a dog without a collar on Spring Street. Sunny stated her business and learned that neither Sergeant Harvey nor Officer Dervich was currently on duty, but Sergeant Harvey would be arriving shortly. Sunny placed an envelope on the counter.

"Could you give this to Sergeant Harvey when he arrives?"

"I'll see that he receives it," said the woman, turning back to her computer.

"It's important."

"I understand."

"What time did you say he'll be in?"

"Some time this morning."

Outside, the birds had started to welcome the day. Sunny glanced at her watch. Bismark's wouldn't be open for another twenty minutes. It was tempting to wait. The cozy atmosphere of the café was addicting, and she could use the comfort of its scarred wooden tables, the morning paper, the aloof camaraderie of the espresso jockeys, and the predictably salty and chewy bagel with cream cheese and tomato. But there would be no relaxing until this business with Nathan Osborne was resolved, and she was going to see it resolved. She cast a last longing look up the street and got in the truck.

The kitchen at Wildside was icy and dark when she arrived, but there was plenty to do and the ovens would heat the place up in no time. She thought with relief of having to prepare the chickpea purée that she'd added to the menu last week, served with rosemary olive oil and goat cheese crostini. It would be a fine way to kill time until she could talk with Steve.

She'd only just changed into her work clothes when Steve Harvey rang the mobile line.

"What's this rant you left me, McCoskey?"

"What do you think?"

"I think you've gone off your cracker. Let me be more specific. On page three of five, paragraph three, you reference the witches of *Macbeth*. Shakespeare, I believe. And I quote, 'Double, double toil and trouble; Fire burn and cauldron bubble.' Sunny, have you lost your mind?"

"That's just historical background material, establishing how widely known the poisonous qualities of the yew tree are. That's what the witches say as they toss sprigs of yew into the pot with the eye of newt. Yew is highly toxic."

"I see."

"Didn't you read the important part? How a good dose of
yew causes a sudden heart attack, often with no other signs or
symptoms? It's a powerful cardiac depressant. Steve, there's a
yew tree right in the backyard at Vinifera and plenty of people
on staff knew about its poisonous properties. Dahlia even mentioned it the night I was there. You don't have to eat very much
of the stuff, and if you made some kind of extract, which is not
very difficult, you'd need even less. You could figure out how to
do it from a book or online, or you could pay somebody to do it
for you. Since the poison takes effect within a few minutes and
Osborne had just ingested a glass of wine when he died—the
source of which is coincidentally very much in question—my
guess is you're going to find a great big dose of taxine in that
glass. That's the toxic element in yew. Taxine A and B. You guys
keep that sort of thing, right?"

"You mean the wine left in the glass."

"Yeah."

She heard the creak of him leaning back in his chair. A tell-
tale thump indicated he'd put his feet up on the desk. "Well, as I
stated before, in a case like this, we don't necessarily treat the
area as a crime scene, since no crime is known to have been committed. When it's fairly clear that the victim has succumbed to
natural causes with no signs of injury or foul play apparent, it
wouldn't be automatic protocol to collect extensive material evidence from the scene of death."

Steve sometimes had a way of sounding like a legal document
spoken in triplicate with footnotes. She stepped up the volume
on the mobile and held it out from her ear, hoping to minimize
the radiation.

"So you didn't keep a sample," she said.

"In this particular situation, we did not have a verified medical history of heart disease. There were no witnesses, and we also had several elements present that might have suggested a more involved scenario."

"So you did keep a sample."

"I believe Officer Dervich thought it prudent to collect samples of the wine on the floor and in the glass, on the off chance they might prove useful."

"That's great. How soon do you think you can find out?"

"We've got two big problems. One is access. Assuming you're right, how do you suppose they got the yew into the wine? Second is logic. Assuming you're right, why wouldn't the perpetrator remove the evidence?"

"I cover that. Page four, I think. All you'd have to do is inject the extract through the foil and cork. And the perp was befuddled after they failed to remove the evidence without messing up the scene. They panicked and got out of there fast. Besides, with what looks like a natural death, they wouldn't need to worry too much about leaving the juice on the scene."

"Sunny, this is exactly the sort of thing I've been meaning to talk with you about. I believe we've talked about it before, but I find myself forced to remind you that it is illegal to practice criminal investigation in California without a license. It is also stupid. You already found out the hard way once. It can land you in serious trouble."

"I'm not investigating anything. I'm just a concerned friend trying to help the local authorities."

"Right now I'm also a concerned friend. I'm concerned that you are far too involved in something that is none of your business."

"But doesn't finding out what happened matter?"

"It does. I'd simply like you to observe the appropriate division of labor. You run Wildside, I'll handle the police work."

"Fine. I'm done. How long is it going to take?"

"This is the situation. I'm going to go out on a limb to check this out for you. Frankly, I don't think there's a chance in hell there's taxine in that wine. But if it will get you off my back, I'm thrilled to do it. As luck would have it, there's an officer driving up to Sacramento later today to testify at the capitol and he can drop off the sample. I had to pull in a few favors up there to get them to stop what they're doing and find a way to identify taxine. Luckily I have a buddy in forensic toxicology who said he'd take a look."

"You mean you already arranged to have the wine tested? You're great, Steve. But why did you give me such a hard time just now? Never mind. Thanks."

"The St. Helena Police Department thanks you for your interest and diligence. You have officially done your duty as a concerned citizen, and now I would like to request that this be our last conversation on the matter."

"This is the last you'll hear of it from me. Except, will you let me know the outcome?"

He sighed and she heard the shuffling of papers on the other end of the line. "I'll have Officer Dervich call as soon as we know."

18

The certainty of the results was a given in Sunny's mind. The toxicology, the opportunity, and the logic fit perfectly. The wine would test positive for taxine. The difficulty now was establishing who did it.

Sunny pulled a lump of pizza dough from the batch she was making and smelled it, then added two more large pinches of kosher salt. She attempted to keep her mind on her work, but her thoughts returned again and again to the facts, or the need to connect them. There was a thread called Marceline running from Nathan's fatal glass of wine to Remy, unfortunately to Andre Moralon, and to Dahlia. There was one more person who might be able to shed more light on these people.

"When do you think you'll hear?" asked Rivka, breaking into Sunny's thoughts.

"I don't know."

"What if it's positive?"

"I'll leave it to Steve and I can get back to work. I want to tackle all those projects we talked about, and put together a bunch of menus for special Tuesday lunches. I thought about Monty's idea of offering a faster, cheaper prix fixe option every day, but that's not what Wildside is about. I want people who come here to do something they don't normally do. I like that it takes a couple of hours to eat. I don't want to change that. But I do want to make it possible for people who only have an hour for lunch to come here. I'm thinking Tuesdays. On Tuesday, you're not in Pays Basque or Perugia or Haute Provence. You're in Milan or Paris or London and you've got an hour to eat a nice, hot bistro lunch and get back to work."

"Power Tuesday," said Rivka.

"That's getting there," said Sunny.

"Upwardly Mobile Tuesdays."

"Maybe it should be Monday."

The two of them worked in silence. Rivka put the lid on a pot of braised greens. Over the white noise of kitchen appliances, soft piano cords announced the imminent arrival of a Puccini aria.

Sunny was restless, but she couldn't possibly get away until the last of the butternut squash ravioli were made. They took more time than most of the other entrées and she couldn't leave Rivka with that kind of challenge. She needed to leave soon, though. She was cutting it close. Andre seemed to come in around noon. The later it was in the day, the more likely he was to be at work, and she didn't want to risk running into him with no good excuse for being at his restaurant.

"You're intense this morning," said Rivka, watching her.

"I need to get everything done. I have an appointment at eleven, but I'll be back before twelve, I promise."

"Oh no. I thought you were satisfied now that Steve Harvey is testing your theory. Don't tell me you're going to go stir up more trouble."

"Not trouble. Answers."

Years of practice paid off at times like this. Her hands glided from task to task, and she moved with such speed and focused attention that the clock on the wall seemed frozen. By ten minutes to eleven, the day's preparations had advanced far enough that she felt comfortable turning the kitchen over to Rivka for the last half hour before they opened. Rivka gave her an imploring look as she opened the door and stepped outside.

Eliot Denby turned from the window in his office at the sound of three gentle knocks on the open door.

"Can I come in?" said Sunny, attempting to sound as casual as possible, as if this surprise visit were a social call compelled only by the desire to strike up a friendship with a fellow restaurateur.

The initial look of annoyance on Eliot's face was swiftly replaced by a charming smile.

"Come in, come in, of course," he said in a voice too richly mannered to be sincere. "This is a pleasant surprise." He stretched out a well-manicured hand and gripped hers briefly in welcome.

"I hate to bother you. I know you are in the middle of a busy morning," said Sunny, "I have an important matter to speak with you about. It shouldn't take long."

"Again! We seem to share so many important matters lately. Have a seat and tell me about it."

She registered his condescension and pulled up one of the minimalist steel-and-leather chairs set up on her side of the desk. Eliot sat down on the other side, and they stared at each other momentarily across the slab of polished cherry wood. A clear iMac sat at one end next to a high-tech telephone, an architect's lamp, and a designer calculator with stylishly oversized buttons. The only paperwork in sight, a stack of brown accounting ledgers and a yellow notepad scored with computations, stood out like relics from a bygone era.

The telephone emitted a triple pulse. Eliot glanced at the display and said, "Excuse me for one moment. I've been trying to reach this person for days."

The break was a relief. Sunny wanted to start with Remy but she needed to be cautious, since she didn't know how close the relationship was between Eliot and Remy, and she wanted to seem to be helping Eliot, not pointing out his mismanagement. And certain as she was that Remy was guilty of selling forged wine, she wasn't certain enough to be his accuser. What if she was wrong? Even if she was right, was it her place to bring his deeds to everyone's attention?

Eliot was describing a conversation he'd had with someone named Tom, and what he understood to be the prospects of some future project. She looked around the room. A matching cherry cabinet with two glass doors displayed artifacts from Eliot's professional life. There was a framed photo of him with Clint Eastwood in front of the Silverado country club, both of them windblown and dressed for tennis. Based on the length of their shorts, it had been taken sometime in the early eighties. She perused the collection of awards and certificates of official recognition handed out by local auxiliaries, city councils, and commissions. Eliot had been Napa City Businessman of the Year in 1985. There was a photograph of him and another man— Nathan?—looking young and elated, arm in arm with Governor Brown circa 1978. Eliot wore a lush mustache and a velour shirt. Another shot showed the two of them standing proudly to either side of a wooden box labeled "Denby's Coastal Ridge Pinot Noir 1988." Next to this photograph stood a bottle of Bandol Rouge from 1991.

Eliot said, "I think that would be wise. I'll bring him along. Right. Two o'clock on Tuesday. See you then." He hung up the phone and finished making note of their appointment in his computer. When he was done, he looked back at Sunny with businesslike enthusiasm. "Sorry about that. It's a shame Nathan didn't live to see this next phase of the business. It's going to be very exciting."

"Things are going well?"

"Very well. We're starting our own line of gourmet products. They'll be in all the high-end markets. Dean & DeLuca, Oakville Grocery, Andronico's. We're shopping a cookbook around, and there's interest in a television show on the Food Network. They can't get enough of Andre."

"That's terrific." She was losing her nerve. Eliot met her eyes, waiting for her to speak. She looked at the cabinet, searching for an entrée to the topic on her mind.

"That's one of my favorite wines," she said, indicating the bottle of Bandol.

"That bottle is special." He stood up, walked over to the cabinet, and removed the bottle, handing it to Sunny with ceremonial reverence. It was a wine she had served dozens of times at dinner parties, and she instinctively held it by the punt—the indentation in the bottom of the bottle—casually, familiarly, as if about to pour herself a glass. She stopped and looked more closely at the label, reading each word. Nothing seemed to have changed since 1991. She rubbed her thumb against the end of the punt, tracing its contours, then handed the bottle back to Eliot, who gazed at it for a moment before putting it back.

"Nathan and I had a wine bar together called Denby's," he said, with obvious pride. "It was in a beautiful old building downtown in Mill Valley, by the theater. We had more fun running that place. Everybody would come in. It was like having a party seven days a week, in both the good and the bad sense. I hardly slept for five years. Nathan had just started Osborne Wines, and he gave me that bottle the day Denby's opened. He said we would drink it on the ten-year anniversary. We never got to."

"It burned down, didn't it?"

"Stupidly. There was a gas heater with a grate in the floor in the office. Somebody put a stack of newspapers on top of it. We never found out who. They caught fire and the place was a heap of smoldering wreckage within half an hour. That bottle was the only one that survived intact. It was in the safe, not the cellar."

"That's terrible. You didn't have insurance?"

"We did. The fire put us out of business all the same. It's a long story." He went back around the desk and sat down, thinking. Finally he said, "The business was heavily in debt to Osborne Wines. We were in it for the long haul. We had invested in an extensive inventory of new wines, which we planned to age in the cellar at Denby's. It was a risky strategy. We bought fantastic stuff. At that time, not that many people knew about the very good Rhône wines and the really great wines from Provence. It was all still fairly new here. You could introduce people to it. After the fire, the insurance payment was just enough to keep Osborne Wines in the black. We walked away with almost nothing. After all those years in business, our only profit was memories."

"And the two of you teamed up again to open Vinifera."

"We thought we'd give it one more try."

"Was Remy Castels the wine steward at Denby's?"

The vertical line between Eliot's eyebrows deepened. "Only for about the last year. We didn't have a sommelier before that. Nathan handled the cellar and the servers sold and poured." He checked his wristwatch. "What was the important matter you wanted to discuss? I need to leave for a meeting in about five minutes."

"It's a hard topic for me to bring up," she said, "and I think it's going to take more than five minutes to explain. I'd rather wait and discuss it later."

"I don't understand."

Sunny stood up. "It's okay. Humor me. I'll give you a call to set up a better time."

Eliot looked doubtful. "Are you okay?"

"Fine. Completely fine. I'll be in touch."

"You do that," said Eliot.

She left him and stepped out onto the catwalk overlooking the dining room. She was almost eye level with the aluminum dragonfly hanging from the ceiling like a light aircraft. She turned and looked back. A single glass block was embedded in the wall between the walkway and Eliot's office. As she watched, a shadow passed in front of it, then back again: Eliot pacing from one side of the room to the other.

19

Rivka didn't say a word when Sunny walked into the restaurant, a sure indication that she was not pleased to have been left to sink or swim in a small but demanding sea of hungry diners. Sunny fell to work firing salmon fillets and rib-eye steaks, sautéing chicken breasts, panfrying trout with bacon, warming duck legs, and coaxing the delicious charred black edge onto leeks, slabs of fennel, and marinated portobello mushrooms. Three hours later she plated the last order of grilled polenta and walked up front to check the dining room. Half the tables were full with parties near the end of their meals. A familiar face caught her eye and she noticed Pel and Sharon Rastburn sitting at a two-top by the French doors. Sharon waved. Sunny took off her apron and went over to say hello.

"Marvelous!" said Sharon. "That was a marvelous meal. Exquisite. You're going to be seeing a lot of us from now on."

Sunny expressed her pleasure that they'd enjoyed their meal, and her appreciation that they'd stopped by. Bertrand appeared bearing digestifs.

"It isn't the 1944, and it isn't Domaine de Mahu," he said, "but it is Francis Darroze Bas-Armagnac. This one is a Domaine de

Pinas 1981, which I find very enjoyable. You can see it is very deeply colored, rich. It's younger, but just as virile."

"I'd be more impressed if it was older but just as virile," said Pel.

Sharon gasped happily and laid a hand on his. "You read my mind."

"Pull up a chair and have a glass with us," said Pel to Sunny. "We're just indulging in a little tribute to Nathan. He loved his Armagnac even more than wine, but not any Armagnac, mind you. He got sentimental in his middle age and developed a strong attachment to Francis Darroze Bas-Armagnac made the year he was born, 1944. His favorite was the one from a little patch of land called Domaine de Mahu. Terribly expensive stuff, of course. He always had a glass of it after dinner. A ritual commemoration of the passing of another day."

"It's understandable," said Sharon. "Each birthday marked another year of his life, but also another year that his father had been dead. His father died the same year Nathan was born, fighting the Nazis in Normandy. He was a draft card baby. His father married his high school sweetheart when he was eighteen, took her on a furlough honeymoon, then shipped out. Four months later she got a telegram, five months after that a baby."

"Join us, Sonya. Nathan would like it," said Pel.

Bertrand slipped away and returned a moment later with another glass and a bottle half full of liquor the color of honey.

"To the joy of life, and the inevitability of death. May it bring release," said Pel.

"To Nathan," said Sharon, "and the velvet flame."

They toasted and Sunny took a sip of the fiery brandy. It smelled and tasted of spice and fruit. Fruitcake in a bottle. Then came wood and hazelnuts, vanilla and leather, British libraries and French restaurants.

"Heavenly," said Sunny. "I don't know why we don't drink this more often."

"It's best to observe moderation with the hard liquors, I always think," said Sharon. "Wine is one thing, brandy another."

"I never developed a taste for it," said Pel. "I stick to red wine."

"Eliot doesn't go in for brandies either," said Sharon. "He agrees with me. Too strong."

"Nathan swore by it. Said it brought him good luck. Besides, he was too much of a Francophile not to adopt the postprandial habit of Cognac and Armagnac. The French love their digestifs."

"That's true," said Bertrand, still standing beside the table. "A small digestif is beneficial to the heart and digestion. Like the name says. A small drink in the evening after a good meal. I don't think it does any damage." He showed the label to the three of them. "This one is good, but the other, the one your friend drinks, is exceptional. And very difficult to find. I would imagine there is an extremely limited supply by this time. And it is very expensive. Close to a thousand dollars a bottle, perhaps."

"Money was no object with Nathan," said Pel.

"There was a time when we half expected him to end up living in our guest room," said Sharon candidly. "Needless to say, I was relieved when Osborne Wines turned out to be a success." She sighed and gave Sunny a resigned smile. "He will be missed."

Hearing a familiar voice, Sunny turned around and was surprised to see Sergeant Harvey standing in the kitchen talking to Rivka. Their eyes met and he lifted his chin at her. She took leave of the Rastburns.

In the kitchen, she laid a finger on Sergeant Harvey's sleeve and said, "Let's go in the office."

She closed the door behind them and leaned against her desk. Steve remained standing. "Well?" she asked.

"Normally it takes at least three days to get results on this kind of request, but I was able to pull some strings and get ours priority."

She nodded. "And?"

His eyes sparkled fiercely. "Negative. There was nothing in that glass that wasn't supposed to be there."

"I don't believe it! Is it possible they made a mistake?"

"They didn't, but I did. I hate to admit it, but you just about had me convinced. Now the guys in Sacramento think I've got an overactive imagination, and I have one hell of an interesting report to write."

"I'm sorry, Steve. I thought for sure that was it. Everything seemed to fit so well."

Steve shook his head. "No, there was nothing. I should have known. It was all conjecture. There is no evidence that Nathan was murdered."

She stared out the window at a row of olive trees flanking the parking lot. "Well, that's it then."

He gave her a curt nod. She followed him out.

"Bye, Sunny. See ya, Chavez," he said.

"Bye, Steve."

Rivka watched him close the door behind him, then turned to Sunny. "Well?"

"Negative."

A trio of chits had stacked up at the dessert station. Sunny went to work on them, grateful for busy hands.

Steve's news was a shock, but it didn't take long to realize what it really meant. By the time the restaurant closed, Sunny knew what she needed to do. It was easy enough to reach Sharon Rastburn, who had no difficulty remembering that Nathan had requested his usual after-dinner brandy on Saturday night from Remy Castels. She believed, but was not certain, that Dahlia Zimmerman had brought the drink to the table.

"And you didn't join him?" asked Sunny.

"We did not. We'd had a good deal of wine with dinner and the last thing I wanted was more alcohol. And we're not really brandy people."

"And Nathan, would you say he was drunk at that point?"

"Not drunk, but he was pleasantly tipsy."

Sunny said casually, "It's such a special drink. Do you think he could really appreciate it at the end of the night like that?"

"Hardly. But he wouldn't savor it anyway. Nathan was not a sipper. He knocked the whole glass back in one go."

"So he would drink it like a shot?"

"Exactly. Usually with an espresso chaser. It wasn't just the flavor he liked about that particular Armagnac, though I'm sure that was part of it. It was the tradition. It was a tribute to his origins. He liked the fact that it had been aging in a barrel in France for as long as he'd been alive."

Sunny hung up the phone and stared at the wall of cookbooks in her office. There was just enough time to catch Monty before he left work.

The parking lot at Foley's Wine was mostly empty. Inside, Monty Lenstrom was busy with a customer. Bill Foley wandered over to welcome Sunny, tickling her nose with a beardy kiss.

"What brings you to these parts, McCoskey?" he said gruffly, as though "these parts" referred to the Indian-ravaged plains of western Wyoming.

"The usual."

"Lenstrom?"

She nodded.

"He has all the luck."

Sunny patrolled the bins and racks while she waited for Monty. The sight of each familiar label hefted an old memory to the surface, an evening or an era.

"Sunny!" said Monty, coming over. "I'm glad you're here. I have something to show you."

They went around back to one of the tasting rooms.

"This just arrived." He put two bottles of 1998 Marceline on the table. "You see how they're packaged differently? I can swap the labels, but the foil is still different."

"Actually, it's amazing there aren't more distinctions," said Sunny. "Essentially, all I have to do is swap the labels and nobody but the experts can tell the difference."

"The system, like most systems, relies upon the honesty and good intentions of the participants. And the fact that if the seller gets caught they're out of business and into jail."

Sunny nodded. "You don't think the foil colors could be different for a very old bottle? Maybe they changed it back in the sixties?"

"I don't think so. Nothing else has changed in fifty years. Michel Verlan has been the winemaker at Marceline since he inherited the job from his father. His son runs the place now, but they are very much in agreement on maintaining a strict traditionalism. You get mavericks when there's no history. When you have a legacy to protect, you get traditionalists. They're standing on the authentic article. Their job is to keep doing it exactly the way their family has for five hundred years. Change could only jeopardize that legacy."

"I want to do a little test," said Sunny. "We have to go into the stockroom to do it."

Once they were there, she told him to stand still and close his eyes. Then she hunted around for a bottle of Bandol Rouge and one of Green and Red Zinfandel, hiding them behind her back in case he peeked.

"Don't open your eyes," she warned.

"I won't. What's the surprise? Are you going to hand me a kitten?"

"A kitten?"

"As long as it's not a snake."

"It is not a kitten or a snake. I'd think it's fairly obvious it's going to be wine since we're in the stockroom. But now that I know you want a kitten, I'll see what I can do. Maybe for your birthday."

"That's nice of you."

"Now imagine we're just sitting down to dinner and we've cracked open a bottle of Bandol Rouge. You're serving."

She put the bottle of Green and Red in his hands and he did what she'd done in Eliot's office. He put his thumb in the punt and held the bottle from the bottom.

"I'm pretending, right? Or is this the test?"

"This is the test. Do you notice anything?"

"Well, this isn't Bandol Rouge."

"How can you tell?"

"Because the punt is too shallow. I've served it a thousand times. The bottle always has a nice, deep punt. This is probably a California wine."

"Very good. You can open your eyes now. You weren't cheating?"

"No. I love this kind of game. Did Andre serve you a bogus glass of Bandol too?"

"It's a long story, but I had the same reaction as you. I've served that wine so many times, and I always hold it by the punt. It's easy because it's so deep. It's also very smooth inside, which is distinctive too. The punt on the Green and Red I handed you is sort of scored. I'll fill you in, but first, what can you tell me about Francis Darroze Bas-Armagnac, specifically Domaine de Mahu 1944?"

"I can tell you that you have very good taste in Armagnac."

"What else?"

"What do you want to know?"

"Everything."

"Well, Francis Darroze is generally considered the best *négociant* of Armagnac."

"Which means?"

"Okay, let's back up. First the difference between Cognac and Armagnac. Cognac is French brandy that comes from the Cognac region and is twice distilled. Armagnac is French brandy that comes from the Armagnac region and is distilled only once. Cognacs are generally made by big companies and are blended for a consistent flavor. That means they'll use a variety of vintages, and those vintages may be made from grapes grown here and there in the region. Armagnac is usually produced by some little guy and done by vintage and estate so you know that you have a brandy made with the grapes of this particular piece of land in this particular year. That means you can get a sense of *goût de terroir,* just like with vintage estate wine. Still gets me all tingly. There's something incredibly exciting about knowing that an Armagnac is the specific production of this little corner of Gascony at this particular moment. I love that."

"From the home of the Three Musketeers and more duck fat than anyone likes to admit," Sunny said.

"True. The Gascons love their duck. Anyway, so the big difference between wine and brandy, other than the fact that brandy has been distilled, is that it's aged in the barrel the whole time. You'd normally age a Cabernet Sauvignon for a year on French oak, then put it in a bottle and let it mature from there. With Armagnac, it only develops flavor and color in the barrel. Once you bottle it, it's over. It's frozen in time after that. So instead of buying a few cases of Armagnac and sticking them in my cellar, I might call up Francis Darroze and say, 'Pull a bottle off of the 1944 barrel.' He does that, writes '*Mise en bouteille* this month and this year' and ships it to me. Once the barrel is empty, that's it for that vintage."

"So the labels are handwritten."

"Usually just the note about when they were bottled. You've got the vintage on the front with the place where the grapes came from, then the month and year it was bottled on the back. The *négociant* goes around to the farmers in the area and finds out what they've got tucked away in barrels in the barn. Stuff grandpa made sixty years ago. He buys the lot of it and acts as the distributor."

"It's like *vins de garage*."

"Exactly. *Les garagistes d'Armagnac*. When you by a bottle of VSOP Cognac, it's been blended and colored for consistency of flavor, color, and style. Nicely predictable, but not so nice for exploring. The vintage estate Armagnacs are entirely unique. The quality depends on the quality of the harvest that year, just like with wine, and when it gets pulled off the barrel."

"And Domaine de Mahu?"

"I don't know it specifically, but we're talking about a very small region. You could go there and take a picture of the particular vines that made your brandy." Monty's eyes twinkled at the thought. "I would imagine the supplies of 1944 are extremely limited, given what was going on in the region at that time. Armagnac is much more like history in a bottle than wine is, actually, since you can age the stuff in the barrel more or less indefinitely. And once you bottle it, it keeps forever."

"Okay, what if you chucked back a glass of the stuff?" asked Sunny. "Would you taste anything other than alcohol fumes?"

"What a waste! You'd suck up some nice exhaust through the nasal passage's back door, but that's about it. It's really meant to be sipped. Armagnac is a digestif. You drink it after dinner to settle your stomach, savor the moment after a fine meal, and promote conversation. Now what's this all about?"

Sunny checked her watch. "It has to do with the Nathan Osborne discussion, as you probably guessed, but I don't have time to explain now. I'll fill you in later."

"Oh, fine. Pick my brain and abandon me."

"I'm not trying to be coy. I have a lunch. If I'm going to get to the bottom of this, I'd better hurry."

PART THREE

The Last Supper

20

Sunny knew where she would find Nick Ambrosi. No bartender worth his margarita salt would give up a weekend shift once he'd earned it. They made more money on Friday and Saturday nights than the rest of the week combined. Since Nick was top dog behind the bar at Vinifera, he was sure to be working. The big question was how Sunny was going to get in and out of there without an awkward exchange with Eliot or Andre. She'd already crashed Eliot's party once today, and she was due back at ten to meet Andre for their long-awaited second date. She was turning up so often the staff at Vinifera was going to start wondering if she needed a job.

She could hardly believe her luck when she pulled into Vinifera. Nick Ambrosi was standing outside, smoking a cigarette. She fought the urge to run over to him before he could go back inside. She'd use the casual approach. There was an old pack of smokes in the glove compartment, used to prove to herself that she could smoke if she wanted to, but didn't want to. She grabbed them and walked over. Nick grinned when he saw her.

"Mind if I join you?"

"Please. You're early for your date."

"And you're well informed, as always."

"I try."

Sunny lit the smoke. It was a shame to use up one of the few nicotine allotments she allowed herself these days, especially when she wasn't even in the mood. "There's something I wanted to ask you."

Nick nodded as though he wasn't surprised.

"A small thing," she said. "I was thinking about Nathan again. How long does it take to drive to his place from here? I mean, how long do you think it took you to drive him home Saturday night?"

"About half an hour, maybe more. Why?"

"That's sort of a burden, isn't it? At the end of a busy night?"

"It wasn't exactly a pleasure, but it's not that big of a deal. We took turns. I only did it once every couple of weeks." He looked across the parking lot at a stretch of vineyard. "You didn't have to drive down here to ask me that. You could have called Andre or anyone. Or waited until you're back here in a few hours. You could have asked me then. What did you really want to talk to me about?"

She fastened her eyes on Nick. "You're right. There's more." She took a drag on the cigarette, letting the nicotine go to work. "Late on Saturday night, Remy Castels took an order from Nathan Osborne for a glass of Armagnac."

A flicker of something, she wasn't sure what, passed over Nick's face. He recovered quickly, resuming a bemused expression. He didn't say anything.

"Do you remember?" she asked.

"Nathan always has a glass of his Armagnac after dinner."

"His Armagnac?"

"We keep a private bottle of 1944 Francis Darroze Bas-Armagnac behind the bar for him. That was his drink. Made the year he was born. That's how he ended every meal. It's insanely expensive stuff."

"Did you pour it, or did Remy?"

Nick's eyes widened slightly, surprised at the question. "I'm pretty sure I did. Why?"

"I'm just trying to picture it. So Remy takes the order and walks over to the bar. You pour the drink from a bottle you keep right there, yes?"

"It's behind the bar."

"But you don't have to go anywhere to get it."

"No. Sunny, what's this about?"

"Bear with me. What happens next? Does Remy take it to Nathan?"

Nick rolled his eyes. "I feel like I should be in a room with a bare bulb. Yes, Remy takes it to him. No, wait, I'm pretty sure Dahlia took it to him."

"If she didn't put in the order, how did she know to pick it up?"

"It's pretty obvious what it is. It was late and most of the tables were empty. You can spot that snifter a mile away. She knew whose it was."

"So she spots the snifter and knows its Nathan's Armagnac. She comes by the bar, picks up the drink, and walks over to the table with it. Do you remember where they were sitting?"

"They were sitting at Nathan's usual table, the corner booth. He was like a mobster. He liked to sit where he could see the door."

"Dahlia would be facing you when she picked up the drink, and facing him when she turned around to take it to him."

"Yeah, I guess so."

Sunny took one last hit, then stepped on the edge of her cigarette and slipped the butt in her pocket. She exhaled. "I'd like to
take a look at that bottle."

Nick laughed nervously. "So would I. I've actually been meaning to mention it to Eliot. Somebody swiped it after Nathan died."

"The bottle is gone?" she exclaimed, forgetting to temper her
reaction. "Do you know when it was taken?"

"Not exactly. It was there Saturday night and not there
Monday afternoon. Remy asked about it after the police left on
Monday, and when I looked for it, it was gone."

"Any idea who might have taken it?"

"It's hard to say. We keep the really expensive stuff in a locked
cabinet behind the bar, but it's not exactly one hundred percent
secure."

"Was the lock broken?"

"No, it wasn't broken," he said, "but it wouldn't have to be. It's
only locked at night after we close, and several people have keys.
There's also a key in the register. I might have even left the key in
the lock. It's possible. I don't really think it's necessary to lock up
the good booze. That was Remy's idea, not mine. Personally, I
think it conveys a sense of distrust to the employees. Who's going
to steal from behind the bar other than one of our own people?
Nobody is going to break in for a bunch of open bottles of alcohol."

"Somebody did, apparently."

He looked away. "I need to get back. Are you coming in?"

She shook her head. "I have to get going. I'll be back at ten."

"When you'll tell me what this is all about."

"I will." She sighed. "A favor? Don't mention this conversation
to anyone?"

"No problem."

Back at home, the light outside Sunny's house did a good job of blinding her and a bad job of lighting the front yard, but she could see well enough to identify purslane among the other weeds. She could almost identify it by touch alone. It had a robust, plump feel, almost like a succulent. Sunny pulled up enough for a large salad and went inside. If all else fails, forage for weeds. There was nothing in the refrigerator and she didn't want to go out. She needed to think.

Based on what she knew about Vinifera and what Nick had said, it would have been difficult but not necessarily impossible for someone, especially Nick himself, to slip a lethal concoction into Nathan's drink. With a little sleight of hand, Dahlia could have done it. Or Nick could be lying—he was obviously hiding something.

Regardless of who did it, it would have been extremely risky. The tall mirror behind the bar, the stairway leading to the upstairs seating, the catwalk to the offices, and the open floor plan all made for maximum visibility in the restaurant. It would have been next to impossible to be sure no one was watching at any given moment. How much easier to stop at the bar at the end of the night on Friday, dose the bottle only Nathan drank from, then get rid of it after service the next night. Or they could have done it at the beginning of the Saturday shift, when no one was around. It would be so easy, especially if they knew Nathan would be coming in with the Rastburns that night. Remy and Dahlia would both know that the Rastburns never joined Nathan in his Armagnac. The fact that the bottle was missing shouted confirmation of this theory. Whether the poison was in the glass or in the bottle didn't really matter.

Sunny let out a loud sigh. There was one huge problem. The only way to confirm her suspicions was to convince Steve Harvey to test the body for taxine. That was going to be a tough sell. If she hadn't been so sure about the wine, he would be much easier to convince now.

She tossed the purslane with what was left of a warm bacon vinaigrette and ate it standing up in the kitchen.

Rivka rang the doorbell at eight-thirty sharp. She was dressed for a party in tall boots and a red jersey dress cut low. A long scrap of indiscriminate black fur was draped around her neck and her hair was pulled back tight.

"Zow, you look hot. Part biker chick, part flamenco queen," said Sunny.

"And you aren't even dressed yet. I thought we were going to go early so we could relax."

"I've been thinking."

"Let me guess. Wait, I have news. I can tell you while you get your body on."

Rivka followed her into the bedroom and reclined against a heap of pillows while Sunny rifled through her closet.

"I went over to Dahlia's after work."

"More secret potions?" said Sunny without turning around.

"Do you want to hear this or not?"

"Of course," Sunny said, choosing a pair of low-slung tweed pants and a clingy paprika sweater. She slipped them on, then sat on the bed and zipped into a pair of suede boots.

"I don't know how you wear those things," said Rivka.

"No pain, no gain." She went over to her dresser and rummaged among the earrings in a little box for a pair of tiny gold hoops.

"Dahlia went to the reading of the will this morning."

Sunny looked up. "And?"

"Osborne didn't have any relatives. He left Dahlia his car and the contents of his house, including his art collection."

"This could be key. He breaks her heart, then leaves her his furniture. Anything substantial?"

"Uh, yeah. You might want to sit down."

Sunny finished putting on her earrings. She turned to her friend with her hands on her hips. "I'm ready."

"It's not a big collection. He only bought art when a friend or a friend of a friend needed money back in the seventies. He was one of the few guys in the early days of that whole hippie artist Marin scene who had what you'd call discretionary income."

"And his friends of friends were?"

"Well, not all of them became famous, but Roy and Wayne did okay for themselves."

Sunny's eyes widened. "No. He has paintings by Roy De Forest and Wayne Thiebaud?"

"Two original dog paintings by De Forest and some kind of pastry by Thiebaud."

Sunny whistled. "They're worth millions," she said breathlessly.

"Maybe. It depends on exactly what they are, but it's a fortune no matter what. Dahlia says it doesn't matter what they're worth because she won't sell them."

"You'd only have to sell one of them to live on the proceeds for a long, long time. What else was in that will?"

"He left instructions to sell the house and use the proceeds to settle his personal debts, which were evidently substantial. Remy Castels inherits Osborne Wines. Eliot Denby gets Nathan's half of Vinifera."

"Very tidy. Everybody's got a motive," said Sunny. "Eliot, Remy, Dahlia. Even Andre, since Eliot owning all of Vinifera will have a direct and substantial impact on his peace of mind and the success of his career."

"I'm sure Eliot knew he would get Vinifera," said Rivka. "Remy might have known about his take, and Andre could reasonably assume that removing Nathan would mean he only had to deal with Eliot, but Dahlia had no idea she was going to inherit a fortune in art."

"You don't think he would have told her?"

"No way. She's in a state of shock."

"What about Pel and Sharon Rastburn?"

"She didn't say anything about them. I don't think they were part of it. The only people at the reading were Dahlia, Eliot, and Remy."

Sunny put on a long camel jacket and ruffled her hair. "How do I look? Ready for date number two?"

"Classic textures, sexy lines. Nicely understated. Well done," said Rivka. "Before we go, I want to show you something."

She dug around in her bag and produced a digital camera. "Sit. I want to show you something Dahlia made. I know you're still sleuthing, but you have to believe Dahlia would never harm anyone, especially Nathan. I took these at her house."

Sunny sat on the edge of the bed and peered at the little screen on the back of the camera. It showed a wooden box open on one side, taller than it was wide, elaborately painted in crimson, orange, yellow, and purple.

"You can't tell because it's so little, but that's a portrait of the seated Buddha floating in the top half of the box," said Rivka. "Really beautiful."

A ruby fringe hung down from the top edge. In front of the box, arranged on a scrap of orange silk, was a collection of votive candles, an ornate brass urn full of sand with the remains of incense sticking up from it, a copper bell of the sort that comes from India or Nepal, and a vase holding one white lily. There was a framed photograph that looked to be Nathan with his arm around Dahlia. A candy necklace was draped over a corner of the photograph, and a Hershey bar and a fat navel orange sat in front of it. Standing in the corner in back was a bottle.

Sunny handed the camera to Rivka. "Look at the bottle in back. Can you tell what that is?"

Rivka shook her head.

"We need to get a better look at this."

Sunny stomped into the front room and turned on the computer before Rivka could protest. She popped the tiny flash card out of the camera and into a port in the side of her printer, scrolled through to the frame she wanted, and hit print.

"So much for going early," said Rivka, watching impatiently.

"It's a test print. It'll just be a second."

The printer spat out a grainy eight by ten. Sunny examined it. In back, standing under the floating Buddha, was a clear glass bottle of liquor, shaped like a wine bottle, less than half full, with the distinctive tan label and rounded cursive font of Francis Darroze Bas-Armagnac.

"That's it," said Sunny. "I can't see the bottom of the label, but that has to be the bottle of Armagnac Nathan kept behind the bar at Vinifera. Have a look." She handed the print to Rivka. "Nick told me somebody swiped it between Saturday night and Monday afternoon. Obviously, it was Dahlia. We need to go out there and get that bottle."

"Hang on," said Rivka. "I'm having déjà vu. We went through this with the wine. If Dahlia put the poison in the bottle of Armagnac, she would have disposed of the bottle afterward. She wouldn't have left it hanging around in a shrine at her house waiting for someone to come along and have it tested."

"Absolutely true. So Dahlia might be off the hook. Maybe the real killer didn't expect the victim's ex-girlfriend to lift the bottle before they had a chance to get rid of it. Regardless of how it happened, there is the bottle in Dahlia's shrine."

"I still don't think there was a killer," Rivka said.

"Riv, I want that bottle. It may have poison in it. We can't risk alerting Dahlia, just in case she is involved, so we're going to have to go out there and remove it ourselves, and the sooner the better. If Steve Harvey wasn't hostile to my suggestions we could call him and he could get a search warrant. She's at the restaurant tonight, right?"

"Are you insane? What are you talking about search warrants for? Dahlia hasn't done anything. If you want the bottle of Armagnac so badly, ask her for it. She might think you're an obsessed weirdo, but if you tell her you think it's important, she'll give it to you. She only took it because it's something Nathan liked."

"That's one theory," Sunny said.

Rivka took a lipstick out of her purse and went over to the mirror above the dresser. She coated her lips in fiery red and pressed them together once. Satisfied, she turned around and faced Sunny. "Let's strike a bargain. I will call Dahlia right now. If she agrees to let us go out there and pick up that bottle, you relinquish all suspicion of her, both because it makes sense and as a personal favor to me, your best friend."

"And if she doesn't?" asked Sunny.

"I'll change into my camos and we commit some breaking and entering."

"The bottle's worth enough, it will be a felony."

"Deal or no deal?"

"Deal."

21

"**Now what?**" said Rivka, examining the bottle.

They sat down on the sofa in Dahlia's cabin. The quiet crept up around them. They still felt like intruders, even though Dahlia had given them her permission. Sunny took the bottle and held it up, letting the light from the lamp shine through the dark auburn liquid. She half expected to see murky signs of tampering.

"So?" Rivka asked.

"Well, I think it needs to be tested."

"You think Steve Harvey's going to go for it again?"

"No, and I wouldn't ask him. I don't have anything concrete. I was thinking I'd call Charlie Rhodes. I checked it out and they have a diagnostic laboratory down there at Fresno State. If he can't do it himself, I'm sure he knows somebody who can do the test for us. The only other way is to send a sample to the veterinary lab all the way out at Purdue in Indiana, and then it takes three days to get the results."

"When was the last time you talked to Charlie?"

"Right after he moved."

Rivka stood up and smoothed her dress. "Do you think he'll do it?"

"I don't know. He hasn't been teaching there very long. It's a big favor to ask, but he owes me one."

Rivka checked her watch. "Let's get going. I don't want to leave Alex sitting at Vinifera alone. He already feels weird about tonight because we're supposed to be not seeing each other and getting a fresh perspective on our relationship."

"So why are you doing it?"

"I miss him."

They drove back down the mountain in silence with the bottle riding between them like a prisoner in custody. When they arrived at Vinifera, Sunny said she'd be in after she made a quick call. She wanted to try to reach Charlie before it got too late. Rivka gave her a look. She knew Sunny was more focused on getting the bottle tested than she was on meeting Alex and Andre. Rivka shut the truck door meaningfully and gave Sunny another wary look through the glass.

Charlie Rhodes picked up quickly. "Sunny! This is a pleasant surprise."

They exchanged the usual greetings of friends who hadn't spoken in several months.

"Are you at work at this hour on a Friday night?" asked Sunny, hearing the murmur of professional voices in the background.

"Yeah. I've got a project on the fast track. I'm practically living at the lab these days."

"That's exactly what I wanted to talk with you about," said Sunny. She explained what she needed.

"An alkaloid screen. That's not too big a deal. I think they can do it over at the avian diagnostics lab. Did somebody's horse die?"

"Horse?"

"It's usually horses and cows that get yew poisoning, sometimes dogs."

"How does that happen?"

"The grazers seem to like the way yew tastes and it's widely available. People plant all kinds of yew trees and shrubs in their yards. The typical scenario is a friendly neighbor brings over the lawn and hedge clippings as a treat for the livestock. It only takes a few mouthfuls and they drop dead. It's a fairly common problem, especially in the transition zones between ag use and suburb, when you mix horse and cattle ranches and semi-rural ranchettes. The horse nibbles on a hedge for five minutes and that's it for the horse."

"That's not exactly the situation here." Then she explained what exactly the situation was. There was silence on the other end of the line. After a while she said, "Charlie?"

"I'm here." He cleared his throat. "Is this at all legal?"

"What?"

"Testing this stuff?"

"A friend gave me a bottle of brandy. I'd like to test it for the alkaloids taxine A and B. What could be illegal about that?"

"Right. I suppose that's okay."

"How soon do you think you could do it?"

"It's too bad you couldn't have made the afternoon Fed Ex pickup. If it was here tomorrow morning we could do it first thing. The lab is open from eight to eleven on Saturday mornings. After that they're closed until eight on Monday."

"What if I brought it down myself tonight?"

"You'd drive it down? It's that urgent?"

"If I'm wrong, time's not an issue, but if I'm right, there's a murderer strolling around Vinifera right now."

There was another silence, then he said, "You can stay at my place."

"Great."

Charlie explained how to find his house and where the key would be so she could let herself in if he was already asleep or not back from the lab yet.

"Are you sure you can stay awake that long?" asked Charlie skeptically. "There's a mind-numbing stretch on Interstate 5."

"Sleeping is the problem. Staying awake is my specialty."

There was still the issue of what to do about the rest of the evening. The drive would take four or five hours at least, and it was already past ten o'clock. If she was going to make it there tonight, she needed to leave right now. The bottle was right there on the seat beside her, and her purse contained everything she really needed other than a toothbrush. All she had to do was find some way out of her date with Andre and she could hit the road. The trouble was, she couldn't tell him where she was going or why, and what possible explanation could there be otherwise? There wasn't one. She'd already feigned illness. This was it. This was the end of the world's briefest romance. Could it even be called a romance? It would have to be recorded as a one-night stand. What else could you call it? And was there any hope Andre would have any desire to see her again after she stood him up twice? She would be lucky if Rivka would talk to her. Going inside would only make matters worse. She started the engine and pulled out of the parking lot, feeling like a criminal escaping the scene of the crime. She waited until she was on the highway to call Rivka's mobile.

"No," Rivka said, picking up. "No, no, no. You have to come in here."

"I can't," said Sunny. "I'm on the road already."

There was a pause, the sound of heels striking the floor, then the susurrus of diners in the background stopped. Rivka must have walked outside. "Where are you?" she hissed.

"I'm headed to Fresno. The lab opens at eight in the morning. I can be back by tomorrow afternoon. I'm sorry, Riv. I couldn't think of any excuse that would get me out of there in a timely manner and I needed to get started. I can't stay up all night driving."

"Yes, you can. You stay up all night all the time. You are the world's most dedicated insomniac. You've stayed up all night to bake cookies, to make sausage, to cure salmon, make wine, devil eggs, knit a scarf, read a book, and wallpaper your bedroom. This is not about Nathan Osborne. This is about your terror of facing Andre Morales. I don't care if you're halfway to Denver, turn around right now and get back here or I will never, and I mean *never*, speak to you again, except perhaps to point out what a weasel maneuver this is."

"Let me get this straight," said Sunny. "You expect me to spend the next two hours sipping wine, then drive five hours to Fresno."

"Yes, I do. If it was anyone else, no, of course not. But you, yes." Sunny heard the unmistakable sound of a match being struck. A moment later there was a long exhale, then: "In the first place, you are totally inured to a lack of sleep. In the second place, you are in desperate need of a boyfriend exactly like the man who is about to walk out of his kitchen expecting to see you waiting for him. And third, you can drink a couple of triple espressos. Now turn around and get back here right now or I am going to throw a Jewish-Latina hissy fit that's gonna make you wish you never knew such a thing existed."

Sunny pulled off where 29 met 121 and headed back the other direction. Minutes later she walked into Vinifera, where Rivka leaped up to give her a delighted embrace.

"So, did you leave it on?" she asked a little theatrically but convincingly. "Every time I think I left a burner on, it turns out I actually didn't. So, did you?"

"No, you were right," said Sunny. "It wasn't on after all. But I feel much better that I checked."

"Good. Now you can relax."

Alex Campaglia, Rivka's boyfriend, stood up from the bar and gripped Sunny's shoulders like he was going to head-butt her. Instead he gave her a loud kiss on each cheek. He seemed even taller than usual and towered over her.

"We thought we lost you," he said, casting a shy glance around the room.

"Not a chance," said Sunny. Nick Ambrosi was working the crowded bar farther down. There wouldn't be time for him to ask her why she'd been so interested in Nathan's missing bottle of Armagnac. One of the other bartenders came over to Sunny and held up an open bottle of Acacia Pinot Noir. She nodded. When all of them had a drink, Alex raised his glass. "Safety first."

They toasted and drank. "Has Andre checked in?" asked Sunny.

"He said he'd be out in about ten. That was about fifteen ago," said Rivka.

Alex yawned. "I can't keep up with the late-drink crowd anymore," he said. "I'm ready for bed."

"It's the restaurant life," said Sunny. "You get off work at eleven and it's time to go out."

"Not if you wake up when the sun comes up."

"Do you?" asked Sunny.

"Every day," said Alex. He and his brother Gabe were fourth-generation St. Helena natives. Their family had been growing grapes and making them into wine on the same land for over a hundred years. He was a farmer at heart.

Andre came out of the kitchen in his white jacket and long apron. He gave Sunny a solid, unhesitating kiss and took a drink from her glass of wine.

"You're okay if I'm back in five? I want to change." He held up his hand, reaffirming the five-minute count.

When he came back out he was wearing a white linen shirt and tan pants. Oh so easy on the eyes, thought Sunny. She'd spent the week obsessing over a theoretical murder and had forgotten. The contrast of white linen on gold skin was working nicely.

"I hear you came to see Eliot today," he said.

"Yes," said Sunny. "I needed to talk with him. Or I thought I did."

"What about?"

Andre, Rivka, and Alex looked at her with interest.

"I had an idea," said Sunny. "As it turns out, it was not a very good one."

"What was it?" asked Andre.

"It was silly. I'd rather not say."

"Oh, come on. It can't be that silly. You thought it was good enough to drive down and tell it to Eliot."

"I'll tell you later."

Andre frowned. Rivka said, "Is anyone else hungry? I didn't get dinner and Sunny ate a pile of weeds."

"That wasn't just weeds, that was purslane," said Sunny, mentally thanking Rivka Chavez, patron saint of those suffering an awkward silence.

"You find purslane in salads in Greece all the time," said Andre. "I like it, but there's some resistance to putting it on our menu. People don't want to pay at a restaurant for something they spend all day yanking out of their garden, and they don't want to eat it at home because they're afraid they'll eat the wrong weed and end up with a stomachache."

"We just need some time to get used to it," said Sunny. "When I was a kid, I thought garlic was a kind of salt. I didn't see a clove of garlic until I was about eight and one of our neighbors started showing me how to cook. Now you wouldn't think of an American kitchen without whole garlic. Purslane will be as common on menus as arugula before too long."

Andre gestured to the bartender. "Can you have the kitchen send out something? A few appetizers and things to share." He looked back at the dining room. "We're going to sit at twenty," he said, standing up and leading them to a table.

A dozen small plates from salt cod to lamb shanks arrived over the course of the next hour. Remy came by several times with wine. He was all poise and grace, though he avoided making eye contact with Sunny. He poured a new wine in their glasses whenever he passed by, saying, "You taste the spice in this one," and "Now we have something with chocolate and blackberry notes. You see if you can taste it." Gradually, the frozen moment at the bar and Sunny's refusal to explain her meeting with Eliot were forgotten, or at least overlooked. Their talk migrated to a discussion of farmed salmon versus wild salmon (no comparison), the best place to eat roasted chestnuts (in front of the Met in New York), and how botrytis wine was discovered (most likely because the harvest in Hungary's Tokaj region was interrupted one year in the mid-1600s by the possibility of a Turkish invasion). They speculated what Napoléon's last days on the island of St. Helena were like, prompted by Rivka's account of the film *The Emperor's New Clothes* and the parallels she drew between his exile on the island prison and her life in St. Helena. The stroke of midnight found Andre describing the first time he read *The Unbearable Lightness of Being.*

"The title is enough," he said. "Those five words say everything. He could have stopped right there."

Rivka looked at Sunny across the table as if to say, "Didn't I tell you he was perfect? Aren't you sorry you nearly blew it?"

Espressos and a trio of desserts arrived. Sunny thought what a fine evening it would be if a five-hour drive wasn't waiting for her. Andre caught the surreptitious flicker of her eyes to her wristwatch and checked his own. "It's getting late. We'll go soon."

It was over quickly. A few minutes later he had signed for the bill and they were standing outside, watching Rivka and Alex walk away. Andre stepped closer and slipped an arm around her waist, grazing her cheek with his lips. "I brought the car. We could go for a drive," he said.

She bit her lip. "I have to go."

"Right now?"

"Yes. I have to meet a friend early in the morning."

"It's not that late. I can have you home in bed by two," he said, grinning.

"There's nothing I'd like better, believe me, but I can't." Adding an apology or making up an excuse would only make it worse, she thought. The less she said now, the less there would be to explain later.

His expression hardened. "You're sure?"

"Unfortunately, yes."

"I guess, if you have to go, you have to go."

She nodded. He went with her to her car, gave her hand a squeeze, and walked back inside the restaurant without turning around.

22

Sunny was south of Chowchilla when the sun
came up over the flatlands. It was the kind of morning that gave
sunglasses and aspirin a reason for being. The truck was no way
to ride the long Central Valley miles. All night she'd wondered
if this was the trip when some aging pin, belt, or piston would
finally give out, leaving her stranded by the side of the road in
the middle of the darkness. Otherwise, her mind had been
surprisingly quiet.

If she was right, she would hand everything over to Steve
and be done with the matter. And if she was wrong, she vowed—
again—to shut the topic out of her thoughts and this time she
meant it. As for Andre, she vacillated back and forth between
annoyance for his assuming she would spend the night with him,
and regret that she hadn't done so. It didn't take long to decide
not to think about that topic either. The rest of the trip was spent
almost pleasantly listening to CDs.

An hour after sunup, she pulled into a Denny's, where the
parking lot was full of shiny new pickups that dwarfed hers.
Inside, the place was spotted with ranchers in stay-pressed pants
and Western shirts. At the counter, she ordered pancakes and

eggs fried over-medium, orange juice, and coffee. She thought how not sleeping is as addicting as sleeping. The fuzzy head like a mild hangover relaxed her, made her care less. She didn't need anything to read or anyone to talk to. It was nice just to sit there and listen to the waitresses calling orders back to the kitchen and snippets of conversation from two truckers down the counter. She was back on the road quickly.

Charlie Rhodes was sitting on the front stoop of his house drinking coffee and reading the paper when she pulled up.

"I wondered if you'd make it," he said. "I worried about the truck."

"Me too, but she did fine."

They exchanged an enthusiastic hug. Charlie hadn't changed much, not that she'd expected him to in the few months since he'd been gone. He looked every bit as tan and easy as she remembered. He had flaws, but they were endearing and only served to increase his good looks. He was smiling and bright eyed.

"You're dressed pretty swank for a road trip."

"Chavez insisted I join her for a fancy dinner before I left." She realized for the first time she must have stuck out at the Denny's.

"It's nice to know Rivka is still calling the shots. Have you eaten?" he asked. "You want coffee?"

"I stopped on the way. I needed pancakes to make sense of the morning. I'd drink a cup of coffee."

"Come inside. You can tell me what you've got yourself into this time."

They sat at his kitchen table and Sunny went over everything again, relating what she'd learned about Nathan Osborne's death, and her theory about the taxine.

"I've got a friend who's a professor of clinical diagnostic tox-icology. He'll be at the avian diagnostic lab all morning. I gave him a call last night and he said we could swing by and hopefully get your alkaloid screen done in a couple of hours. Are you going to stick around after?"

"I'd love to, but I think I'd better head back. If it's positive, I'm going to need to talk to Steve Harvey, and I'd like to do that in person. If it's negative, I'd like to take off these shoes and get some sleep, then try to forget any of this happened."

"We've got some beautiful mountains around here," said Charlie. "I was hoping I might get to show you around. I haven't had a chance to make too many friends down here yet."

"You will. I mean you will get to show me around. And I'm sure you'll make friends, too." She sighed. "I'm so tired. What I mean is, I'd like to come back when I'm not attempting to make a tremendous ass of myself based on the most threadbare evi-dence of malicious activity directed at someone I never even met."

"The timing could be better, I guess."

"Can you imagine me hiking in the mountains in these shoes?" She held up a stiletto-heeled boot.

She dropped Charlie off at his office, thanked him for his help, and made her way back to Highway 99 and eventually Interstate 5, headed north. The security was tight at the lab and she hadn't been allowed in. Charlie came out and said they might as well go relax somewhere. It would be a couple of hours. The results were there when they checked back after a ramble around campus: no trace of taxine A or B. That was it. Sunny was going to keep her bargain with herself. Nathan Osborne died of natural causes.

She'd wasted a week worrying herself and others to the contrary, but it was over. The nagging voice that suggested Dahlia or someone else might have swapped out the contents of the bottle was to be ignored. It was Saturday and she would be home by mid-afternoon. There was still plenty of weekend ahead. She could relax, get some sleep, and forget about all of this. On Monday, she would turn her attention back where it belonged: her own life and Wildside.

The drive home seemed to take forever. She was genuinely tired now, and her spirits dragged her down. The radio played generic country music, nothing with soul, and the bleached yellow sky seemed to suggest despair. A white haze gathered during the drive north, culminating in dense blue-gray clouds as she reached the Bay Area. The first drops fell at Oakville just before three, a lonely rain that seemed to promise nothing.

At home, she lay down on the couch and fell into a restless sleep, haunted by dilemmas. If the poison wasn't in the wine Nathan drank at home, why did someone go to the trouble of removing it? The poison could have been put directly in the glass of Armagnac at Vinifera, only there was no good way to get it in there unseen. If Dahlia was in love with Nathan, why did she sleep with Andre, and why was she kissing Nick? If Nathan was dealing in phony wine way back when Denby's was opened, why would it matter if he found out about Remy's work on the wine club's Marceline? Wouldn't he have taken it in stride? Or would Remy have been careful to keep it secret, lest his boss have even more leverage over him?

Gradually she came to the idea that none of it mattered, and that Rivka was right. It was possible the entire obsessive act of chasing theories and details had been an elaborate ruse by the subconscious in an effort to protect herself from falling for Andre Morales and risking getting hurt.

It was no use trying to sleep anymore. She'd never been good at naps. Besides, if she took one now it would throw off her inner clock even more. It was getting close to time for dinner. She went over to the phone and dialed the number written on the pad beside it. Andre's mobile line rang. After six rings, it went to voice mail and she hung up. She stood over the phone, thinking, then opened her planner and found Steve Harvey's number.

"McCoskey," said Steve. "I hesitate to ask. What can I do for you?"

She paused but was not deterred. "Well, I had an idea."

"Which is?"

"A much more direct route than checking possible delivery mechanisms of the poison. It makes much more sense to check the repository. Then we know if there's any point in checking for sources. I don't know why I didn't think of it before."

"Let me make a note of this. You would like me to dig up Nathan Osborne and test his body for yew tree," said Steve.

"He's already buried?"

"This morning. And I'm not real excited about exhuming the body just because you had a brainstorm—another brainstorm."

"I can understand that."

"Thank you. Is there anything else I can help you with?"

"No, I think that's it."

"Good. Nice talking with you, Sunny."

"You too, Steve."

Disappointed but not surprised by Steve's response, she checked her messages. One from Monty, nothing from Andre. She felt both exhausted and agitated. A bath might help, or food, but she wasn't hungry. She looked up at the clock in the kitchen. If she hurried, she could make the last yoga class of the day in Calistoga. That, at last, was a good idea. She needed peace, control, and a nice mellow workout. Yoga was the answer.

The sound of rain on the Quonset hut's corrugated metal roof blended with the soft chanting music and the participants' intentionally loud, slow breathing. Gradually the noise of her own thoughts lifted and everything began to come together. She could let all of it go. The insatiable desire to know what had happened to Nathan Osborne could be held over the cliff of oblivion and released, to drift away, never to be thought of again. She sank deep into the practice, listening only to the language of tendon and muscle. A feeling of safety washed over her, encouraged by the instructor's final words. *Peace.* The equilibrium reestablished, she stepped into rain boots in the yoga studio's foyer, filled with renewed confidence and a sense of security, her faith in the prevailing benevolence of the universe restored.

Outside it was raining hard. She ran across the street to the truck with her yoga mat tucked under her arm, clutching her umbrella, purse on the other arm, keys in hand. There was a note under the windshield wiper. She grabbed it, collapsed the umbrella, and hopped in the truck as fast as she could. Several pages had been torn out of a college-ruled notebook and the blue lines ran. Inside them, another page had been folded up. She unfolded it, smudging the pale blue lines with wet fingers. A single sentence had been scratched out in awkward back-slanting angles with heavy black ink, probably written with the left hand. A drop fell from her chin and hit the word *hurt*. She read the note again. *Stop snooping around and leave well enough alone before you get hurt.*

The paper on the inside wasn't wet, so it hadn't been there very long. She got out of the truck and stood in the rain, scanning the darkened street. A few others exited the Quonset hut and dashed toward their cars. She studied the row of parked cars on either side of the street. They sat empty as far as she could see. The real estate agency she'd parked in front of was locked up, lights off. Whoever left the note was gone, and so was her tranquillity.

23

She locked both doors, put her mobile in her pocket, and ran a bath as soon as she got home. She sank into the hot water, staring straight ahead, and distractedly ran her fingers over the star-shaped keloid scar on the back of her thigh. The note did not necessarily have to be premeditated. It could have been left on impulse. That would be good. It was nicer to think someone had seen her car and had a sudden nasty idea rather than had a nasty idea and followed her, waiting for their chance to leave their threat.

All the locals recognized the Ranger with the root beer–colored side panels. She'd driven it for five years, and her father drove it for twenty before that. Maybe the killer saw it parked outside yoga and decided to give her a scare, since they just happened to be passing by. It didn't have to mean they were watching her every move. More important, it didn't have to mean they were watching her house now.

She stepped out of the bath and toweled off. She could stay home and wonder who was threatening her, or she could go to Vinifera and face them, whoever them was. The note had been left some time between quarter to six and quarter to eight. It was therefore unlikely to have been anyone working tonight, since anyone on staff couldn't have been hanging around Calistoga when dinner service was starting in Yountville, twenty-five minutes away. Nick and Andre would have been at Vinifera by then for sure, as would Dahlia, assuming she was working tonight. That left Eliot, and to a lesser extent Remy, who had more freedom to come and go as they liked, but whose absence would be noted.

Of course, who was to say that the note had been left by a Vinifera staffer? There was still so much she didn't know. Who was to say that Pel and Sharon Rastburn didn't have more to do with Nathan's last hours than they let on? And there were others at Vinifera—bussers, barbacks, waiters, line cooks, a hostess, even a PR person and executive assistant. Any of them could be involved. No, thought Sunny, it's someone close to me, somebody aware of my investigation of Nathan's death.

Based on what she'd seen in Andre's eyes last night, he was not capable of murder. She was clearing him of all suspicion. She wanted to see him again, but not to grill him about his relationship with Nathan or his knowledge of Marceline.

The note intended to frighten her off had only renewed her conviction that a murderer lurked at Vinifera.

"Dressed to kill," said Nick when she walked up to the bar.

"It's just a skirt," said Sunny.

"It's never just a skirt," said Nick. "Want me to tell him you're here?"

"Please."

It was getting late and the restaurant was slowing down. A handful of tables were occupied. A few more customers sat at the small tables near the bar. Nick waved over a busser and spoke to him. Sunny waited. She watched Remy help himself to two glasses down at the other end of the bar. He filled one from an open bottle of Mason Sauvignon Blanc, emptying it in the other. He pulled up each of the open bottles sitting on ice to check the label, but none was Mason. Finally, after a second's hesitation, he topped up the glass with a bottle of what looked like Cakebread and carried the two glasses out.

Nick came back and busied himself nearby.

"Is anything what it seems around here?" said Sunny.

"What do you mean?"

"Oh, nothing," said Sunny, looking away. "That star. I never noticed it before."

Nick turned to look at a star of light striking the wall between the kitchen and the tall mirror behind the bar. It sat near the middle of the wall and was well proportioned, with slender arms and a fiery center. "It's funny, isn't it? It almost looks like it was put there on purpose."

"Wasn't it? I assumed it was art," said Sunny.

"Nope, accident. When the light is on in Eliot's office, it shines through the glass brick, hits the dragonfly, and gets refracted over there. I've been meaning to make it part of the usual setup to turn that light on when we open. We never noticed it until a couple of weeks ago, because Eliot doesn't usually work in there at night."

Sunny contemplated the burst of light. "He's been working longer hours lately?"

"Trying to save our skins. Things were bad enough before Nathan died. Eliot's been up there trying to find some way to make the numbers work."

"I thought Vinifera was doing well."

"We serve plenty of food, we just don't make any money. I don't think Eliot is even taking a salary right now."

"Ouch. Has he been here all evening?"

"I think he's been here all day. He was here when I got here at three. Just between you and me, I have a hunch it's sink or swim for him right now. Make this place go or shut it down."

"He seemed so casual."

"Eliot doesn't let on. It's not good for business."

The busser came out of the kitchen and waved to Nick from down the bar. He went over, listened for a moment, then came back. He braced himself in front of Sunny.

"Andre says he's busy and won't be able to see you tonight, but he'll call tomorrow."

Sunny frowned. "Ouch, that doesn't sound very good. Isn't he even going to pop out for a second?"

He shook his head. "What happened with you two? He was walking around like he won the lottery all week, now he gives you the big blowoff."

"Thanks for clarifying," she said, laughing. "I was still sort of clinging to the hope that he might actually be busy."

"What do you think? So what happened?"

"Not that much. I wasn't entirely honest with him last night and I guess he could tell."

"Lies already? You two are on the fast track."

"I didn't lie, I just didn't say where I was going."

"Careful there. He's the sensitive type. Passionate artist kind of guy. Like all you chefs."

"I'm more of a pragmatist than an artist. I cook because I like to eat. Do you think he'll change his mind?"

"You mean tonight? I doubt it. Maybe tomorrow."

Well, she'd done it. She'd messed up the best chance at love she'd had in years, not to mention making a fool of herself, driving halfway across the state to test a perfectly pristine bottle of French brandy. "I guess it's a fitting end to the day."

"You don't want that to be the end. Hang out and relax for a little while. Let me pour you something." He surveyed the open bottles. "How about a nice, juicy Stag's Leap Cab?"

"Okay, but I want to watch your hands. Looks like you never know what's going to be in your glass around here."

"Excuse me?"

"I just watched Remy mix Mason and something else, Cakebread maybe. I wouldn't mind drinking either of them, but I'm not sure they're good as punch."

Nick frowned his disapproval. "He's terrible. He says most of the people who come in here can't tell grape juice from soda pop and don't deserve to drink good wine."

"Even if they can't say what's wrong with a glass of wine, they might just notice that they aren't thrilled. That's a great way to lose customers," said Sunny. "Besides, what if somebody other than me saw him do it? In addition to being bad business, it's illegal to swap out the goods on your customers. He's crazy."

"Not crazy, just arrogant. Imagine if you knew in your heart that you were a superior being, but you were stuck here waiting on a bunch of ignorant Americans. He does that stuff all the time. I'll tell you something else." He put his elbows on the bar and leaned close. "He loves to mess with people. He used to mess with Nathan constantly. I don't know how Remy lives with himself, now that Osborne's dead. Osborne almost never got what he thought he was drinking. It was a game with Remy. He'd bring in crappy wines we don't even serve here and pour them for Nathan like they were some big deal. I don't think Nathan ever guessed. He couldn't taste much of anything when he was loaded."

"And you didn't say anything."

"It's not my job to squeal. I just pour what they tell me to pour and stay out of the funny business. Besides, it wasn't always just for fun. There was a practical aspect to it. Nathan treated this place like a candy shop; enough to have a fairly serious impact on the bottom line. He'd come in with a group of his cronies, drink Manhattans for three hours, then start ordering the most expensive wines we serve. It drove Remy crazy to have his cellar hit like that. He called it enological vandalism. Remy got in the habit of decanting Nathan's wines for him at the bar. So they'd have a chance to breathe, he said, which was bullshit. He'd pour a good enough wine, we don't have any bad wine on the list, but he wouldn't always open every six-hundred-dollar ego booster that Nathan wanted."

Sunny made an effort not to betray her excitement. She said casually, "What about Nathan's fancy Armagnac? I'll bet Remy loved to see him toss back a shot of that without even tasting it."

"That was the worst. That even made me shake my head. Especially since that stuff is my favorite. I could make a meal out of a snifter of really good Armagnac."

"He wouldn't know the difference if that was switched on him by that time of night anyway, would he?"

Nick busied himself with tasks behind the bar. Sunny took a drink of the wine he'd poured her and let the question linger in the air. After a while she said, "How long have you had a thing for Dahlia?"

He didn't look up. He was matter of fact. "Long time. Why?"

"Even when she was dating Nathan?"

"We met her right about the same time. When she started working here. There's never been much between us. Or at least nothing mutual."

Sunny thought for a moment and then said, "What did you serve Nathan when you didn't give him his 1944 Francis Darroze?"

Nick smiled. "Again with the Armagnac. You're obsessed."

"Yes, I am. Humor me."

He sighed. "Fine. I almost told you the other day when you were asking about it anyway. I don't see what harm it can do to admit it now. The only person who would be mad is Nathan. Eliot would thank us."

Sunny put on an intrigued but not overly eager expression, hoping to encourage him without betraying the intensity of her interest.

Nick glanced up the bar to see that no one needed help, then settled in. "It was Remy's idea. He said the next time we emptied a bottle, I should keep it and refill it with our cheapest Cognac. This was quite a while ago. A couple of years, I guess. I thought it was risky because they don't taste alike to me, and the color is pretty different, but Remy said he'd take care of that. He'd be sure to always be the one who ordered Nathan's Armagnac, and if he was still sober enough to notice a difference, he'd let me know. If someone else happened to put in the order, I poured the real thing, just in case."

Sunny had to remind herself to breathe. "There were two bottles of Armagnac that looked exactly alike," she said.

"I always kept one real bottle and one of the old empties refilled with cheaper—but still quite good Cognac. On the rare occasions when Nathan was sober at the end of the night, Remy would ask for a glass of Francis Darroze and I would pour the real thing. Most of the time he asked for 'our finest Armagnac,' and then I'd pour from the decoy. I still don't see the harm in it. We must have saved the restaurant thousands of dollars, and Nathan still got his nightcap."

"But the bottles looked exactly alike. If you weren't familiar with the contents, you wouldn't notice the difference, right?"

"Oh, I could tell the difference. The Cognac has a glassier, crisper look to it than the Armagnac, and it's much yellower, not as red."

"You could tell, but that's because you know what it's supposed to look like. Could Eliot tell, for example?"

"I don't think so. Besides, Eliot only drinks wine. And Nathan never noticed."

"So only you and Remy knew there were two bottles."

"I think so. I certainly never told anyone. It's not the sort of thing you'd want known. There was another reason for the decoy. Somebody had been nipping out of the bottle fairly regularly. Enough that I noticed. We went from ordering a bottle every couple of months to needing a new one every month. It was probably the cleanup crew after hours. It was starting to add up, so I'd leave the decoy out and lock up the real stuff. Then during business hours I'd swap them in case I wasn't behind the bar when Nathan wanted his drink."

"Do you think Dahlia knew?"

"I don't see how she would. Like I said, I never told anybody, and Remy isn't the type to share confidences, especially when it comes to pulling a fast one on his boss."

She took a deep breath and a drink of wine before she asked her next question. She exhaled, making a noise like steam in a pipe the way they did in yoga, *ujjayi* style, without meaning to, trying to stay calm. "Nick, where's that second bottle now?"

"You mean the decoy? It's gone. They got 'em both."

"They?"

"Whoever stole it. They've both been gone since I checked on Monday afternoon."

Both bottles were gone on Monday. Dahlia took one of them, as a remembrance of Nathan. That bottle did not contain taxine. The other was still missing. "Oh, shit," she said. "Oh, shit."

"What?"

"Are you having family meal tonight?"

"Every night. If you're hungry, you're welcome to stay. You can be my guest. Things are winding down. They'll probably do it pretty soon."

"What would you say if I told you I know where one of the bottles of Armagnac is? I think I ought to go get it and we can make a toast to Nathan."

"How the hell do you know where it is?"

"I have my ways. I think it's a good idea, don't you?"

"I suppose it is. It would be a better way to finish off the bottle than it just disappearing. Did you get hold of the real stuff or the decoy?"

"I'm not sure. You can tell me when you see it. Listen, Nick, there's more to this than seeing Nathan off. I know who took one of the bottles. I think it's very important that we find out who removed the other one, but we'll have to be tricky about it. Whoever it was, I don't think they realized there were two of them. I can't explain everything, but we may be able to tie up all the loose ends around Nathan's death if we do this right."

"You mean who broke the bottle at Nathan's place?"

"Among other questions. Would you be willing to tell your story about swapping out the Armagnac? You could make it funny."

"I could do that, I guess. I've definitely been curious about that broken bottle."

"If you do this right, we'll get it all. I'm convinced of it. I need to make some calls and get everyone here before the key players go home. Can you sell the idea of toasting Nathan to Andre, Eliot, Remy, and Dahlia so they'll stick around? Once we have everyone together, you tell your story about the double life of the Armagnac, including how both bottles disappeared after Nathan died, and how one reappeared today. Oh, and after you give your speech, make sure you suggest that Eliot offer the final toast.

That part is crucial. I'll explain everything to you later. I have to go get the bottle."

"I don't know about Eliot. He almost never stays for family meal."

"It's just for the toast before. Tell him that Pel and Sharon Rastburn are coming down specially for it. One more thing, don't be too clear about where each bottle was kept and when you moved them back and forth. It will be better to leave the impression that they were both just hanging around and only you could tell the difference."

"This sounds like a setup. I don't like theatrics, and I'm not a snitch."

"You won't be snitching. You're just going to tell the truth. If there's nothing to be learned, we'll all have a shot of brandy, wish Nathan well, and forget about the whole business. However, if my hunch is right, somebody at this restaurant is going to be very upset when they hear about your economizing."

"I think I need to know where you found the bottle," said Nick. "People will ask."

"Just say it reappeared as silently as it disappeared."

"That's not true."

"Okay, say that a certain individual removed it for sentimental reasons, then thought better of it and asked me to return it. When you saw it, you had the idea to use it to say bon voyage to Mr. Osborne."

"Another lie."

"That's not a lie, that's spin. I'm just trying to give you credit."

"What's this really about?"

"It's about finding out what happened last Saturday night. Trust me."

Nick shook his head. "Those are the two most dangerous words I know."

24

The Rastburns did not need to be persuaded. They were touched by the sentiment and more than happy to get up from their video, drive forty-five minutes down Valley, and join the party, despite the hour. Sunny thought it was testimony to their devotion to Nathan, or perhaps Eliot.

Rivka was a different story. "Why do you need my help? Can't you have your inquisition without me?" she said.

"I could, except I need the Armagnac. It's sitting on my kitchen table. Be a good lass and bring it down here? The key's in the usual spot."

"Inside the faux dog turd around the side of the house."

"*Exactement.*"

"Mind explaining what you've got up your sleeve?"

"I would, but I don't want to spoil the surprise."

"Throw me a bone."

Sunny pinched the tiny phone awkwardly against her shoulder and opened her umbrella. She walked across Vinifera's parking lot through the downpour to make sure she was out of earshot.

"Details later, but I think the only way to solve this is to force the guilty party to step forward, and I think I've found how to do it. This toast may be our last, best chance."

There was a brief silence, then Rivka said, "I'll be there as soon as I can."

Sunny hung up and dropped her phone back in her pocket. That was it. All she had to do now was wait until everyone arrived. She huddled under her umbrella and watched the rain strike the blacktop. She dug in her handbag for a mint, turned it on her tongue for a count of twenty, added five more for extra credit, then crunched it up, wondering what she would say to Andre when this was all over.

A few customers left the restaurant, no one arrived. The Rastburns pulled up sooner than she would have expected. They must have dashed for the door. They were more jovial than the occasion seemed to merit.

"A fine idea," said Pel, striding up with hands in his pockets like a student. "Eliot must be coming to terms if he feels up to this. It's a lot to lose your best friend."

Sharon followed behind, beaming from under an umbrella. She stood beside them and shook off the water. "We wouldn't miss it," she said.

They lingered under the awning, the Rastburns lulled briefly by the rain, Sunny stalling for time. A moment later, Rivka drove into the lot, then walked up carrying a brown paper bag. Sunny introduced her.

"Shall we join the others?" said Pel.

Inside, the restaurant stood empty except for a foursome chatting over coffee in one of the booths along the far wall and another couple talking softly at the bar. A collection of staff from the front of the house had pushed a string of tables together and were serving themselves from platters of polenta, roasted root vegetables, and a pork loin. Family meal was going to be indoors tonight. Sunny led the way to the bar, where Nick was waiting.

"Are we ready?" she said.

"I'm ready if you are," said Nick. He handed her a tray of empty glasses and took up another himself. He gestured to Remy, who walked to the kitchen door and leaned in. A few minutes later, several of the kitchen staff collected around the group seated at the long table. No one knew exactly what was going on and they whispered to each other, waiting for whatever announcement was to take place. Nick stood at the head of the table. Andre came out of the kitchen looking somber and sat down. Dahlia was already seated at the far end of the table, talking to one of the other servers. The Rastburns sat across from them with Rivka. Remy came over and Nick whispered something to him. Remy went to the phone by the bar and made a call. Soon after, Eliot appeared at the top of the staircase. He took in the group below him. A flash of surprise was swiftly replaced by annoyance, and just as quickly glossed over by enthusiasm. He jogged down the stairs with a gracious smile.

"What's going on?" Eliot asked Nick.

Nick made eye contact with Sunny and she nodded. "We all know how Nathan liked his Armagnac," he began in a toast-master's loud voice. "Straight up and the more expensive the better." Everyone chuckled. He went on. "Someone, and it seems we may never know who, took the liberty of removing Nathan's favorite bottle after he died." The chuckles stopped. "I assumed it was gone for good, but today it happens to have reappeared." He put the paper bag on the table and pulled the bottle out of it. He took a moment to examine the label, then put it back down. "Which brings me to something of a confession. Since Nathan's death I've suffered a guilty conscience for my complicity in a ruse originated by our own Remy Castels."

The group turned to Remy, who stood stone-faced. Andre flicked his eyes to Sunny. She thought she detected more than a hint of irritation. Pel and Sharon looked at Eliot, smiling slightly with anticipation of a heartwarming anecdote. Nick continued. He seemed to relish the opportunity to make a presentation. "It started a couple of years ago. Eliot, you'd been complaining about the comp tab at the bar. Remy pointed out that about half of it could be eliminated if we could persuade Nathan to drink a VSOP instead of his usual. As there was little chance of that, we decided to take matters into our own hands." He explained about the two bottles. The group shifted nervously. Sunny looked at Dahlia, who stared at Nick with an amused look on her face. She turned to Eliot. His face had drained of color.

Nick held up the bottle. "As luck would have it, we've been blessed with the real stuff. Personally, I am going to assume it was the ghost of Nathan Osborne who returned it, and the fact that he chose to return the genuine article is his way of saying no hard feelings. Wherever he is, I hope Nathan will forgive me. It was, mostly, for the greater good of Vinifera."

There was another round of chuckles. Most people seemed comfortable with the story. Nick pulled the cork and poured a splash in each glass. "Everyone take a glass and we'll have a toast," he said, as the glasses circulated. "Eliot, would you do the honors?"

Eliot stood rigid with his glass stiffly in hand. He looked around the table, his eyes darting from one face to another in a mute display of panic. All eyes on him, they waited, glasses at the ready. He looked from one end of the table to the other, woefully, then turned back to Nick. All the while he said nothing.

Andre cleared his throat nervously and put on an over-gracious smile. He shot Nick an icy look. "Maybe Eliot needs a moment to think," he said. "It's been a difficult week for all of us. It's usually better to give people a little notice before they're going to be put on the spot." Nick looked suddenly deflated and a deep blush spread across his cheeks.

Sunny avoided Nick's eyes and pinched the foot of her glass, swirling the splash of golden liquid. Andre continued. "Nathan and I had our differences," he said, "but we shared an appreciation for authenticity and craftsmanship. Nathan was a perfectionist, and if we differed in our opinions on what constituted perfection, we shared the belief that satisfaction was to be found in attention to detail. Nathan was exactly the kind of man who would have been deeply annoyed by the prank Nick has just described, if it weren't for his sense of humor, the trait that saved him from being boorish. He will be missed."

Andre raised his glass and around the table others stood, waiting to drink as soon as his toast was finished. "Good night, sweet prince, and flights of angels sing thee to thy rest. To Nathan."

"Stop!" yelled Eliot. "No one drink. Do not drink." Eliot cast a pleading look around the table. "No one must drink the Armagnac."

"What is it?" asked Andre.

"Osborne," choked Eliot. "That son of a bitch. You have to understand. He ruined me. He destroyed Dunby's, destroyed my dreams. But that wasn't good enough. He had to play the same game all over again." He turned on Andre ferociously. "He drained the restaurant. He didn't even need the money, Andre. Do you know what's in those precious alcoves downstairs? Nothing. Most of that wine is practically worthless. Everything I ever worked for was a big joke to him. When I confronted him, he just laughed."

25

Monty heaved an armload of vine canes onto the fire. He stared into the heart of orange embers and watched the flames lick up around the new fuel. Sunny picked up a stray cane and poked at the blaze, flicking errant stalks back into the heat. They'd been burning vine trimmings all morning in a light drizzle. Rivka stood meditatively testing the toe of her rubber boot against the fire, seeing how long it could tolerate the heat.

Monty tossed another armful of cane onto the fire and pushed the wheelbarrow back into the tool shed. He came back looking pleased with himself. "That's it. That's the last of it."

"I still can't believe you were right," said Rivka.

"Neither can Steve Harvey," said Sunny. She shivered. "He was still shaking his head when I met him this morning. Remy has been talking a blue streak. They're going to test Osborne's body today. I hope those guys in forensics make good money."

"Forget the guys in the lab, what about the folks who have to dig him up?" said Monty. "You couldn't pay me enough."

They sat silently watching the bonfire until it had burned down to a circle of white ash with a marmalade core, then walked up to the house to make a late lunch. Monty and Rivka stood out on the deck, staring at the fog sitting low on the bare vineyard. Wade Skord, whose home they were enjoying like it was their own, would be back in a week. The burning could have waited for his return or his return from the next year's vacation for that matter, but the day had been perfect for it and Sunny had craved it: the smell, the mesmerizing undulations of flame, the crackle of the dry canes, the heat on her face and cold day at her back. Monty and Rivka felt the same way. They'd jumped at the first mention of the word *bonfire*.

Sunny came out of the house onto the deck carrying a bottle of wine. She splashed some into Monty's glass. He wrinkled his nose. "Not the Safeway Red again."

"You're always so snobby about my *Falcon Crest* special," said Sunny. "I think it's entirely drinkable, especially for the price. You should give it a chance. Just taste it once without expecting to hate it."

"I've been thinking," he said. "You were extremely lucky. What if you were wrong and the poison wasn't yew tree? All you tested that Armagnac for was taxine. What if it had arsenic or ant poison or who knows what else in it? What if Eliot hadn't snapped? You could have killed off the whole staff at Vinifera in one blow."

Sunny filled her own glass. "It frightens me to admit that I hadn't thought of that."

"You think it frightens you. I'm the one who'd have to deal with the ramifications. Who would I have dinner with on Friday nights if you two weren't here?"

"Your girlfriend?" Sunny said.

"Annabelle? I should be so lucky. The woman spends more time on the road than Mick Jagger."

"I suppose if no one had come forward I would have had the sense to stop everyone from drinking," said Sunny. "At least I hope I would have. Except it honestly hadn't occurred to me that

that bottle might have something else toxic in it. I was so focused on the yew tree aspect."

"Can we stop poking around other people's affairs now?" said Rivka. "I just want everything to get back to normal."

"I'm still shocked that Nathan Osborne never guessed he was being duped by Castels serving him whatever wine happened to be around, let alone Cognac in place of Armagnac," said Monty. "The guy knew everything there was to know about wine and brandy."

"He was so busy practicing his own deceit he probably never had time to wonder what other people were up to," said Sunny. "He spent more than a decade defrauding Eliot Denby."

"What made Eliot suspicious in the first place?" asked Rivka. "He hadn't figured it out in ten years."

"I wondered that too," said Sunny. "Apparently Eliot stumbled across one of Nathan's phony invoices by accident. It was marked received with a date that was still a week away and he got suspicious. He confronted Remy, Remy confessed everything he knew to save his own hide, and they cut a deal. Eliot said he'd let Remy off if he kept quiet and didn't tell anyone he had figured out what was going on. Eliot said he would straighten things out with Nathan; Remy didn't know how. He thought Eliot was keeping quiet because he didn't want the press to get hold of the story."

"We nailed that whole broken bottle fiasco early on," said Monty. "I'll take credit for that, if you don't mind. I knew it was Remy."

"Uh, I think that was me, but you can take credit if you want," said Sunny.

"And why did he do it? Why not just leave it there?" said Rivka.

"Remy was terrified," said Sunny. "He had all the pressure he could handle worrying about whether or not Eliot was going to turn him in. The last thing he wanted was for Nathan to see his bit of handiwork with the wine-club Marceline. He probably knew Nathan well enough to guess that he would use it in any way he could. Blackmail, for example. So, in a panic, Remy decided to sneak into Nathan's house and swap the fake Marceline with the real stuff, just like we guessed. Everything was fine until he spotted Nathan and was so startled he dropped the bottle he was carrying."

"While we're hashing through all this, how did Eliot manage to leave the note on your car? Wasn't he at the restaurant the whole time yesterday?" asked Rivka.

"He didn't, Remy left it. I assumed it was about Nathan, but it wasn't. Remy was afraid I was going to expose his wine-club fraud. He had no idea Nathan hadn't died a natural death."

"It's a shame he'll go to jail," said Monty. "One less Master Sommelier on the continent. We'll have to make due with forty-one of them now."

"He and Nathan had so many scams running at Vinifera it was a full-time job keeping track of them," said Sunny.

"And what about the Bandol you came to see me about. How did that figure in?" asked Monty.

"That was what first got me thinking it wasn't Remy after all," said Sunny. "When I went to see Eliot on Friday, he showed me his prize possession, a bottle of Bandol that Nathan had given him when they opened Denby's back in the day. It was in the safe with the accounting ledgers, so it survived the fire. It predated Remy's employment. When I felt the punt and realized it was a fake, I knew everything couldn't be Remy's doing and Nathan wasn't what he seemed. It would take a genuinely mean spirit to start a partnership with a lie. We'll never know for sure, but I think it's pretty clear that the Denby's fire was arson. Nathan had been filling the cellar at Denby's with cheap wine for five years. He needed to get rid of the evidence so he could start again."

"You figured if Eliot had found out about Nathan, he had a motive," said Monty.

"The worst kind, revenge," said Sunny. "I wasn't sure he knew until Nick told me Eliot had been working late, trying to find a way to save the business. That didn't fit with what Eliot had said in our meeting. He'd given me the impression that business was booming. I realized he was lying because he didn't want anyone to know the business was in trouble. That could lead to all kinds of unpleasant questions, such as *why* it was in trouble, considering the place was busy every night. Eliot had to keep Nathan's fraud a secret and play down the restaurant's financial problems in order to keep his motive hidden.

"Then I remembered the stack of old ledgers on his desk and figured they dated back to the Denby's era. It was true that he'd been working late making computations, but he wasn't trying to save the business. He was calculating how much Nathan had taken him for over the years. It was an obsession. He kept doing it even after he'd killed him."

"And all that wine locked up at Vinifera was fake," said Rivka. "I still don't see how they did it."

"Not fake, just wrong," explained Sunny. "Remy would place an order for a bunch of high-end wines. Nathan would intercept it on his wholesaler end and replace it with an order for less expensive stock. Osborne Wines would deliver that order, and the regular guy at Vinifera would receive it so everything looked legit. Then when the invoice went to Remy, he'd swap it out with the original invoice, lock up the stock in the alcoves so nobody was the wiser, and they'd split the take."

"Sounds complicated," said Rivka. "And risky."

"I think fraud usually is," said Sunny. "If people put half as much effort into doing things the right way, they'd probably make just as much money and they wouldn't have to worry about getting caught."

"A nice sentiment, but untrue," said Monty. "Let's say a wholesaler buys a bottle of wine for ten dollars. Using Osborne's strategy, the wholesaler sells it for a hundred dollars to the restaurant, but then switches invoices. On paper it now looks like the wholesaler sold a ten-dollar bottle of wine for twenty—the usual hundred percent markup. Since he actually sold it for a hundred, he just made eighty dollars more than he should have, tax free. Well, forty, since he has to give the guy on the inside his cut."

"You're probably being more generous than Nathan was," said Sunny.

"I still don't get how Eliot knew which bottle of Armagnac to poison," said Rivka.

"He didn't, since he never knew there were two. He was just lucky. Or unlucky, depending on how you look at it," said Sunny.

"Hang on, I need to sort this out," said Rivka. "All of this bottle switching still has me confused."

"It's actually very simple," said Sunny, swirling her wine. "Last Friday night Nick put the fake bottle out, locked the real one in the cabinet, and went home. Eliot sneaks in and doses the one that's out. On Saturday, Nick comes into work and switches them around like he always does. He puts the real stuff out and locks the fake stuff in the cabinet. Later that night, Remy orders a glass for Nathan. He evidently gives Nick the sign to use the fake stuff. Nick takes that bottle—the one with Eliot's little present in it—out of the cabinet and pours it. Nathan drinks it, goes home, and dies. Meanwhile, at the end of his shift, Nick does the usual. He locks the real bottle in the cabinet and puts the fake one—the one with the poison in it—on the shelf before he leaves. Eliot nabs the bottle off the shelf late that night and gets rid of it. The real bottle stays in the cabinet until Monday, when they find out about Nathan's death and Dahlia uses a key to make off with the real bottle."

"I may never order a digestif again," said Monty.

"I keep thinking of what Catelina told me," said Sunny. "'It's not what they say is in there that's the problem, it's what's in there that they don't say.'"

"Enough with the Portuguese aphorisms," said Monty, "and for the love of god, let's open a decent bottle of wine. Life is too short to drink mediocre wine, especially on Sunday when there's a cellar not fifty yards away stocked with great Zinfandel hoping for a visitor."

He marched to the railing and dumped the contents of his glass over the side. Sunny winced.

"What?" Monty asked.

"Oh, nothing," Sunny said.

"What?"

She picked up the bottle and scraped at the label with her fingernail, eventually separating the top label from the one underneath. She peeled it away and handed the bottle to Monty, who took one look and said, "You bitch."

"Takes one to know one."

"That was really low."

"It wasn't meant to be a joke," said Sunny, laughing. "It was just an experiment. I wanted to see if you could really tell the difference."

"Let's see," said Rivka, taking the bottle. "Oh Lenstrom, that's gotta hurt. 1991 Shafer Hillside Select Cabernet Sauvignon. If you hurry you can probably still suck a few drops off the grass."

Monty made a sour face. Sunny poured another glass and handed it to him. He took it without looking at her.

"What about Andre?" said Monty, trying to recover. "You haven't said a peep about him."

"I figure I'll let the dust settle, then give him a call and see where we are."

"He'll be there for you, don't worry," said Rivka. "And that reminds me. Dahlia gave me something to give to you." She took a little parcel wrapped in tissue paper out of her pocket and handed it to Sunny. She unwrapped it and spread out the tissue on her palm. Inside was a leather cord with a forest green pouch attached, just big enough to hold the tiny glass vial inside. "What is it?" she asked.

"An amulet," said Rivka. "It's called New Beginnings."

"New beginnings," said Sunny, putting it around her neck. "I like the sound of that."